MW00573359

Also by the Author

Kamikaze

The Erin O'Reilly Mysteries
Book Twenty-One

Steven Henry

Clickworks Press • Baltimore, MD

First publication: Clickworks Press, 2023
Release: CWP-EOR21-INT-P.IS-1.0.2

Sign up for updates, deals, and exclusive sneak peeks at clickworkspress.com/join.

Ebook ISBN: 979-8-88900-011-2
Paperback ISBN: 979-8-88900-012-9
Hardcover ISBN: 979-8-88900-013-6

For Poppy, my dauntless, abundant, joyful golden girl.

Kamikaze

Pour 1.5 oz. vodka, 1 oz. triple sec, and 1 oz. lime juice into a cocktail shaker filled with ice cubes. Shake and strain into a chilled cocktail glass. Garnish with a lime wedge and serve.

Chapter 1

"This is going to be a disaster. They're never all going to fit. We're going to crash and burn."

Michelle O'Reilly surveyed the room, hands on her hips, shaking her head.

"Nonsense, dear," Mary O'Reilly replied briskly. "It's only a few more guests than usual. We'll have plenty of room."

"It isn't the square footage I'm worried about," Michelle said. "It's the chairs. We don't have enough."

Erin O'Reilly looked from her sister-in-law to her mother, then back at the O'Reilly living room. She believed in adapting and overcoming whatever obstacles life threw in her way, but she had to admit Michelle had a point. Michelle and Sean Junior's Midtown Manhattan brownstone was looking awfully full.

"Let's see," Michelle said to Mary, ticking off names on her fingers. "There's you and Sean Senior; Michael and Sarah; Tommy; Erin and Carlyle; Ian, Cassie, and Ben; and of course Junior, Anna, Patrick, and me. That's twelve people, and that's not even counting the dogs. Rolf, Miri, and Lucy."

"The dogs don't need chairs," Erin said. Rolf was lying on

the carpet in the middle of the living room. The German Shepherd wore an expression of long-suffering patience. Erin's niece Anna was on one side of him, braiding little colored ribbons into his fur. On the other side, a fluffy Newfoundland puppy was tugging on one of his large, upright ears.

"Lucy! Stop that!" Anna scolded. "You can't chew on Rolfie!"

Lucy took no notice, continuing to pull. She growled low in her throat, thinking it sounded fierce. It didn't.

"Let's see," Mary said, tapping her chin. "We've got eight chairs in the dining room set. That leaves four. You've got one in the kitchen..."

"Another two folding chairs in the front closet," Michelle said. "And I guess we can use the swivel from Junior's office."

"There!" Mary said. "That wasn't so bad, was it? Just think, I raised twice as many children as you've got. We always found room for them."

The shrill beep of an alarm cut through the air.

"Oh no!" Michelle exclaimed. She spun and dashed into the kitchen to tend to an unspecified culinary emergency. At the same moment, a crash came from the living room. Patrick O'Reilly and Ben Jordan had been building a castle out of wooden blocks. They had apparently neglected a major structural support and the whole thing had come tumbling down. Miri, Ian's scruffy, nervous dog, twitched and scooted under the couch. Her snout protruded, quivering. Ian got down on one knee and began talking soothingly to her.

"Good thing Thanksgiving only comes once a year, eh, Mom?" Erin said with a smile.

"Get used to it, dear," Mary said. "One of these days this might be you."

"Give me a police station on a Saturday night," Erin said, but she was still smiling. The O'Reilly house was full of people she loved. She might complain, but she wouldn't be anywhere else in the world.

The O'Reilly clan always got together for the holidays. It was one of the only times Erin saw her brothers Michael and Tommy. She ran into Sean Junior more often than either of them would have liked; trauma surgeons and police detectives had an uncomfortable amount of overlap in their professional lives. But Erin's mom and dad had moved upstate after her dad had retired, and it was always good when they came down to visit.

This year, however, things had gotten a little out of hand. Inviting Morton Carlyle, Erin's boyfriend, was the obvious thing to do. Ian Thompson, Carlyle's driver and bodyguard, needed to be included. That would have happened anyway, as Ian had been made an honorary O'Reilly after he'd nearly died protecting Michelle and her kids. But now Ian had a girlfriend, and that girlfriend had a son from her first marriage, so Cassie and Ben Jordan were roped in, too. Next thing anybody knew, they had a dozen people crammed into the house.

Mary bustled out to the kitchen to help Michelle get the food on the table. Erin started corralling her brothers, collecting furniture, putting the extra leaf in the dining table, and trying to keep Lucy from eating Rolf's ears. By the time the turkey was placed on the table, golden-brown and steaming, the friends and family were seated. The dogs lurked under the table; Rolf and Miri at the feet of their respective humans, Lucy wandering from one set of ankles to another, begging for treats.

After a few moments, Sean Junior took advantage of a pause in the hubbub. He cleared his throat loudly.

"We're going to say grace in a minute," he said. "But first, I just wanted to say how glad and... and grateful Shelley and I are to have you all here with us."

Erin heard the hitch in her brother's voice and caught the look in his eye. He and Michelle hadn't fully recovered from the events of the previous summer. Their marriage had strained to the breaking point, but it hadn't quite come apart.

"It's been a difficult year," he went on. "For all of us. But we've made it through. Now we're here together, enjoying what looks to be a fantastic Thanksgiving feast. I want to thank my mom for her famous pies—remember to save room, everybody—and Sarah for her sweet potato casserole, and Cassie for... what's this again?"

"Macaroni pudding," Cassie said. "It's one of Ben's favorites. It's kind of like mac and cheese's big brother."

"It looks delicious," Sean Junior said. "And I want to thank Carlyle for the wine. I have to say, it's pretty great having a pub owner in the family. You took your time, kiddo, but you know how to pick 'em."

Erin smiled and shook her head. Carlyle wasn't quite in the family, not technically. But he certainly had a well-stocked cellar. He gave her a sly, subtle wink and squeezed her hand under the table.

"And as for all the rest of you," Sean finished, "you brought yourselves, and that's what matters most. We're so very thankful all of you are with us. And I hope all of us will be together again next year, and for many years to come."

"Hear, hear," Michael said, raising his wine glass.

Erin nodded. But looking at Carlyle and Ian, she was thinking about all the narrow escapes, the fear, the bullets, the blood, and the pain. They'd dodged death this past year and had only scraped past it by a razor-thin margin. They'd passed through a lot of dangers and close calls, but they weren't out of the woods yet. Her own hopes were much more modest than her brother's. She hoped they'd all live to see New Year's Day.

"If you'd like to say grace, Dad?" Sean said, turning to his father.

Sean O'Reilly Senior cleared his throat. His mustache shifted. "Bless us, O Lord, for these, Thy gifts, which we are about to receive from Thy bounty," he said. "Through Christ, our Lord. Amen."

"Can we eat now?" Ben asked loudly.

"I think we'd better," Erin's dad said.

*　*　*

"No offense, but I prefer my family gatherings to yours," Erin said as she steered her Charger through the Manhattan streets. Ian would normally have driven them, but he'd borrowed Carlyle's Mercedes to transport Cassie and Ben.

"You're referring to our meeting with Evan next week?" Carlyle replied.

"Yeah. Any idea what he wants to talk about?"

"I presume he'll be discussing some organizational changes, on account of recent headcount reduction," he said dryly.

Erin swallowed, feeling the two slices of Mary O'Reilly's homemade pie shift in her overfull stomach. Unable to choose between pumpkin and apple, she'd compromised and had one of each. She knew Carlyle was thinking about Veronica Blackburn. Neither of them had liked the streetwalker-turned-madam, but they hadn't wanted her to die the way she had, either.

"The O'Malleys are running out of bosses," she said. "First Liam, then Mickey, now Veronica. That just leaves you, Evan, Corky, Finnegan, and Pritchard. If things keep going like this, we won't need to do anything. The whole gang's going to self-destruct."

"I've heard evil contains the seeds of its own destruction," Carlyle said. "But that's no great surprise. We're all of us rushing toward death, when you get down to it."

"That's a cheerful thought," she said. "Aren't we supposed to be feeling thankful today?"

"Oh, I'm grateful, darling," he said, laying his hand on her thigh. "Not least to your kin, who've welcomed me as one of their own. When your brother said I was one of the family, does he know something I don't?"

"No!" Erin said sharply, glad she wasn't a blusher. "I mean... we can't rush into things. With everything that's going on."

"Of course not," he agreed. "I'm merely glad your da's decided not to shoot me."

"He never would've shot you."

"You're certain of that? A gangster stepping out with Sean O'Reilly's only daughter?"

"Okay, he probably wouldn't have shot you. At least, nowhere vital. Maybe in the leg or something."

"That's a great comfort, darling."

* * *

The holiday season was a time of light, joy, and family. Sappy movies appeared on TV. Multicolored lights were hung from just about every horizontal surface. New York's drab concrete and asphalt were festooned with red and green. And the crime rate went up by about twenty percent.

Criminologists theorized this was because people carried more cash and crowds got bigger. Americans also liked to travel, visiting their relatives. That meant more empty houses and apartments, which made prime targets for burglars. But none of that explained why the murder rate also spiked on major holidays.

Vic Neshenko's theory was as terse and straightforward as Vic himself. In the Precinct 8 Major Crimes office the following morning, when Erin mentioned the uptick in homicides that came with Thanksgiving and Christmas, his answer was a single word.

"Family."

"Maybe your family, Vic," she said. "Not mine."

"I'm serious," he said. "Take your average American family. Chances are, two or three of them aren't on speaking terms. Maybe one guy is boinking his brother's wife. Maybe another guy borrowed money and never paid it back. Whatever. But they're going on with their lives, everybody's basically fine, until wham! It's Christmas and they're all gonna be under the same roof for a few days. To get there, your average Joe's gotta go through a crowded airport full of bullshit security, the airline loses his luggage, he's tired, he's stressed. Now he's in a house with eight screaming kids, two of which are his own, he's using Aunt Edna's toothbrush because his suitcase got flown down to Fort Lauderdale or some damn place, he's sleeping on the fold-out bed with a metal bar across his spine so he wakes up with a backache. Then he's sitting next to his asshole brother-in-law, who he hates and who won't shut up about the Democrats or the Republicans or whoever. There's alcohol, lots of it, so he's more than half drunk. And right there at his fingertips is a nice, fresh-sharpened carving knife. Yeah, I got no idea why people get stabbed during the holidays."

"Wow," Erin said. "You've put some thought into this."

"I call 'em like I see 'em," Vic said.

"Neshenko's right, sorry to say," Lieutenant Webb said from behind his desk. "But we don't need to worry about any of those homicides. They're open-and-shut. The Homicide boys can sort them out in an hour or two, tops. I'd be surprised if we get anything big on our plates. Even gangsters like to go home for the holidays."

"Where they can murder their wives, girlfriends, and in-laws," Vic said.

"Right," Webb said.

"Black Friday," Vic said darkly. "Watch. We're gor̄ some sort of weird-ass murder case. Some psycho'ᵴ offing people in the Walmart checkout lines."

"You drink a lot during the Christmas season, don't you," Erin said.

"I drink a lot year round," he replied. "That doesn't make me wrong."

"Let me tell you what makes you wrong..." Erin began.

"Hold that thought," Webb said, raising a hand. In the sudden silence, the tinny notes of canned music drifted through the office air.

"Oh my God," Vic said. "I don't believe it. The Lieutenant changed his ringtone to 'Jingle Bells.'"

"Shut up, Neshenko. I need all the Christmas cheer I can get." Webb thumbed his screen and put the phone to his ear, mercifully cutting off the chorus. "Webb."

He listened to the voice on the line for several moments. "Copy that," he said at last. "Wait a minute. How come this is ours? Shouldn't it be NTSB? Oh. Yeah, I copy. Okay, we'll get right down there."

Webb put his phone back in his pocket. "Saddle up," he said.

"Where are we going?" Erin asked.

"Jamaica Bay Wildlife Refuge," Webb said.

"What's up?" Vic asked. "Are the waterfowl forming gangs? Ducks versus geese?"

"Plane crash," Webb said.

"Oh my God," Erin said, echoing Vic's words but leaving out the ironic humor. That explained Webb's question about the NTSB. The National Transportation Safety Board was responsible for investigating crashes. If they were calling in Major Crimes, it meant they'd already found signs of foul play.

"From JFK?" Vic asked.

Webb shrugged. "We'll find out when we get there."

"How many passengers?" Erin asked. She felt sick to her

stomach, her thoughts filled with passenger planes packed with holiday travelers.

"That's the weird thing," Webb said. "None."

"Just the pilot?" Vic asked.

"Not even that," Webb said. "The plane was empty."

Chapter 2

"You ever heard of the *Mary Celeste*?" Vic asked.

"Wasn't that a ship?" Erin replied. She wasn't really listening. She was concentrating on her driving.

"Ghost ship," Vic said. "Way back in the 1800s, they found her drifting in the middle of the ocean. Plenty of food on board, cargo untouched, everything where it was supposed to be. Except for the crew. They never found any trace of them."

"So that's your theory? This is a ghost plane?"

"It's easy to get out of a plane," he said. "All you gotta do is jump."

"Okay," she said. "So your theory is that somebody took a perfectly good plane and jumped out of it?"

"You're the one who said the plane was perfectly good," he said. "Suppose the engine quit?"

"You don't jump out of a plane if the engine stops working," she said. "You try to land it, like Chesley Sullenberger did on the Hudson."

"I'll bet you Sully didn't have a parachute," Vic said.

"You're saying he would've bailed out of a plane full of people if he'd had a way to save himself? You really do have a dim view of human nature."

"I'm a cop. It comes with the shield. I'm telling you, Erin, the world is going straight down the toilet and humanity is pulling the flusher. That's not pessimism; that's the truth."

A Patrol car directed them onto the Cross Bay Boulevard and across the North Channel Bridge. The road took them to an island in the middle of the wetlands, in the center of which was a little cluster of houses, insulated from Long Island by the surrounding water.

"I bet this is the most exciting thing that's happened here since... I dunno, forever," Vic said. "You know where you're going?"

"I figured I'd make for the flashing lights and smoke," Erin said. She cocked her head to the right, where a column of black smoke hung on the air.

"Must still be warm," Vic said. "I'm surprised the Transportation Safety boys called us this fast. Five bucks says Homeland Security shows up, too."

"No bet," Erin said. "They probably beat us here."

"Looks like you didn't manage to lose the Lieutenant," Vic said, glancing in the rearview mirror. "Can you believe that piece of junk he's driving? Somebody ought to tell him fake-wood bodywork was never in style, even when it was in style. The only good thing about that station wagon is, nobody would ever think a cop was driving it. You could take it on undercover jobs and get away with it, just because nobody would want to look at it."

"Why didn't you give him a lift in your Taurus?"

"It's in the shop. Transmission. What, you think I'd ride with you by choice?"

On the far side of the little town, Erin spotted another Patrol car. She rolled down her window and flashed her shield to the uniform, who waved her to the right. A short, winding access road brought them to the Broad Channel Pump Station, an unassuming cluster of pipes and valves behind a chain-link fence. The surrounding parkland was scraggly grass and shrubs. A short distance away, something shiny and metallic lay crumpled in the field. Smoke drifted lazily up from the wreckage. A cluster of people were in a huddle near the crash site.

"I'll be damned," Vic said. "Here we are, not five minutes from Brooklyn, and it looks like the ass-end of nowhere."

The parking lot held three Patrol cars, a fire engine, an ambulance, and a matched pair of black SUVs with government plates. Erin parked next to one of the squad cars and got out, unloading Rolf as Webb brought his beat-up old station wagon to a stop beside the Charger.

Vic pointed a thumb at the SUVs. "What'd I tell you?" he said. "Feds."

"Looks like it," Webb agreed. "But which Feds?"

They met a pair of EMTs on the way. The medics, in the absence of casualties, were going back to their ambulance to head to the next emergency. That left half a dozen cops, a team of firefighters, and four guys in black topcoats and suits.

Erin recognized one of the suits. "Agent Johnson," she said. "Keeping the homeland safe?"

"O'Reilly," Agent Johnson said, smiling and offering his hand. "Lieutenant. Neshenko. Glad you could make it. You know Agent Smith, I think."

Johnson's partner gave them a polite nod. As Homeland Security agents went, they were decent enough guys.

"And this is Don Warner and Oliver Brickles, NTSB," Johnson went on, indicating the other two suits.

Warner and Brickles shook hands with them. Erin reflected that in every pair of guys, there was always a tall thin one and a short fat one. In this case, Warner was the tall one and Brickles was the short one, while Johnson was slender and Smith was stocky. Neither one looked like they'd ever smiled in their lives. They also looked cold. The wind was raw, coming off Jamaica Bay right into their faces.

"Lieutenant Overlin, from the 100," the highest-ranking uniformed officer on the scene said.

"Lieutenant Webb, Major Crimes," Webb said, moving in for another handshake.

"Heard about your squad," Overlin said. "You've got quite the reputation. Glad you could make it."

"What're we looking at here?" Webb asked. "Accident or deliberate?"

"Too early to tell," Brickles said. "We won't have a cause for the crash until we've made a detailed examination of the wreckage."

"And it has to cool before we can even start looking," Warner added.

"Then why are we here?" Vic asked.

Everybody looked at him.

"Someplace you'd rather be?" Johnson asked.

"No, I'm fine with it," Vic said. "I'm just wondering what puts this on our desk? Is there something weird about this plane that makes it an obvious job for Major Crimes? Or is this something NTSB wants to shove off onto somebody else?"

Warner and Brickles weren't amused. "We take our job seriously, Detective," Warner said.

"So what's the deal?" Vic asked.

"The plane is a Beechcraft G36 Bonanza," Brickles said. "It's a very common aircraft."

"In production since 1947," Warner added. "Longest continuous production of any aircraft in history. About seventeen thousand have been built. We're not sure how many are still flying."

"One fewer than this time yesterday," Vic observed.

"The Model 36 Bonanza redesigned the tail," Brickles said. "The V-tail on the older models was a source of accidents among inexperienced amateur pilots."

Erin exchanged looks with Vic. This was probably useless trivia, but it was pointless to interrupt professionals while they were talking about their field of interest.

"The G36 has an upgraded EFIS," Warner continued.

"A what now?" Vic asked.

"Electronic Flight Instrument System," Brickles explained. "It's a popular and reliable system. It's unlikely to have failed."

"A possible failure point is the elevator control cables," Warner said. "A couple years ago, Australia grounded older Beechcraft until the cables could be inspected. They can fray, causing trouble on takeoff or landing."

"Excuse me," Erin said. "This is all really interesting stuff, and I understand you guys really know your technical info, but what about the human element?"

"Detective O'Reilly is politely referring to the fact that the pilot does not appear to be in the aircraft," Webb said. "That has been known to cause planes to crash."

"That's true," Brickles said.

"So where is he?" Vic asked.

"We don't know," Warner said.

"Could he have been ejected from the vehicle?" Erin asked. She didn't know much about airplane crashes, but she'd responded to a lot of car accidents. A driver who wasn't wearing a seatbelt could be thrown a surprising distance on impact, usually straight through the windshield, and cars moved a lot slower than planes.

"Unlikely," Brickles said. "The windshield is cracked, but there's no hole large enough for a human body to pass through."

"But the side door is open," Lieutenant Overlin said.

Erin squinted through the drifting smoke. It appeared the smoke had come from a grass fire around the plane, not the plane itself. The door in the fuselage was, indeed, open.

"The first responders didn't open it?" Webb asked.

"No, sir," one of the Patrol officers said. "Busby and I were first on the scene. It was like that when we got here."

"So our guy survived the crash-landing and got out," Webb said. "Then he fled the scene. But why?"

"That's nuts," Vic said. "A guy might abandon his car if he wrecks it, but an airplane?"

"Now that, I can answer," Overlin said. "Landon, show them what you found."

"Busby and I were on patrol about half a mile north when it came down," Officer Landon said. "Made a hell of a noise. We called it in, then we laid rubber and got here as fast as we could. Minute or two, tops. I didn't see anybody running away, and the guy would have to have been on foot. I don't see where he could've gone. Anyway, we came up on the crash. The grass had lit up, and we were afraid the gas tank was gonna go, so we climbed in to see if anybody was hurt. We didn't find anyone, injured or not. But here's what we found."

He pointed into the interior of the plane. The detectives peered inside.

"Looks like sacks of coffee," Vic said.

"Yeah," Landon said.

"So?" Vic asked.

"So who transports coffee by single-engine prop?" Overlin asked, raising his eyebrows.

"Geez, I'm an idiot this morning," Vic said. "That's not coffee, is it."

"It's packed in coffee," Overlin said. "But Landon and Busby found half a dozen bricks of what's probably coke hidden in there."

"And that's why a guy would run," Vic agreed. "Especially if he heard your siren. Six kilos is serious weight."

"Except that doesn't answer the question of where he'd go," Erin said. "And why he'd leave his cargo behind. If you're right, that's a very valuable delivery."

"There's a gun in the cockpit, too," Landon said. "MAC-10 submachine-gun with suppressor."

"Okay, this plane obviously belonged to a drug mule," Webb said. "But I'm still not hearing an answer to the main question. Where's the pilot? There's two roads out of here. You gentlemen came in on one. Could the guy have escaped on the other?"

"On foot?" Landon was doubtful. "I'm pretty sure we would've seen him."

Webb turned to Erin. "I think we can do better than 'pretty sure.'"

She'd already been thinking of that. "Absolutely, sir," she said. "Is it safe to go into the plane?"

"Yes, ma'am," one of the firefighters said. "We sprayed down the engine. What you're seeing is just residual smoke. The fire's out."

"Rolf, *komm*," she said, climbing into the little airplane. Rolf scrambled up alongside her. She led him to the pilot's seat and pointed to it. "*Such!*"

Human beings were smelly. Most people didn't know that they had two different kinds of sweat. There was the kind that came from physical activity or overheating, which wasn't particularly strong-smelling, and there was the kind that came from intense emotion. The second kind was musky, reeking of fear and tension. Everybody smelled different, and that was before taking into account the clothes they wore, the places they went, the foods they ate, their general health, and their emotional state.

Rolf didn't analyze all the factors in a conscious way. All he knew was that his partner was pointing him toward a smell and telling him to track the person who matched it. The slits on the sides of his nostrils were an adaptation placed there by nature, allowing his olfactory receptors to follow a scent without needing to draw a breath. But Rolf inhaled deeply, nostrils flaring, getting a nose-full of his target. In a matter of moments, he knew the missing pilot's emotional condition and a great deal about where the man had been and what he'd been doing. The K-9 couldn't explain what he was smelling to Erin, but that wasn't his job anyway. His job was tracking.

The Shepherd snuffled at the pilot's seat. Then he whirled and pulled back the way they'd come, tail wagging eagerly. The smell was fresh and clear. Rolf was excited and happy, knowing that if he successfully tracked down his quarry, his rubber Kong ball would definitely be waiting for him.

He pulled Erin to the side door and hopped down to the smoldering grass. Then he stopped short. His tail kept wagging a moment longer, but he became suddenly uncertain. He raised his snout and sniffed the air, getting a breath of smoke. He snorted, shook his head, and tried again. He went in a slow circle, inspecting the ground. His tail became hesitant and then drooped. He whined softly. It didn't look like he'd be getting the Kong.

"No good," Erin said to the onlookers.

"Maybe the smoke is screwing with him," Overlin suggested.

"Not a chance," Erin said. "If this guy came through here, Rolf would know. Our boy got out of the plane before it came down."

Rolf whined again. Erin rubbed the base of his ears. Her own nose picked up nothing but smoke and the heavy reek of aviation fuel, together with an unpleasant burnt smell that reminded her of her confrontation with the late and unlamented Mickey Connor. It was a sickly-sweet odor, like scorched cotton candy. With all the fuel fumes in the air, they were lucky the plane hadn't exploded.

"You mean he jumped before it crashed?" Brickles asked.

"Or he got thrown out," Vic said. "Maybe there was another guy, a passenger, and he pitched the pilot out."

"A midair hijacking?" Johnson asked. "Interesting thought. It would explain why the plane crashed, if our hijacker didn't know how to land it."

"Pretty stupid guy if he chucked the pilot out of a plane he didn't know how to fly," Vic said.

"This was your theory," Erin reminded him. "And criminals can be pretty dumb."

"Who owns this plane?" Webb asked the NTSB guys. "I'm sure you've checked the registry."

"It's registered to Arthur Wilder," Warner said. "He's a resident of Philadelphia."

"Do you have his flight plan?" Webb asked.

"He was flying from South Jersey Regional Airport to JFK," Brickles said. "He was scheduled to land at 0630 this morning."

"Any passengers?" Erin asked.

"None listed," Warner said.

"What time was the crash?" Webb asked.

"The plane hit the ground about six-forty," Officer Landon said. "We called it in right away; Dispatch will have the time stamp."

"So he was running a little late," Webb said.

"Is that important, sir?" Erin asked.

"Maybe," Webb said.

"What sort of autopilot does this thing have?" Vic asked the NTSB guys, thumping the fuselage with his hand.

"It's not a drone," Brickles said. "It doesn't have fancy AI. This is an old aircraft. It has a basic autopilot."

"It can follow the flight path," Warner said. "It'll maintain stability and altitude."

"Doesn't seem to have done a very good job," Vic said.

"Could our guy have abandoned the plane mid-air?" Erin asked. "What would've happened to the plane if nobody was flying it?"

"Assuming no mechanical malfunctions, it would have kept going on autopilot," Brickles said.

"Until it ran out of fuel," Warner said.

"Or landed," Brickles added.

"A plane can land on autopilot?" Webb asked.

"Possibly," Warner said. "It depends on how the pilot set it up."

"But it isn't a good idea," Brickles said.

"Dangerous," Warner said.

"Yeah," Vic said. "You could crash your plane into an island or something."

"According to your information, Wilder was on the plane when it took off?" Webb asked.

"Correct," Brickles said.

"And according to Rolf, he wasn't on the plane after it hit the ground," Webb went on.

"That's right," Erin said, scratching the ruff of fur on Rolf's neck.

"You're sure of that," Webb said.

Rolf stared up at Erin with his intense brown eyes.

"He is," Erin said. "So I am too."

"That's good enough for me," Webb said. "That means Arthur Wilder left this aircraft somewhere between South Jersey and here."

"There's a good chance he's in Jamaica Bay," Vic said. "Or Sandy Hook Bay. Either way, he's probably getting acquainted with the local marine life right now. Crabs eating well today."

Erin made a face. "Thanks for that."

"He's right," Warner said. "Parachuting into water without a survival raft is pretty much suicidal."

"And that's assuming he had a parachute," Brickles said.

"He'll wash up on the beach in a day or two," Warner predicted.

"Or not, depending on tides and currents," Brickles said.

"In the meantime, somebody's going to be wondering where their coke shipment went," Webb said. He turned to Lieutenant Overlin. "It's in your AOS. You want it?"

"Isn't this a Major Crimes case?" Overlin asked. "That supersedes our Area of Service."

"Not yet," Webb said. "Without a body, we can't even make the determination whether it's a homicide or not. If it's just drugs, that's under Narcotics jurisdiction. But this flight crossed state lines, so maybe it's Federal."

Johnson held up his hands. "Whatever this is, it doesn't look like a matter of national security," he said. "Homeland's washing our hands of this one. The DEA might want a piece of it. I'll be filing a report with them."

"I hate departmental turf wars," Vic muttered. "It's like street gangs, only with more paperwork and less shooting each other."

"Agent Johnson," Erin said. "Why did Major Crimes get called so quickly?"

"Call it a hunch," Johnson said. "Plane full of drugs, mysterious disappearance. I don't think Arthur Wilder was suddenly overcome by suicidal thoughts and decided to play paratrooper without a chute. I think something happened on this plane that would fit your definition of a major crime."

"You think he was murdered," Erin said.

"Like I said, it's a hunch," he said. "I'll contact the DEA and they'll work with local law in Philly and South Jersey Regional. It'll take some time. Sorry for dragging you all the way down here for what's probably nothing. Chances are, this is the last you'll hear of this."

"So that's it?" Vic said. "We turn around and go home?"

"Disappointed?" Erin asked.

"A little, yeah," he said. "It's like when you're watching a sex scene in a movie and they fade to black right before you get to the good stuff. It's a... whaddaya call it? An anticlimax."

"If that was a pun, it should be taken out and shot," Webb said. He shook hands with Overlin again. "Let us know if there's anything you need, Lieutenant."

"Copy that," Overlin said. "We'll keep you in the loop."

"Come on, kiddo," Erin told Rolf. "Back to the office."

Rolf nosed at her hand. Vic was right; this wasn't how this was supposed to end. He hadn't gotten even one good chew on his Kong ball.

Chapter 3

"Have I got this right?" Vic asked from behind his desk. "We're investigating a crime that might not be a crime, with a missing person who may or may not be dead."

"There's the drugs on the plane," Erin said. "That makes it a crime."

"Right," he said. "And if I was on the Narcotics squad, that much coke would give me a serious hard-on. But I'm not a narc, so it doesn't."

"We're talking about cocaine, Vic, not Viagra."

"Johnson is right," Vic went on. "This is interstate drug smuggling. That makes it a DEA problem."

"True," Webb said. "And like Johnson, I'll be forwarding my report to them. But in the meantime, since you clearly don't have anything better to do, I'd like you to develop some background on Arthur Wilder."

"I knew we shouldn't have closed that last homicide," Vic grumbled. "The problem with being good at shoveling shit is, people just give you a bigger shovel and a bigger pile."

"And you've got to keep digging," Erin agreed absently. She was looking at her computer screen. "Arthur Wilder's got a jacket, but not much of one."

"What've we got on him?" Webb asked.

"Drunk and Disorderly, a couple of DUIs," she said. "Looks like Philly PD busted him for solicitation of a minor a couple years ago, but it didn't stick. Victim's family dropped the charges."

"Sounds like a classy guy," Vic said. "But that doesn't exactly scream 'drug dealer' to me. Who was the girl he went after?"

"Patience Goodspeed," Erin said.

"Sheesh," Vic said. "Sounds like some chick that came over on the *Mayflower*. How old is she?"

"Sixteen."

"That's legal," Webb said. "Creepy, but legal. Sixteen is the age of consent in Pennsylvania."

"She's sixteen now," Erin said. "She was fourteen when Wilder got arrested."

Webb, who had two teenage daughters of his own, shuddered. "How old is this dirtbag?"

"How old are you, sir?" Vic retorted. "Nobody calls them dirtbags anymore."

"I'll call them whatever I damn well please," Webb said. "Answer the question."

"Wilder's forty-one," Erin said.

"I agree with the Lieutenant," Vic said. "This guy's a creep. I'm starting to hope he fell out of that plane and screamed all the way down."

"I still want to know what he was doing with half a dozen bricks of coke in his private plane," Webb said. "I've got his financials here. I see a bank account with a seven-figure balance. He's got a nice house in Philly. This guy's got plenty of money."

"Is he married?" Erin asked.

"Spouse is Regina Wilder. Married twelve years. No kids."

"You think wifey knows he was playing around with one of the Daughters of the American Revolution?" Vic asked.

"She would've found out when he got arrested," Erin said.

"But she didn't file for divorce," Webb said. "Interesting."

"Prenup," Vic said. "I'd bet a week's salary on it. If they split up, she doesn't have a golden parachute."

"And just like that, we're back to parachutes," Erin said. "You know, a golden parachute wouldn't actually be much use."

Vic snickered. "Yeah, it'd be like jumping with an anvil tied to your back. You'd hit the ground just as hard, and then a big chunk of metal would smash you flat. Serve all those CEOs right."

"O'Reilly, get on the phone with Philadelphia," Webb said. "I want you to talk to Mrs. Wilder."

"Yes, sir," Erin said gloomily.

"Cheer up," Webb said. "This isn't a family notification. For all we know, Wilder's still alive."

"Yeah," Vic said. "Maybe he's made of rubber and he bounced when he hit the ground."

"You have an interesting definition of optimism, Neshenko," Webb said.

"I'm Russian," Vic said. "For us, that counts as optimism."

Erin looked up the phone number. Fortunately, there was only one Regina Wilder listed in Philadelphia. She dialed the number.

"Hello?" a woman said. She sounded polite, well-educated, and calm.

"I'm trying to reach Regina Wilder," Erin said.

"This is she. Who's calling, please?"

"My name is Erin O'Reilly, ma'am. I'm a detective with the New York Police Department." Erin let that hang in the air.

Most people got uncomfortable when the police contacted them. Sometimes they let things slip without intending to.

"I'm sorry, you said the New York Police?" Mrs. Wilder said. "There must be some mistake. I'm not in New York. I'm in Philadelphia."

"Yes, ma'am," Erin said. "I'm calling about your husband."

"Is Arthur all right?" Mrs. Wilder asked. "Oh dear, I should have thought of that at once. He was flying to New York this morning. Did something happen?"

"What was the purpose of his visit?" Erin asked, deliberately avoiding the questions.

"Business."

"What business is Mr. Wilder in?"

"He's an importer. Ms. O'Reilly, what is going on? Where is my husband?"

"We're trying to ascertain that right now," Erin said.

"What do you mean?" Mrs. Wilder asked. "Why would you be looking for him?"

"Ms. Wilder, was anyone else on your husband's plane when it took off?"

"I don't know. I wasn't at the airport. I've been here, at home, all morning. Ms. O'Reilly, you're frightening me."

"Where does your husband's business import from?" Erin asked.

"All over the place. Europe, Asia, South America... What does that have to do with anything? Please tell me what is going on."

It was time to stop dodging. Erin gave it to her straight. "Ma'am, your husband's plane crash-landed near JFK Airport a couple of hours ago. He wasn't on board. We don't know where he is or what's happened to him. I'm going to give you my phone number. If you hear anything, either from him or from anyone who knows anything about what's happened, please call me immediately."

Regina Wilder was silent for a moment. Then she said, "Of course, Ms. O'Reilly. I have a pen here. I'm ready for that telephone number. I'll let you know if I hear anything."

*   *   *

"I've got nothing," Erin announced after ending her call. "The guy's an importer, according to his wife."

"We knew that already," Vic said. "He's importing nose candy."

"I'm going to take a closer look at his financials," Webb said. "This is really looking like a drug-related death. I'm going to be interested in what those two guys from NTSB determine to be the cause of the crash."

"You thinking sabotage?" Vic asked.

"Maybe," Webb said thoughtfully. "Either that, or there was a passenger on that plane."

"Some Navy SEAL or Special Forces badass," Vic said. "We're talking serious James Bond shit here. He sneaks on board the plane, knifes the pilot, tosses the body out, parachutes down to a waiting speedboat, or maybe a submarine..."

"Vic, do you even hear the words coming out of your mouth?" Erin said. "That's half Eighties action movie and half bullshit."

"What do you mean?" he asked indignantly.

"I mean, if he knifed Wilder, where's the blood?" she asked. "That cockpit was pristine. And why get rid of the body if you're going to crash the plane anyway? That makes it more suspicious, not less. You'd leave the corpse on the plane and hope the crash messed it up enough so cause of death wasn't clear. And don't get me started on the getaway submarine."

"It would've been a cool way to do it," Vic sulked

"This is going to take a little time," Webb said. "I expect the Transportation Safety folks will need a few days to examine the wreckage. Without a body, we don't have a lot to go on. It's not even officially a homicide, so whatever this is, I wouldn't call it a Major Crimes case, no matter what Homeland Security has to say. Not yet, at any rate. We can do some of the investigative legwork, but if anything else comes up, we're putting this on the back burner. Besides, there's a better-than-even chance the DEA will pull it out from under us."

"Interstate drug trafficking," Erin agreed. "But it really might be some sort of accident. The drugs could be incidental."

"That's an incidental quarter-million dollars or so in product," Vic said. "The narcs are going to think it's a pretty big deal. But you're right, even bad guys have accidents sometimes. I still hope it was James Bond."

"Let's not put Sean Connery on the whiteboard just yet," Webb said.

"Or Pierce Brosnan," Erin said. She'd grown up in the Nineties.

"I'm thinking Daniel Craig," Vic said. "He's my kind of Bond. I always thought I looked a little like him."

"Maybe," Erin said. "From the back."

"Okay," Vic said.

"If the lighting isn't too good..."

"I said okay."

"If I'd been drinking..."

"Enough already!"

*　　*　　*

One of the unfortunate truths of being a detective was that not every case got neatly wrapped up. All too often, something new came along and pushed an ongoing case to the back of the line. They might be waiting for DNA lab results, or for another agency to get back to them, or for a legal challenge to work its way through the courts. The Wilder case wasn't unusual, except in its absence of a body.

Erin put it out of her mind and concentrated on other business. She had a lot on her plate. In addition to her normal job, she was trying to snip off the loose ends on her sprawling, months-long undercover assignment with the O'Malleys. Finally, after too many close calls, gunfights, explosions, and deaths, they were within spitting distance of shutting Evan O'Malley down.

They had everything they needed: dozens of hours of incriminating conversations, recorded on hidden microphones; insider knowledge and testimony from Carlyle about the workings of the Irish mob; names, dates, and details of innumerable major felonies; and the bow on top of the package, Evan's ledger.

The ledger hadn't been a physical document. Evan had entrusted his financial records to the photographic memory of an unusual, gifted young woman who never forgot a number. But Erin and her allies had figured out Evan's secret, and Corky Corcoran had worked himself into Maggie Callahan's good graces. He'd convinced Maggie to commit the records to paper as an emergency backup, so the police had a window into Evan's dealings to ensure they rolled up the entire organization at one go.

Or at least, they'd be able to do that once Corky came back to New York. The last Erin knew, he'd been on his way out of the city, and probably the country, in the company of a terrified murder witness. He'd be back someday, but Erin wasn't clear on exactly when. In the meantime, she was prepping the rest of the case. Her case officer, Lieutenant Phil Stachowski, had a file bulging with incriminating information, but they were constantly adding to it. They'd had a few setbacks on account of the shifting nature of the O'Malley upper management. Erin really wished Evan's associates would stop getting murdered long enough for things to settle down.

And then there were her other extracurricular activities. After the Street Narcotics Enforcement Unit had tangled with a crooked squad of cops from the Organized Crime Task Force, Erin had found herself wondering just how deep the rot went in the NYPD. Vincenzo Moreno, the late head of the Lucarelli Mafia family, had definitely had someone inside the police, someone with access to Internal Affairs files. Erin had gone to her own Internal Affairs contact for help.

Kira Jones might not be working Major Crimes anymore, but she was still a friend, and she'd agreed to see what she could find out within her own department. So far, nothing had turned up, but Erin was trying to juggle that investigation along with all the rest.

As if that wasn't enough, it was now the Christmas season and Erin was a member of a sizable family with a lot of shopping to do. She had three brothers, a young niece and nephew, her parents, and a few in-laws to find gifts for.

Then there was the inevitable departmental paperwork and the constant training sessions with Rolf to keep him sharp and well-exercised. It was amazing how the hours could fill up, even in the absence of new crimes to solve.

All things considered, she was just as happy to forget about Arthur Wilder. The importer from Philly disappeared from her world over the following week and she didn't miss him. Time slipped past her, almost unnoticed, until the dead body washed up on Brighton Beach. Then Wilder became her problem again.

Chapter 4

Erin, Vic, and Webb stood on the Brighton Beach boardwalk, waiting for the Medical Examiner to finish. It was a cool, clear morning, the temperature hovering around thirty-five. Their breath steamed on the air. Rolf, at Erin's side, was sitting mostly still, but his paws tapped the boards impatiently as he shifted his weight from one front foot to the other.

"Who found the body?" Erin asked.

"A woman out walking her dog," Webb said.

"Tide must've brought it in overnight," Vic said.

"They're sure of the ID?" Erin asked.

"Wallet in his pocket," Webb said. "Driver's license, pilot's license, credit cards. The wife's coming up, but I don't know if they're going to want her to confirm. That'd just be a formality anyway. It's Arthur Wilder."

"I wouldn't want the wife seeing him," Vic said. "The guy's been in the water almost a week. And he came down pretty hard. Son of a bitch must've hit the waves like a goddamn meteor. I'm surprised we didn't get a tidal wave from the impact. I don't think she'd know her own mom in that situation."

"He was wearing a parachute," Webb said.

"Which didn't open," Vic said. "Landing in water wouldn't have done him any good. From that height, it's like face-planting on concrete."

They watched the proceedings on the sand for a few moments in silence. Sarah Levine was working with her usual clinical, emotionless competence. The two men who drove the coroner's van were smoking cigarettes and waiting for permission to move the body. Hank and Ernie were two of the least pleasant guys Erin knew. She was trying not to look at them or to listen to their conversation, but it was hard.

"You a Megadeth fan?" Hank asked Ernie.

"I'm a fan of all kinds of death," Ernie replied. "If people stopped dying, we'd be out of a job."

"You know the song *High Speed Dirt?*"

"Enlighten me."

"Oh, Jesus," Vic muttered. "Here they go again."

Hank started singing, if you could call it that. "See the Earth below, soon to make a crater. Blue sky, black death, I'm off to meet my maker."

"The crater would've filled in right away," Ernie pointed out. "Water impact."

"Still made a crater, though," Hank said. "That's physics. Like the apple falling on Newton's head."

"That's if the apple was going at terminal velocity," Ernie said. "Now that would've made a crater right in Newton's cranium. Say, you ever heard of anybody getting killed by getting hit by an apple?"

"Nope," Hank said. "Knew of one guy who got offed by a potato gun."

"No shit? I didn't think they had the force."

"Absolutely. MIT did a study. If a spud hits you in the head at close range, you've got a better than fifty percent chance of a skull fracture."

Ernie shook his head sadly. "Death by potato? Hell of a way to go."

"You think peeling the potato makes a difference?" Hank wondered.

Erin was done being near those two. She hopped the railing onto the beach and walked toward the body. Rolf easily jumped to the top rail, planted his paws on it, and sprang down to accompany her.

"Good morning, Doc," Erin said. "What've you got?"

"Decomp isn't as bad as if the body was dry," Levine said without looking up from her work. "Cold water causes adipocere to form on the tissues. See the soapy-looking residue there? It's formed from body fat. However, the skin has become fully waterlogged and is beginning to slough off the flesh."

"Thanks," Erin said, swallowing. She was glad the salty smell of the ocean covered up most of the stink of death.

"Time of death is difficult to determine," Levine said. "Preliminary COD appears to be massive blunt-force trauma, likely from high-velocity impact with the surface of the water. The sudden deceleration shattered most of the bones and ruptured several internal organs. Death was instantaneous."

"I would hope," Erin said. "I heard he was wearing a parachute."

"The parachute wasn't deployed," Levine said.

"Why not?"

"That's not a medical question. The parachute was not open, so the victim died."

"Was he conscious before he hit the water?"

Levine finally looked up at Erin. "I have no way of knowing that," she said. "In fact, I can't absolutely state that the impact was fatal. If he was dead or unconscious beforehand, it would explain why he didn't deploy his parachute. I'll know about toxins when I run his bloodwork, but the nature of his injuries will make it difficult to determine whether he sustained any prior damage."

"Okay," Erin said. "Anything else you can tell me?"

Levine stared at her for a long moment. "About what?" she finally asked.

"About the victim."

"It will be in my report, which you will receive when I file it."

"Right. Thanks."

Erin left the Medical Examiner and the CSU team to work their magic and returned to her squad. Rolf, unconcerned, sat back on his haunches and vigorously scratched an ear with his hind foot.

"Homicide?" Vic guessed.

"They didn't find a knife sticking out of him, if that's what you're asking," Erin said. "It's way too early to tell. All Levine knows so far is that Wilder came down fast and came to a sudden stop in the bay, and we already knew that."

"At least we know where he ended up," Webb said. "It makes sense. His flight path took him right over the bay. The only question was whether he'd wash up here or on Breezy Point." He nodded across the water.

"He could've drifted all the way back to Jersey," Vic said. "Then he'd be their problem, which maybe he should be anyway. The state line runs straight across the water. Depending on where this happened, it might be something for the New Jersey State Police, or the Coast Guard, or maybe the Port Authority. That's in addition to the DEA. Homeland Security doesn't want him. They said so."

"Mrs. Wilder will be here soon," Webb said. "Are we in the Six-One or the Six-Oh?"

"Pretty much right on the line," Vic said. "But we're in the Six-Oh." He'd grown up in Brighton Beach and knew the precinct Areas of Service from his Patrol days.

"Then we'll meet her there," Webb said. "It's time to start building a timeline and find out why this idiot jumped out of a plane, with a parachute, and didn't bother to use it."

*   *   *

Regina Wilder was a tall brunette, five-foot ten in her bare feet, six-one in her heels. She was dressed stylishly in a beige pantsuit and broad-brimmed hat. Her hair and makeup were perfect, her complexion flawless. Erin thought she looked like she'd walked right off a movie set, or maybe a fashion runway. All she needed was a long-handled cigarette holder to twirl between her fingers.

They met the new widow in the lobby of the Precinct 60 house. It would've been hard to picture a less appropriate setting for her. The station was a blue-collar brick-and-concrete lump that looked like it hailed from the height of the Cold War. It probably still had an old fallout shelter in the basement.

"Mrs. Wilder?" Webb said.

"Yes," she said, favoring him with a polite smile.

"Lieutenant Harry Webb," he said, offering his hand. "I'm in charge of the investigation into the circumstances surrounding Mr. Wilder's unfortunate incident."

She arched a perfectly-sculpted eyebrow and gave his hand a cool, brief shake. "That's a great many words, Lieutenant," she said. "You mean that you're looking into Arthur's death?"

"That's correct, ma'am," he said. "My sympathies for your loss."

"Thank you," she said. "It did come as something of a shock, though perhaps not entirely a surprise."

"Why do you say that, ma'am?" Erin asked.

"I think we should discuss this in a more private setting," Webb said.

"Interview rooms are this way," Vic said. He'd been in the 60 before and led the way down a back hallway to a dreary concrete room with three metal chairs and a matching table bolted to the floor.

"Oh, my," Mrs. Wilder said. "I've never been behind the scenes at a police station. Do you really work in this drab, dingy place?"

"We're with Major Crimes, ma'am," Webb said. "We operate out of Precinct Eight in south Manhattan."

"It's pretty drab and dingy there, too," Vic said. "But we don't complain. It keeps us acclimated to the street. Murder isn't pretty."

"Murder?" Mrs. Wilder repeated. "I thought Arthur's death was an accident."

"We're still collecting information," Webb said. "Please, sit down."

Mrs. Wilder sat in the lone chair on one side of the table. Erin and Webb took the seats opposite her. Vic remained standing, leaning against the wall by the door, arms crossed. Erin had left Rolf in the break room down the hall, with the K-9's sullen acquiescence.

"What do you know about your husband's business dealings, Mrs. Wilder?" Webb asked.

"Very little, I'm afraid," Mrs. Wilder said. "I'm kept quite busy with my own affairs and I really have no head for business."

"To your knowledge, were all his dealings legal and aboveboard?" Webb asked.

"What are you suggesting, Lieutenant? That I might be complicit in some manner of underhanded commerce?"

"I'm suggesting no such thing, ma'am," Webb said calmly. "I'm just trying to get a sense of Arthur's situation."

"I don't know anything about any crimes Arthur may have committed," Mrs. Wilder said.

"Including Patience Goodspeed?" Erin asked.

Mrs. Wilder's eyes flashed angrily. It was only for an instant, but all three detectives had been looking for it and all of them saw it. "That is a personal matter," she said in icy tones. "I have nothing to say on the subject."

Interrogations were not polite interactions. They might be civil on the surface, but they were the process of digging through layers of defensiveness, half-truths, justifications, and outright lies. Erin was good at getting the truth out of interviewees; Webb was a master. The Lieutenant nodded as though accepting her stonewalling, but Erin knew he had no intention of letting it go at that. He was preparing to try again, from another angle, once Mrs. Wilder had been softened up a little.

"Private planes don't normally carry parachutes," Webb said. "Why was Mr. Wilder wearing one?"

The sudden shift of subject accomplished its goal. Regina Wilder was startled and, for the first time in the interview, her composure cracked a little. She blinked twice in rapid succession and uncrossed her legs.

"What?" she said. "I thought... that is, Arthur led me to believe..."

"Most accidents happen on takeoff and landing," Webb said. "A chute would be useless in those situations. And they're harder to use than people think. You need special training and skydiving experience. But you knew that already, didn't you?"

"Yes, of course," Mrs. Wilder said, recovering. "Arthur was an accomplished skydiver. He always insisted on having a parachute in his airplane."

"What were his other hobbies, ma'am?" Webb asked.

"Rock climbing, bungee jumping, stock-car racing, that sort of thing."

"I see. Your husband was a bit of a thrill-seeker, would you say?"

Mrs. Wilder pressed her lips together and nodded.

"Did you participate in any of these activities?" Webb asked.

"Of course not!" she exclaimed. "It's all so silly. Grown men running around in the wilderness, jumping off rocks and bridges, driving cars as fast as they can. Nonsense!"

"Adrenaline junkies are like that," Vic said. "They get off on the action."

Mrs. Wilder frowned at Vic's choice of words. "Crude," she said, "but not inapplicable."

"Is that why he bought the Beechcraft?" Webb asked.

"It's why he got his pilot's license," she agreed. "In truth, as I said, I'm not terribly surprised this is what happened. You can only roll the dice so many times before they come up snake-eyes."

"Are you a gambling woman, Mrs. Wilder?"

"Only in a casual, social sort of way."

"Did you ever meet Miss Goodspeed?"

"Only once, at the farm," Mrs. Wilder said.

"What farm was that?" Webb asked, keeping his voice mild and encouraging, giving no indication that they were now discussing the topic she'd previously refused to talk about.

Mrs. Wilder's eyes flashed again. "Her family farm, if you must know," she said. "That's where Arthur met the little minx. She played the innocent, but I saw the way she was looking at him. Wide-eyed, disingenuous, and all the time fishing around for a way to get into his pockets."

"His pants, you mean?" Vic asked.

"I mean his bank account!" Mrs. Wilder snapped. "The little tramp was looking for a payout. Why do you think her parents didn't want to take her to court? Talk to them, see what they say about her. Are we done here?"

"For the moment," Webb said. "Thank you very much for coming in the middle of this difficult time."

Mrs. Wilder got to her feet and started for the door.

"Just one more question, ma'am," Webb said.

Erin and Vic exchanged glances and tried to hide their smiles. It was cliché, but that was because it worked.

"Yes?" Mrs. Wilder replied sharply, obviously eager to get out of the room and on her way.

"If Arthur was an experienced skydiver, why would he have a malfunction with his parachute?" Webb asked.

"You'd have to ask him," Mrs. Wilder said coldly. "Not that you can."

Chapter 5

"That is one cold, hard bitch," Vic said, watching the Precinct 60 front door swing shut behind Regina Wilder.

"I didn't ask for your opinion, Neshenko," Webb said.

"With all due respect, sir, that's not an opinion," Vic said. "It's a fact."

"If my husband had just died, I'd be a lot more upset," Erin said.

"On the other hand, your husband hasn't been screwing an underage girl," Vic said. "Your hypothetical husband, I mean."

"We need to talk to the Goodspeed family," Webb said.

"You think some teenage farm girl is really an evil mastermind?" Vic said doubtfully.

"I think we need to get the whole picture," Webb said. "But we're getting ahead of ourselves. For all we know, this wasn't a homicide. If Wilder's plane malfunctioned and he tried to jump, screwed up somehow, and killed himself in the bay, none of the rest of this matters. Before we go traipsing around the Pennsylvania countryside, let's get back to the Eightball and see what else we can find on Wilder."

"I like the drug angle," Vic said.

Erin nodded, but her thoughts were elsewhere. The meeting with Evan O'Malley was set for eight o'clock at the Barley Corner. She needed to be ready for whatever was going to happen. It was on Carlyle's home turf, which was good, but she still didn't know the agenda, which was bad.

"This is gonna be one of those cases, isn't it," Vic said.

"One of which cases?" Webb asked.

"One of those cases where the victim's a complete asshole and everybody who ever knew him wanted him dead. I hate those."

"You'd rather the victim be popular, a good guy, a terrible loss to humanity?" Webb replied.

"No, if this guy really was a pedophile, I'm glad he's dead and I wish it'd been slower and hurt more. I just hate having too many suspects. It's like throwing darts at the phonebook."

* * *

A man was waiting for them in the Major Crimes office. He was a silver-haired Latino with a complexion like old leather. He had on a plain black suit that made him look like an undertaker, and a .357 magnum on his hip that made him look like an Old West gunslinger. He was talking with Captain Holliday.

"Here they are now," Holliday said, seeing the detectives come up the stairs. "Lieutenant, this is Special Agent Julio Lorcas, DEA. Agent Lorcas, allow me to introduce Lieutenant Harry Webb and Detectives Erin O'Reilly and Vic Neshenko."

"Pleasure," Lorcas said, shaking hands with each of them. "I've heard a great deal about you."

"Oh crap," Vic muttered.

Lorcas smiled with the left half of his face. "Nothing to worry about, I assure you," he said. "I understand you've been liaising with the Street Narcotics unit."

Vic blinked. "Where did you hear that?"

Erin elbowed him. "We've worked some busts with them," she said.

"Gotten a lot of smack off the street," Lorcas said. "Might be rearranging the deck chairs on the *Titanic*, but every little bit helps. I've spoken with Sergeant Logan in SNEU. He speaks very highly of your team."

"He's got an excellent team of his own," Webb said. "Good police, every one of them."

"I suppose you know why I'm here?" Lorcas said.

"I assume it's got something to do with six bricks of coke on an island in Brooklyn," Webb said.

"Precisely," Lorcas said. "As I'm sure you're aware, that kind of volume is always tied to gang activity."

"Do you know who Arthur Wilder was working for?" Erin asked.

"That's a complicated question," Lorcas said.

"How so?" Webb asked.

"We've had our eye on Mr. Wilder for some time," Lorcas said. "We knew he was moving product for a Mafia family. We believe he was originally connected with a *capo* named Matthew Madonna."

"Mattie Madonna's dead," Erin said.

"Yes," Lorcas said. "He was killed during an internal coup by Vincenzo Moreno."

"Who was killed just before Thanksgiving by Madonna's son," Erin said. "In a New York courtroom."

"Yes," Lorcas said again. "You're well-informed."

"We were there," Vic said. "Watched it happen."

"Control of the Lucarelli family is in flux at present," Lorcas continued. "It isn't clear who's calling the shots right now."

"Valentino Vitelli is probably in the best position," Erin said, not adding that she had enough dirt on Vitelli to bury him. That was need-to-know information.

"We were hoping Mr. Wilder would lead us up the food chain," Lorcas said. "We'd been waiting for him to make a move."

"He's been under DEA surveillance?" Webb asked.

"Correct."

"But he ended up on the sand in Brighton Beach with every bone in his body broken," Erin said. "How'd your guys let that happen?"

"We didn't have an agent on the plane with him," Lorcas said sharply. Then, in a quieter tone, "We were keeping at arm's length. We didn't want to spook him. Unfortunately, he's no good to us dead."

"He's no good to anybody," Vic said. "Dead or alive," he added in an undertone.

"Do you have any idea how he died?" Webb asked.

"I was hoping you could tell me," Lorcas said. "We have several theories. He may have been taken out by a competitor. He may have been eliminated as part of the Lucarellis' internal power struggle. Or it's possible someone made our surveillance, in spite of our efforts, and disposed of him as a security risk."

"Wouldn't they have waited until he touched down and delivered the drugs?" Vic asked. "That was a lot of dollars in that plane."

"You're assuming the crash was intentional," Webb said.

"I've spoken to the NTSB," Lorcas said. "You'll have their report within the hour detailing the cause of the crash."

"Excuse me," Webb said. He went to his computer, logged in, and poked around in his files for a few moments.

"How come you heard this before we did?" Vic demanded.

Lorcas shrugged. "We're both Federal agencies," he said.

"Meaning you scratch each other's backs?"

"Meaning the transfer of information is slightly more efficient," Lorcas said smoothly. "Relax, Detective. I only got the word about an hour ago, and I was badgering them. Nobody's trying to keep you out of the loop. Nobody's out to get you."

"The only people who say that are the people who're out to get you," Vic said darkly.

"Is he always like this?" Lorcas asked Erin.

"No," she said. "He's on his best behavior right now. Most of the time he's much worse."

"Got it," Webb announced. "Let's see... according to the NTSB, the cause of the crash was foreign matter introduced into the fuel mixture, resulting in the engine seizing up."

"Sugar," Erin said.

"How did you know that?" Webb asked.

"I smelled it," she said, remembering. "At the crash site. Burnt sugar."

"Rolf would be proud of you," Webb said. "There's no reasonable way it could have been accidentally mixed with aviation fuel, so as of this moment, we are officially investigating a homicide."

"Any word from CSU?" Erin asked.

"Yes," Webb said. "Just came in. It appears the deceased's parachute malfunctioned."

"No shit," Vic said. "Wonder what tipped them off? The sound he made when he hit the water?"

"The ripcord was pulled," Webb said. "But the chute didn't open."

"Wilder was a skydiver," Erin said. "He knew what he was doing. Don't they prepare their own parachutes?"

"Absolutely," Vic said. "I'd never trust some idiot to pack my chute for me."

"You've been skydiving?" Erin asked.

"Hell yes," Vic said. "It's a rush like you wouldn't believe. When you hit free-fall, that adrenaline is something else."

"Yeah," Erin said. "It's your body screaming that you're about to die. I get plenty of that in my day job. I don't need to go chasing thrills for a hobby. There's something wrong with you. Any idea why the chute didn't open?"

"According to the preliminary CSU report, the chute was sewn shut," Webb said.

"You mean with needle and thread?" Erin asked.

"Apparently," Webb said.

"So he pulled the cord and nothing happened," Vic said. "It takes about ten seconds to fall the first thousand feet. After that you hit terminal velocity and it's about five seconds every thousand. How high you figure he was when he bailed?"

Webb examined the NTSB report. "They don't know exactly when he left the plane," he said. "But he was probably around five thousand feet, give or take."

"So he had half a minute to think about it on the way down," Vic said. "Wonder what was going through his head."

"I bet he was wishing he'd double-checked his parachute," Erin said. "So this is murder twice over. They sabotaged his plane and his chute."

"Definitely," Webb said. "Which means we need to look hard at Arthur Wilder. I'll stay here and work the Mob drug angle. I'm sending the two of you to Pennsylvania, first thing in the morning. I'll coordinate with local law so they know you're coming."

"Road trip!" Vic said. "You pick the tunes, I'll pick the snacks."

* * *

"That's exactly what he said," Erin told Carlyle. "I swear, Vic's half great cop, half rebellious teenager. I think he's just looking for an excuse to get away from our adult supervision for a day or two."

Carlyle chuckled. "How old is the lad, exactly?"

"I'm not sure. Thirtysomething. Younger than I am." She took another bite of her shepherd's pie. "It's a good thing I lead an active life, or Marian would have really fattened me up by now."

"I'll pass that on to her. She'll take it as a compliment."

They were eating supper upstairs at the Barley Corner, unwinding after Erin's shift while they waited for the O'Malley management to arrive. The rest of the workday had passed without incident. Erin had tried to educate herself on the subjects of skydiving and piston-driven airplane operation, with limited success. She'd also looked up the route she was planning on taking to rural Pennsylvania in the morning.

"This may be the wrong time in our relationship to mention this," she said, "but I really don't like hanging out with your friends."

"They're not my friends, darling," Carlyle said gently. "Evan O'Malley is no one's friend."

"Coworkers, then."

"Fair play, darling. No fear, I'm engaged in a change of employment, as you're well aware."

"That reminds me," she said. "What happens afterward?"

"They'll not stay late, I'm thinking," Carlyle said. "I was planning on a wee nip and some quiet time with my bonny colleen before I go back to the pub and conduct some business."

"That's not what I meant. What do we do once this whole thing is over?"

"Assuming we've not been murdered by vengeful gangsters?"

She made a face. "Yeah, assuming that."

"I rather enjoy owning a pub. I think I'll continue doing that."

"They're not going to confiscate the Corner?" Erin was surprised. They hadn't talked about this.

Carlyle smiled. "The Corner's been part of an ongoing criminal enterprise, no doubt about that," he said. "But it's really not a money-laundering front. Oh, that's why Evan purchased it in the first place, but in one of life's little ironies, I've actually turned it into a profitable legitimate enterprise. For all the gambling, smuggling, and whatnot that's been conducted on the premises, the business itself is clean and has been for years. I've not seen those marvelous ledgers we're all fixated on, but there'll be nothing incriminating on their pages about my pub."

"*Your* pub?" she asked.

"The title's in my own name, aye." He was still smiling. "Someone needs to own it, and I convinced Evan that was the best way to avoid suspicion. And I'm not going to be charged with anything."

"So even after everybody goes to jail, you get to keep this place?"

"Aye, free and clear."

"And you've been saving money."

"Yes, unlike most in the Life."

"How much?"

"Beg pardon?"

"How much cash do you have lying around?"

"That's rather an impolite question, darling. You'd not want people thinking you were just after me for my money, would you?"

Erin rolled her eyes. "I think we're way past that. Come on, give me a number."

Carlyle pursed his lips. "I don't know the precise number. I've most of my funds in various investments and a few discreet offshore accounts. I imagine it's in the neighborhood of four, perhaps five."

"Four or five what? Dollars? Thousands? Hundreds of thousands? Four stacks of gold bars? Five sacks of loot? What?"

"Million," he said quietly.

Erin had chosen the wrong moment to take another bite. She choked on a semi-solid mouthful of mashed potato. Gasping and wheezing, she grabbed for her glass of Guinness and took a swig. She set it down again, eyes watering.

"You've got *four or five million dollars?!*"

"Or thereabouts," Carlyle said. "Are you all right, darling?"

"Jesus, I make eighty grand a year. Before taxes."

"I've done well enough for myself."

"But won't you have to turn it all over?" she asked. "I mean, when we roll everything up?"

"Everything they can prove came from criminal enterprise, aye."

"How much is that?" she asked, suddenly suspicious.

He shrugged. "It's all jumbled together, darling. And the offshore amounts can't even be traced to income in America. As far as I can tell, they can't prove any of it's dirty."

"You're not planning on keeping it!"

"I wasn't planning on throwing it away, if that's what you're asking."

Erin spluttered indignantly, to Rolf's interest. His partner didn't usually make sounds like that. He laid his chin on her knee and watched her, wondering what was going on.

"We'll discuss this later," Carlyle said. "Right now, we've a meeting to host. Are you wearing your recorder?"

"Yeah," she said. "You?"

He patted his necktie, which concealed a microphone and thumb drive.

"Okay," she said. "But we're not done talking about this."

*   *   *

Erin and Carlyle settled into their seats in the Barley Corner's back room. Rolf lay down at Erin's feet under the card table. The table had a rack of poker chips and two unopened decks of cards on it, though they didn't know whether they'd be playing. Ian Thompson was minding the security cameras, two of his guys watching the front door, so they were as safe as they could be under the circumstances.

Erin looked at the poker chips and thought, *four or five million dollars!* It didn't feel real. She wondered why her first thought when he'd told her about his savings had been to get rid of it all. Didn't she *want* to be rich?

If she'd wanted to be rich, she thought, she'd have gone to business school like her brother Michael, or into medicine like her other brother Sean Junior. The only cops who got rich were the dirty ones. All Erin had ever wanted was to earn enough money to live in reasonable comfort while doing something that mattered. Too much cash, she believed, was bad for the soul.

But was that really true? Suppose Carlyle did keep his offshore accounts and investments. They could do whatever they wanted. They could take that trip to Ireland both of them had been thinking about. They could have the best clothes, the best food, the best... everything. And what if they had kids someday? Children were expensive, not even counting college. Didn't she want to give hers the best start in life? The world was hard enough if you had money; if you were poor, it was brutal.

Was this what it felt like to get corrupted? Erin wondered who she could talk to about this.

The clink of the doorknob derailed her train of thought. She jolted back into the present moment as Gordon Pritchard, AKA "Snake," came in. He was a small man, about five-foot nine and very thin, but he was dangerous. The right side of his face and body were horribly scarred from a long-ago mishap involving a gasoline bomb. He always wore a glove on one hand to hide the wrinkled scar-tissue, but there was no hiding his face.

"Evening, Cars," he said in his hoarse, rasping voice. He'd inhaled some of the hot gasoline vapor, with predictable results on his vocal cords. "O'Reilly."

"Mr. Pritchard," Carlyle said politely. "Glad you could join us."

Pritchard turned in the doorway and nodded. A moment later, Evan O'Malley and Maggie Callahan came in. Maggie, to Erin's delight, was holding a squirming, fluffy Golden Retriever puppy in her arms.

Carlyle stood up to greet them. "Mr. O'Malley, Miss Callahan," he said. "It's a pleasure, as always."

"Thank you," Evan said. "Good to see both of you. I hope you're well."

"We're good, thanks," Erin said. "Is that Puzzle, Maggie?"

"Yes," Maggie said, and she actually smiled. "Puzzle, say hello to Erin."

The puppy snuffled curiously at Erin's face and licked her cheek. Erin scratched him under the chin. Maggie sat down on the other side of Erin from Carlyle and continued cuddling her dog. Rolf raised his head and sniffed once. Then he rested his snout between his paws with a sigh. He had no time for young pups. They had no work ethic or self-control.

"We'll be having a new guest tonight," Evan said. "He should be here momentarily. Finnegan's bringing him."

"Friend of his?" Erin asked.

"Associate," Evan said.

As if on cue, the door swung open again and Kyle Finnegan entered. Behind him loomed a large, broad-shouldered man with black hair, black stubble on his chin, black eyes, and a black leather jacket. He openly wore a big hunting knife on his belt in a cross-draw sheath. Erin noted its pommel was shaped like a human skull.

"Mr. Finnegan," Carlyle said in carefully neutral tones. He neither liked nor trusted the unstable gangster. "Good of you to join us. Would you care to introduce your comrade?"

"All professions be-rogue one another," Finnegan said. "Fill every glass, for wine inspires us, and fires us with courage, love, and joy. Women and wine should life employ. Is there ought else on Earth desirous?"

"Declan Rafferty," the new arrival said, crossing his arms. "And you'd be Cars Carlyle and Junkyard O'Reilly. Don't think we've met."

"I'm sure I'd remember you," Carlyle said. "What line of work are you in, Mr. Rafferty?"

"Entertainment industry," he said. "Moving up in the world. Call me Red."

"I see," Carlyle said.

So did Erin. This was Veronica Blackburn's replacement. She couldn't prove it, but she was certain Pritchard had tortured and murdered Veronica, on Evan's orders, after the madam had gone behind Evan's back on a drug deal. Red Rafferty was saying he was a pimp. That was probably what Finnegan had meant with his reference to women and wine, though it was always tricky to know exactly what Finnegan was talking about. Red was an unusual nickname for a black-haired Irishman, but she didn't ask about it. She didn't think she wanted to know.

Caitlin Tierney, one of the Corner's waitresses, bustled in to take drink orders. Declan was a beer drinker. The rest of them went with whiskey, with the exception of Maggie, who Evan said would have mineral water.

"I think we're all here," Evan said once they had their drinks in front of them. "I don't expect our business will take long this evening. The first piece of it is already concluded. You've met Mr. Rafferty. He'll be assuming duties surrounding the employment and protection of the young ladies employed by my interests. He's had a great deal of experience in that field and I'm sure he'll do well."

"I won't let you down, boss," Rafferty said. He cracked his knuckles as he said it and gave Erin a casual, sidelong look that made her skin crawl. He probably didn't mean anything by it, but she still had to brace herself not to flinch. A man who made his living selling women as commodities would treat them the same way when he was off the clock. She saw crisscrossing scars on his knuckles. Those were the marks of a man who used his fists a lot, and Erin had the suspicion he was usually hitting people who couldn't hit back. She remembered Mickey Connor and reflected how some things just never changed.

"Next, I'd like to address the current situation regarding our Italian friends," Evan said.

The door flew open and banged against the wall, cutting him short. Pritchard moved so fast that Erin barely saw him. He was out of his chair, a sleek automatic pistol in his hand, before she'd even started to react. Rolf sprang to his feet, startled and alert. Even as she reached for her backup ankle gun, some disinterested part of Erin's brain told her, *watch out if you ever shoot it out with Snake, he's fast.*

A man stood in the doorway, his wild shock of bright red hair outlined by the hallway lights. His hands were empty, but his eyes twinkled with mischief.

"Starting without me, lads?" Corky Corcoran said. "And there I was thinking you'd be missing me."

Chapter 6

A thousand questions died behind Erin's lips, questions she couldn't ask. *What are you doing here? What did you do with Teresa Tommasino? Is she all right? Is she alive? Why didn't you warn me you were coming? Are you out of your goddamn mind? Why did I think I could trust you to do this one simple thing? Is this a damn game to you? How can you stand there grinning, like nothing happened?*

"We weren't expecting you, lad," Carlyle said. "I fear you've caught us all a bit wrong-footed. If you'd put that thing away, Mr. Pritchard, I'd be obliged."

Pritchard, eyes narrowed, slipped his gun back under his coat. His hand came out empty. Erin eased her hand away from her own gun.

"Mr. Corcoran," Evan said. "I hadn't heard you were back in town."

"Just arrived," Corky said breezily. He walked into the room, clapped Pritchard on the shoulder, circled the table, patted Carlyle's shoulder in a more personal, genuine way, slipped Carlyle's whiskey off the table with his other hand, gulped it down, bent over, and planted an impertinent kiss on Erin's cheek.

Erin, too stunned to react, just sat there and stared at him. Up close, she noticed some changes to the Irishman. He'd always been pale, like most redheads, but now his skin was tanned. Wherever he'd been, he'd spent a lot of time in the sun, and he'd probably been somewhere much warmer than New York. She also saw a ridged white line running along the side of his scalp, just above the ear. It was a scar, and she knew he hadn't had it the last time she'd seen him.

"What've I missed?" Corky asked, finding an empty seat between Carlyle and Finnegan. At that moment, Puzzle poked his little snout over the edge of the table. "Dear Lord, that's the sweetest wee beastie I've seen! You brought your pup along, Maggie?"

"Yes, thank you," Maggie said. She caressed the puppy's head. "He's been wonderful. It was so nice of you to get him for me."

"I'm glad he's been a joy and a comfort, love," Corky said. "And here's Red Rafferty, if I'm not mistaken. How's about you, lad?"

"I'm good," Rafferty said, and Erin was startled, but not exactly surprised, to see a smile on the pimp's brutal face. Almost everybody liked Corky, often in spite of themselves.

"But where's Vicky?" Corky asked, glancing around the table.

There was a brief, uncomfortable silence.

"Miss Blackburn suffered a misfortune a short while ago," Evan said. "She's no longer with us. Mr. Rafferty has assumed her position."

"Ah," Corky said, mustering a careless cheerfulness from some inner reserve. "Well, there's some things Vicky could do that I'd not want Red doing, but I suppose there's naught more to be said on the subject. I'm glad you didn't decide to replace me while I was out."

"Where did you go, anyway?" Rafferty asked. "I've heard a couple different things."

"I've been exploring business possibilities," Corky said. "Networking, you ken. Out California way."

"What sort of possibilities?" Rafferty pressed.

"Nothing that concerns a lad of your proclivities," Corky said. "I'd just as soon discuss it with Evan before bringing my thoughts before the committee."

"Enquiring for the rogue, said me Connaught brogue, wasn't much in vogue on the rocky road to Dublin," Finnegan said.

"Still cracked in the head, I see," Corky said cheerfully.

"I became insane, with long intervals of horrible sanity," Finnegan replied.

"Who said that?" Corky asked.

"I did, just now," Finnegan said. "Didn't I? Or did I just think it?"

"I thought you were quoting."

"Every word that's been spoken has been spoken before, and better, by other men," Finnegan said.

"Ah, I've missed this sorry lot of scunners," Corky said. "But I'm interrupting. Please, pretend I'm not here. You'll not even notice me."

"I doubt that," Carlyle said with a smile. "My whiskey seems to have vanished, for one thing."

"If I see it, you'll be the first to know," Corky replied. "It seems drinks and colleagues have a habit of vanishing."

"As I was saying," Evan said, "our Italian friends are experiencing a certain amount of turmoil. This gives us an opportunity for expansion."

"Didn't we just get done fighting with those lads?" Carlyle asked mildly.

"Vincenzo Moreno was a formidable opponent," Evan said. "But with him out of the way, the Lucarellis don't have anyone else of his caliber. Valentino Vitelli is the best of them and he's an old man. He doesn't have the stomach to resist."

Erin wasn't at all sure Evan was right about that. Vitelli might be old, but he was a tough, ruthless street hood from Brooklyn. He wouldn't go down easily, and certainly not without a fight.

"The Oil Man got clipped?" Corky asked, raising his eyebrows. "Now that's a bit of news and no mistake."

"Where the hell have you been, Corky?" Rafferty asked. "It was all over the news."

"I've not been paying attention to the telly," Corky said. "Nothing on it but thieves, liars, and politicians. But I'm repeating myself."

"What is it you're planning?" Carlyle asked. "A full-scale war?"

"Nothing like that," Evan said, shaking his head. "We've been weakened the past few months too. That's why we need to expand. Otherwise we'll get swallowed up by someone else, probably those Colombian cutthroats, or maybe one of the other Mafia families. But in the meantime, we don't have the firepower to shoot it out on the street."

"I'm glad to hear it," Erin said. "My squad has enough work without these guys throwing any more of it my way."

That drew a chuckle from the group. Even Evan smiled.

"I was just thinking we should consider renegotiating our prior agreement with them," Evan said. "Specifically, control over imported pharmaceuticals."

"We're getting back into the narcotics business?" Corky asked.

"I'm considering all options," Evan said.

"Who'd be in charge of it?" Carlyle asked. "It's hardly something in my line, nor Corky's."

"Either Mr. Finnegan, or possibly Richard," Evan said.

"Richard who?" Corky asked.

Corky's question surprised Erin. Not the question itself; she'd been opening her mouth to ask the very same one. But Corky knew *everybody*. It was impossible Evan was suggesting someone Corky hadn't heard of. But then she caught the twinkle in Corky's eye and knew he was winding Evan up.

"Richard O'Malley," Evan said with a flicker of irritation. "My son."

"Oh," Corky said. "Of course. Terribly sorry."

Erin looked around at the other faces at the table. Rafferty, Carlyle, and even Finnegan showed confusion that mirrored her own. This was the first time Erin had ever heard Evan mention his son's name. Richard O'Malley was a nonentity. She couldn't recall him being involved in any part of the massive, sprawling investigation of the O'Malley organization.

"I thought Richard wasn't in the family business," she said.

Evan turned his icy eyes on her. "Why would you think that?" he asked.

"He's never been to any of the meetings I've been to," she said, refusing to be intimidated. "Nobody's ever talked about him. He's not here now, is he?"

"That's true," Evan said, some of the chill dropping away from his stare. "I've been keeping Richard on the fringes of the business. But I think he may be ready for a little more responsibility. It's only a possibility at this stage, but if he does come in, I trust you'll all make him feel welcome."

"Of course," Carlyle said.

"All part of the family," Corky said. "The more, the merrier."

"Your squad recently helped recover a sizable shipment, unless I'm mistaken," Evan said abruptly, his attention snapping back to Erin.

"You mean the plane in Jamaica Bay?" Erin replied.

"Just so," Evan said. "What happened to that product?"

"The plane came down in the One Hundred's AOS," Erin said. "They would've checked it into Evidence down in Brooklyn."

"Is that accessible?" Evan asked.

Erin blinked. "I don't know," she said. "I could check."

"Please do."

She knew why he was asking. Six kilos of coke would prime the pump nicely to help restart the O'Malley narcotics engine. All she had to do was smuggle it out of a police evidence locker. The thought was horrifying, except for the knowledge that she'd just gotten Evan O'Malley on tape, asking her about the possibility of doing it. That was a very valuable recording, one more bar on the cage they'd built for him.

"I'll look into it," she said.

"I think that concludes our immediate business," Evan said, standing up. "The rest of you are free to do as you will, of course, but I'll say goodnight now."

Corky paid no attention. He was trying to coax Puzzle up onto the card table. Maggie was smiling and—Erin could hardly believe it—*giggling* while she tried to restrain the squirming puppy.

"Miss Callahan," Evan said quietly. "If you're quite ready?"

"Yes, of course," Maggie said, reverting at once to her usual mousy shyness.

"Be seeing you," Pritchard rasped. His voice made it ambiguous whether he was saying goodbye or making a threat.

"Have you ever considered how useless eyes in the back of your head would be?" Finnegan said to him. "You couldn't see a thing; your hair would always get in the way."

"Goodnight, lads," Carlyle said, getting to his feet. "Miss Callahan. Always a pleasure."

Erin waited as long as she could after the door closed behind the O'Malleys, leaving just her, Carlyle, Corky, and Rolf in the room. She turned off the microphone sewn into her underwire and saw Carlyle straighten his tie, which meant he was doing the same to his own recorder. Then she exploded.

Corky saw her coming, but she had him cornered with nowhere to hide. She grabbed his shoulders and pushed him against the wall, setting her face inches from his.

"What in God's name happened?" she demanded. "What are you doing back? Why didn't you call? And what the hell happened to your head?"

Corky's smile was rueful. "Things got a mite out of hand," he said. "I can explain."

"Is Teresa alive?"

"She's the picture of bleeding health, last I saw of her."

"The last you saw of her!" Erin echoed angrily. "You promised to look after her! To keep her safe!"

Carlyle put a hand on Erin's arm. She ignored him. Rolf watched the confrontation, ready to intervene with his teeth if it became necessary. The dog's hackles were raised. The Shepherd could feel the heightened emotion in the room and it was making him edgy.

"That's why I'm here," Corky said quietly. "I was putting her in danger, so I did the only thing I could."

Erin let go of his shoulders, but she didn't back away. "Explain," she said between her teeth.

"We got away clean as a nun's conscience," Corky said. "Everything went precisely to plan. I took her out of the city, clear out of the state, and no one suspected a thing. We got along grand for a few days, getting to know one another on the road."

"I'll just bet you did," Erin growled. "I told you what would happen if you screwed around with her."

"It wasn't like that," Corky protested. "Terry's a fine lass, a good girl. But she'd had a bad scare and it took some time for her to calm down. Everything went well until Baton Rouge."

"Louisiana?" Erin asked.

"Aye. It was sheer bad luck, but didn't we run into one of the Lucarellis at a roadside diner."

"You're kidding," Erin said.

"I know," Corky said. "What are the bloody chances? The only good news was, he didn't know about Terry. But he recognized me."

"Who was it?" Carlyle asked sharply.

"Fishhook Lou Andreotti," Corky said.

Carlyle nodded. "Nasty piece of work, that one."

"Never heard of him," Erin said.

"You wouldn't have," Corky said. "He worked out of New Orleans. Anyway, we slipped out of the diner when I saw him, but too late. He made my car and managed to follow us."

"Wait a second," Erin said. "Why would he follow you? Why would he care?"

"Corky killed his brother a few years back," Carlyle said gently. "Left him face-down in the Gulf with a knife in his heart."

"Oh," Erin said. "Oh, shit."

"Just so," Corky said. "He followed us to a hotel further on. I'd stepped out to get some food. He broke into the room and accosted Terry."

"You said she wasn't hurt," Erin said.

"He didn't harm her," Corky said. "He wanted to use her as bait to get to me. I came back and we had a wee scuffle." He raised a hand to his head and ran his fingertips along the new scar.

"He did that to you?" Erin asked. "How?"

"Cargo hook," Corky said. "You didn't think they called him Fishhook on account of his angling hobby, did you? We made a run for it and wound up in a wee town on the west coast, I'd best not say which, and I got Terry settled in. I was meaning to stay with her, as God's my witness."

"Until the trial?" Erin asked.

"At least," Corky agreed.

Erin narrowed her eyes. "You were sleeping with her!" she snapped.

Corky didn't say anything, but he didn't have to. His face gave him away.

"God damn it!" Erin burst out. "That's the one thing I said *not* to do! She's a vulnerable woman, a civilian! She wasn't put there to be your... your plaything!"

"And I'm telling you, it wasn't like that!" Corky shot back. "That's not what happened!"

"So you *didn't* sleep with her?"

"Of course I did! But that's not the point!"

Erin punched him. She hadn't planned on doing it. Her hand moved pretty much on its own in a hard right cross to the cheek. Corky saw it coming and weaved his head as much as the confined space would allow. She still made contact, but it was a glancing blow.

"Erin!" Carlyle exclaimed.

Erin reversed her motion and brought her arm the other direction, aiming a backhand strike at Corky's other cheek. He caught her wrist with a hand that moved much faster than hers.

"I love her!" Corky said.

"I'll bet!" Erin spat. She strained against his grip. "Let go of me!"

"Are you going to hit me again?"

"Probably."

"Then I'll keep my hold, thanks all the same," Corky said. "Listen to me, Erin! This wasn't the plan. It wasn't what I intended. But it's the truth. I love her. I'll take a beating for my sins, Lord knows I deserve it, but not for this. You scarce know the lass. I got well acquainted with her."

Erin's mouth twisted angrily. She considered throwing a punch with her off-hand. "Well-acquainted!" she spat.

"Terry's the finest woman I've ever known," Corky went on in a near-whisper. "She's the only one who's ever truly seen the best in me. Damn it all, I wanted to stay with her more than anything on Earth. I'd have given it all up for her. Everything! New York, my livelihood, my bloody life if that's what it would have taken."

"So why are you here and she's not?" Erin demanded.

"Fishhook Lou," Corky said. "I'd taken a sideline while I was there, bringing in some income, keeping my hand in, you might say. Word got round and my description found its way to him. He'd not stopped looking, you ken. He made another try for us."

"Persistent blighter," Carlyle said. "Where's he now?"

"Under a rock where no one's likely to look for him," Corky said, and Erin flinched at the sudden coldness in his voice. His sparkling green eyes had gone flat and hard, like chips of jade, and she remembered what was too easy to forget about James Corcoran; he was a gangster. For all his cheer and high spirits, he could be a very dangerous man. He'd killed before, she didn't know how many times.

"Sounds like self-defense to me," Carlyle said, glancing at Erin.

"And it didn't happen in the United States," Corky said. "It's nothing for an American copper to fret over."

"Jesus Christ," Erin said. "You murdered a mobster?"

"Aren't you listening yet?" Corky retorted. "He was going to kill the both of us. He was maybe three seconds from doing for Terry when I got to him, and I had to run bloody fast to make it in time. He was a filthy gobshite who needed killing, and if you're waiting for me to apologize, you'll be waiting a long bloody time."

"What happened then?" Erin asked, trying to keep her voice calm and level. She almost succeeded.

"What do you think? I left Terry with plenty of money, a steady job, a house to live in, and food in the refrigerator. Then I got out of there." Corky let go of her arm and shook his head. He no longer looked hard and tough; now he just looked miserable. "I left her, because I was the reason she was in danger. The only place she was safe was away from me. Don't fear for her, Erin. She's fine. It's me who's lost."

"Holy crap," Erin said. "You're serious."

"Aye," Corky said. "That does happen, from time to time. I swear, Erin, I took the best care of her I could. She... she didn't want me to go. Begged me not to. I can get in touch with her by phone, but I'm not going to go to her, because I'll not be the cause of any more trouble for the lass. And if there's anything she needs, anything at all, I'll do it in a heartbeat. Up to and including taking bloody bullets for her, should it come to that."

Erin stared at him. He stared back. Neither of them moved for what felt like a very long time.

Then Erin stepped back and let her eyes slide away from his face. "Sorry I hit you," she muttered.

"I was expecting it," Corky said grimly. "I know what you think of me."

"I ought to know how to reach her," Erin said. "Now that she's alone, wherever she is. What if something happens to you?"

"I've a telephone number," he said. "I'll give it to you."

"Truce?" Carlyle inquired. "Are we all friends again?"

Erin nodded.

"I never stopped being your friend," Corky said.

"Except when you tried to sleep with my brother's wife," Erin reminded him.

Corky looked pained. "I swear, it'll never happen again."

"Damn right it won't. Because then I really will cut your nuts off. With scissors. Rusty ones."

"You were serious about that? I thought you were joking."

Erin just looked at him.

"I'm thinking we all need another drink," Carlyle said. "Something seems to have happened to mine. Corky, would you be a good lad and let Caitlin know we're needing a bit of refreshment?"

"Without hitting on her," Erin added.

"All that's behind me," Corky said. He walked out of the room.

"My God," Erin said to Carlyle. "He actually sounds like he means it."

Chapter 7

"You're quiet this morning," Vic said, half an hour into their drive.

"I've got some things on my mind," Erin said. "People can surprise you sometimes."

"Yeah. Sometimes they've got concealed weapons."

"Anyway, you're being quiet, too."

"I figure it's rude to talk through a mouthful of pork rinds."

"I can't believe you're eating those for breakfast."

"It's a survival thing," he said. "Zofia's on this whole health-food kick. I gotta sneak my junk food when she's not looking. You're not gonna squeal on me, are you?"

"I ain't no rat," Erin said, smiling.

"The dog likes them, anyway."

"Vic! Don't give Rolf pork rinds!"

"Why not? He scarfs them up like nobody's business. You sure you're feeding him enough?"

Rolf poked his head between the front seats and let his tongue hang out. He loved long car rides. He also loved pork rinds. Vic slipped him another one on the incorrect assumption Erin wouldn't notice.

"I shouldn't have let you bring snacks," Erin said.

Vic took a long pull at his Big Gulp of Mountain Dew. "And I shouldn't have let you put on this girlie music," he replied.

"You don't like Rachel Platten?" she asked. The chorus of "Fight Song" was playing in the background.

"She's okay, I guess. In small doses."

"I could say the same thing about you."

"I don't come in small doses."

"And that's my cue to change the subject," she said. "What do we know about Patience?"

"She's a teenage girl, so she's moody and unpredictable," he said. "According to the court filing, the Wilders owned a couple of horses and kept them at her family's riding stable. Did you ever want a pony?"

"I was a little girl once, Vic. Of course I wanted a pony. But they're not exactly practical in Queens and we couldn't afford one."

"You could've gone into the ten-foot cops," Vic said, using one of the nicknames of the NYPD Mounted Unit.

"I got Rolf instead. No regrets." She scratched the K-9 under the jowls. Rolf leaned against her and panted happily.

"Apparently, Wilder came out for a ride one sunny day," Vic went on. "Patience was working in the barn. He thought a little roll in the hay might be a fun way to end the ride."

"With a fourteen-year-old? Sheesh."

"Yeah, I know. Goddamn pedophiles. Anyway, the consent issue is a little murky."

"No it isn't," she said. "Statutory rape is statutory rape. A girl that young *can't* consent."

"Okay, okay," Vic said. "I'm on your side here, Erin. I think the son of a bitch should've been castrated with a pair of pliers. All I'm saying is, nobody said anything violent happened, and the girl might've gone along with it more or less willingly."

Erin rolled her eyes and gripped the steering wheel tightly. She was thinking about her niece, who'd be a teenager all too soon.

"The complaint got dropped long before it came to trial," Vic said. "The reason isn't listed; the family decided to walk away."

"I wonder why," Erin said.

"That's one of the things we're driving all this way to find out," he said. "Man, I haven't been this far from New York in years."

"I have," she said.

"Yeah, I remember. Last time you went out of town, you ended up shooting a woman in your own apartment as soon as you got back and your boyfriend ended up in the hospital."

"Don't remind me."

"You think this teeny-bopper sabotaged Wilder's plane? Out of revenge?"

"Maybe," Erin said.

"Would she even know how?"

"If she grew up on a farm, she probably knows her way around engines." Erin double-checked her GPS to make sure they were on the right road. They were westbound on I-78 across New Jersey. They'd hook north past Morristown to I-80 and follow it most of the way to their destination.

"And she knows all about horsepower," Vic said and snickered. "I guess sugar in the gas tank isn't exactly rocket science."

"There's the parachute, too," Erin said.

"Yeah," he said. "Stitched shut. That sure sounds like a girl to me."

"Some men know how to sew," she said. "Maybe none in this car, but they do exist."

"I can sew," Vic said. "Mom taught me. She said chicks dig a guy who can do domestic chores."

"Well, aren't you a man of hidden depths," she said. "But that wasn't what I was thinking about."

"Share your brilliant deductions, Sherlock."

"Does that make you Watson?"

"God, I hope not. The guy was a putz. But that'd mean Rolf is the Hound of the Baskervilles, right?"

"Vic, have you ever read *Sherlock Holmes*? Do you have any idea what they're actually about?"

"Saw the movie about that ghost dog. You could do it to Rolf. A little glow-in-the-dark paint and the bad guys would piss themselves."

"Anna puts bows in his fur sometimes. That's bad enough. I was just thinking, the killer had to know about the parachute."

"Of course," Vic said.

"Think about it, Vic. Your average pilot, if he's got engine trouble, does he jump out of the plane?"

Vic considered. "No," he said. "He tries to land it. If the engine goes, he does a dead-stick and glides it in."

"But Wilder jumped," Erin said. "And the killer knew he would. They were counting on it."

"Yeah," Vic said. "If he was a decent pilot, he would've had at least a chance of bringing it down in one piece. I wonder why he did jump."

"He was an adrenaline junkie," she said. "Besides, if the engine failed suddenly, he might've figured he had a better chance of surviving on the chute. I agree, it was reckless, but if it fit his personality, that means the killer had a pretty good idea how he'd behave."

"And that means it was somebody who knew him pretty well," Vic said. "Damn. That kind of wrecks my rival-drug-dealer theory."

"It still could be," she said. "It could've been an assassin who did his homework. He could've been following Wilder around, studying him."

"And practicing his needlework," Vic said. "That'd be one weird-ass Mob killer."

"Remember the last hitman we dealt with? He killed people with doorknobs and radiators."

"I don't like thinking about him. I still have bad dreams about falling off things, thanks to that asshole. Hey, you want any pork rinds?"

"No."

"Red vines?"

"Yuck."

"Diet Coke? I know you drink that, I've seen you. I got it especially for you."

"Yeah, sure. Just put one in the cup-holder. What else you got?"

Vic rummaged in the plastic bag at his feet. "Potato chips?"

"What flavor?"

"Potato flavored. What're they supposed to taste like?"

Erin sighed. "We've got another hour to go. Pass them over."

*　　*　　*

Goodspeed Farms was a quaint little stable nestled in the Pennsylvania hills. Erin reflected that they were about as far off the beaten path as it was possible to get. The trees and roofs were thick with fresh snow. Everything was white around them. Her feet sank two inches into the stuff as she got out of the Charger.

Rolf hopped down, thrust his muzzle into a snowbank, and snorted. Then he planted a shoulder, flopped onto his back, and started vigorously rolling, kicking his legs in the air.

"You figure anyone's home?" Vic asked.

Erin wordlessly pointed to the chimney of the nearby house. A plume of smoke drifted into the sky and she could smell a wood-burning fire.

"Right," Vic said. "Sheesh. It's not like we've got fireplaces in Manhattan. I didn't grow up in the Nineteenth friggin' Century."

The front door of the house swung open before they reached it. A gray-bearded man in a flannel shirt stood in the doorway, looking them over.

"Mr. Goodspeed?" Erin guessed.

"Wilbur Goodspeed," he said. "And who might you be, ma'am?"

"Erin O'Reilly, NYPD," she said, pulling up the hem of her jacket to show her shield. "This is Vic Neshenko. We'd like to talk with you and your daughter."

"New York, eh?" Mr. Goodspeed said. "You're a ways from home. Roads treat you all right? They get a bit slippery this time of year, and the plow's not as good as it ought to be."

"We made it okay," Erin said.

"That's good," he said. He considered them. "Well, since you came all this way, you might as well come in and set a bit, warm yourselves up. Prudence can put some cider on the stove."

"Thank you, sir," she said.

The house was rustic but warm and cozy, the furniture obviously hand-crafted, probably by Goodspeed himself. The detectives settled in by the fireplace. A pair of border collies that had been napping on the hearth got up to investigate Rolf, tails wagging. They quickly decided he was harmless and, after he patiently ignored the younger one's invitations to play, lay back down and ignored him.

"I'm guessing this is about Patience," Mr. Goodspeed sighed.

"Yes, sir," Erin said.

"I'd prayed we were done with all that," he said. "Is this really necessary?"

"Yes, sir. Something's happened with Arthur Wilder."

Mr. Goodspeed's pleasant, honest face hardened at the mention of the name. But he just nodded. "I'll fetch Patience. Half a moment, please."

While he was gone, his wife brought them mugs of hot cider, spiced with cinnamon. Erin and Vic gratefully accepted and sat sipping, hands wrapped around the warm ceramic, watching the fire.

"I could get used to this," Vic said. "Maybe I'll retire out here, assuming I live to retirement."

Wilbur Goodspeed came downstairs with a girl in tow. Patience was a brunette in a hand-knitted sweater, a pretty girl with a sprinkling of freckles on a round-cheeked face. She darted a quick glance at the detectives but mostly looked at her own feet.

"Patience, my name is Erin," Erin said, standing up. "This is Vic. We're with the New York Police Department. Can we talk to you for a few minutes?"

Patience looked at her father. Wilbur took her hand and squeezed it.

"Her mother and I will need to be present," he said.

"Of course," Erin said.

Prudence, Patience, and Wilbur sat together on their couch, Patience between her parents. Erin and Vic turned their chairs around to face them. Prudence was holding Patience's left hand, Wilbur her right. Erin was glad of the fire. It made the proceeding feel more homey and comfortable than this sort of interview usually was.

"I understand this may be difficult to talk about," she said. "But I need to ask you some questions about what happened with Arthur Wilder."

"I haven't seen Mr. Wilder in more than two years," Patience said quietly.

"You gave a statement to the police," Erin said, opening the folder she'd brought with them. "You said that on August Fifth two years ago, Mr. Wilder found you in your family's barn and propositioned you. When you refused, he forced himself on you. He was arrested and charged. However, two days later, you recanted your statement and the charges were dropped. He was released. Is that correct?"

Patience hesitated. "You're with the New York police, you said?" she asked.

"That's right," Erin said.

"Then what does this have to do with you? We're in Pennsylvania and that was two years ago."

"No statute of limitations on statutory rape," Vic said. "It could've been twenty years ago."

"I'm only sixteen," Patience said. "I wasn't even born twenty years ago."

"We're investigating Mr. Wilder," Erin said. "Anything you can tell us about him might help us figure things out."

Patience went pale. She lurched in her seat, and for a moment Erin thought she might pass out, or maybe throw up. "Oh God," the girl moaned.

Prudence clutched her daughter's hand. "What's the matter, dear?" the older woman asked. "Are you ill?"

"What did I do?" Patience suddenly cried out, jerking her hands free from her parents. "What did you make me do?"

Vic and Erin exchanged perplexed looks. Even Rolf raised his head from the warm hearth to give Patience a quizzical once-over.

"Patience, that's enough," Wilbur said, softly but sternly. "Get hold of yourself, girl."

Patience had tears in her eyes. "Who was it?" she asked Erin in a whisper.

"I don't understand," Erin said. "I'm sorry. What do you mean?"

"Who else?" Patience asked, getting the words out with obvious effort. "How many?"

"How many what?" Vic asked.

"How many others? How many girls in New York did... did he..."

Then Erin understood. "We don't know of any other girls Wilder mistreated," she said. "That's not why we're here."

Patience sniffled. "It's not?" she asked.

"Mr. Wilder's personal plane crashed last week," Erin said. "His body was recently found on the beach. He can't hurt anyone any longer."

"He's dead," Vic added unnecessarily.

"Dead?" Patience repeated.

"Yes," Erin said.

"Excuse me, ma'am," Wilbur said. "But what does this have to do with my daughter?"

"Where were you eight days ago?" Vic asked.

"I was here," Patience said. "All day."

"Can anyone vouch for that?" Erin asked.

"I can," Prudence said.

"So can I," Wilbur said.

"You were here the whole day?" Erin pressed. "Did you leave at any point?"

"I took Star out for a trail ride," Patience said.

"Can anybody vouch for you?" Vic asked.

"Only Star," Patience said, and there was a light in her eyes that hadn't been there before. "He's a six-year-old gelding, a Morgan. He's my beautiful boy."

"How long was the ride?" Erin asked.

"Five hours, I suppose."

"Have you had any communication with Mr. Wilder since the incident?"

Patience hesitated again. She looked at her father.

"He hasn't been here," Wilbur said. "We kicked him off the property. He's not welcome here."

"That wasn't quite what I asked, sir," Erin said. She gave Patience a calm, long stare. "Is there something you want to tell me?"

"I sent him a text message," Patience said in a low voice.

"When?" Erin asked.

"A couple of weeks ago."

"Had you been in contact with him before that?"

"No. I've... I've been talking with my... therapist. Working through things. She says..." Patience wouldn't meet Erin's eye. "She says I need to forgive myself."

"Patience did nothing wrong," Wilbur said. "Absolutely nothing. That... *man* is the one who ought to be ashamed."

"No, Dad," Patience said. "I needed to forgive him, for what he did. This was for me, for my healing. I couldn't hold on to that hurt."

"Can I see the text, please?" Erin asked.

"Of course," Patience said. She reached into her back pocket.

"Hold it," Wilbur said. "Don't you need a warrant for that?"

"Why would we need one?" Vic asked. "Are you hiding something?"

"I don't have anything to hide," Patience said. She swiped her finger across the screen and quickly brought up her message history. She held it up for Erin to see. The message on the screen read:

Mr. Wilder, what you did hurt me very badly. I can't forget, but through God's goodness I can find it in my heart to forgive you. Someday soon you will know how wrong you were, and I pray you will be able to ask God for His forgiveness. I will never see you again. This is the last you will hear from me. Bless you.

"Patience," Erin said. "Why did you drop the charges?"

"I didn't want to do any of it," Patience said. New tears filled her eyes. "I was so ashamed. Of all of it. If I'd gone to court, I would have had to tell it to all of them... to strangers. And I was trying to be friendly. Maybe I... maybe I led him on, or teased him, or... or something."

"This wasn't your fault," Wilbur said. He glared at Erin. "You know what would have happened. Some lawyer in a fancy suit would have stood in front of her and accused my daughter of being a slut! You know what happens, you've seen it. Tell me I'm wrong."

Erin sighed. "Doing the right thing is often really hard," she said. "I know it wasn't an easy situation."

"He was rich," Wilbur went on. "A man like that can buy anything. Justice is for sale in this country, just like everything else. Why should some rich lawyer get richer off him when—"

He cut himself short, but he'd already said too much. "When the money could go to you instead?" Vic asked, eyes gleaming. "How much did he give you?"

"If you think I'd sell my daughter, sir, you can leave this house this minute," Wilbur said angrily.

"It went into a trust," Prudence said in a low voice. "For Patience, when she turns eighteen. It's not ours, we can't touch it or spend it. How could we?"

"How much?" Erin asked gently.

"One hundred thousand dollars," Prudence said.

"Dad didn't want to," Patience said. "But he also didn't want me to be..."

"'And Joseph her husband, being a righteous man, and not willing to make her a public example, was minded to put her away privily,'" Wilbur quoted. "Matthew 1:19."

"You say you're not ashamed of her," Erin said, speaking slowly and thickly. She was having trouble talking around the sudden lump in her throat. "But you are. You wanted to keep the whole thing quiet."

"Of course I did," Wilbur said. "Why would I want to put my little girl through that? She'd already been humiliated. It would happen again. That evil man would never have gone to jail over this. Never. This was the only way he'd pay for it at all. His sin will pay for my daughter's education. She'll go to college, any school she wants to get into. It may have been the Devil's money, but it's in God's hands now."

"I didn't want his money," Patience said. "But what was I supposed to do?"

Chapter 8

"I'll tell you what she was supposed to do," Vic growled. "She was supposed to tell him to shove that money up his ass. Then she was supposed to help throw his money-stuffed ass in jail."

They were back in the Charger, starting the long drive back to Manhattan. Rolf was staring out the window at the unfamiliar rural scenery.

"It's not always that easy, Vic," Erin said. "She was in a tough situation."

"It just pisses me off that he got away with it by writing a goddamn check," Vic said.

"He didn't get away with it. He's in the morgue right now, with about two hundred broken bones."

"So you think she did it?"

Erin didn't answer right away. She concentrated on the road, steering carefully on the packed snow.

"Five hours unaccounted-for," he went on. "She could've gotten to a car and driven to the airport in two hours. I figure five minutes to dose the gas tank, half an hour to stitch up the parachute, another two hours back to the farm. Plenty of time."

"I know," she said. "But she doesn't seem like a murderer."

"I don't think she's out looking for more guys to kill," Vic said. "But that guy asked for it. Hell, he begged for it. If he raped her, the bastard had it coming."

"That's not really the point, is it, Vic? We don't decide if it's justified. That's up to the DA."

"I know. But he screwed a fourteen-year-old and bribed her family to get out of it!"

"And if that was our case, we'd arrest him," she said. "I'm not defending him! The more I learn about this guy, the more surprised I am that nobody killed him before now. But let's try to think like cops, not decent human beings. You're right about the timeline. The MO fits with what I'd expect from someone like Patience. And there's that text message."

"Yeah," he said. "Funny timing, don't you think? She sends that right before the mope takes his last jump. It's easy to say you forgive a guy when you're about to kill him."

"Nothing easier," she agreed. "Why hold a grudge against a dead man?"

"Hey Erin, New York is that way." Vic pointed to the left.

"We're not going back to New York yet."

"Where are we going?"

"South Jersey Regional Airport."

"I guess we might as well," he said. "I mean, it's only two hours out of our way, in a totally different state. What're you hoping to find?"

"I don't know," she said. "Maybe somebody saw something."

"This is a new one for me," he said. "Amish girl murders a guy by sabotaging an airplane."

"She's not Amish," Erin said. "Amish girls don't have cell phones."

"Okay, Quaker. Whatever. You gotta admit, they were rustic. Full of backwoods folksy charm."

"I don't think I want to take you out of the city again. You get weird."

"You know what she makes me think of? That Tom Petty song."

"I'm a detective, Vic, not a mind reader. Which one?"

Vic started singing. "She's a good girl, loves her mama; loves Jesus and America too. She's a good girl, she's crazy about Elvis; loves horses and her boyfriend too..."

"Okay, that's enough," Erin said. Her singing voice was terrible, but Vic's wasn't much better.

Vic wasn't listening. "And I'm free..." he sang, his voice breaking a little on the high note. "Free fallin'..."

"Time for some more Rachel Platten, I think," Erin said. "Shut up and stick some pork rinds in your noisy hole." She turned on the radio and turned it up loud.

* * *

"It ain't exactly JFK," was Vic's verdict on South Jersey Regional Airport.

"It's Jersey," Erin said. "What'd you expect?"

"It's nicer than I thought," he admitted.

She nodded. The little airport was ringed by woods and consisted of a handful of hangars, a café, and a small museum. The runway was tiny by New York standards, but plenty long for the single-engine propeller planes that populated the hangars.

"Start at the café?" she suggested.

"I could use a burger," he said. "We missed lunch and those pork rinds could use some company."

The café was almost deserted. A pair of guys in greasy coveralls sat by the wall, eating sandwiches. A middle-aged waitress with stringy brown hair and tired brown eyes gave the detectives a smile.

"How's it going?" she said. She took in Rolf with his K-9 vest. "You guys cops?"

"NYPD," Erin said.

"You're a ways from home," the waitress said. "Get lost on the way to Philly, or what?"

"Just looking to grab lunch," Erin said. "What's good?"

"Everything on the menu, hon. Just take a seat anywhere and I'll be right with you."

They slid into the booth adjacent to the workmen. Rolf settled under the table with a sigh. Vic examined the menu.

"They don't have vodka," he complained.

"Or whiskey," she said. "This is a diner, not a bar. Besides, we're on duty. Deal."

They ordered hamburgers and fries. Vic got a Mountain Dew, Erin a Diet Coke. Then they sat and waited, casually listening to the other two customers.

"So this guy wants to know if I can fix it," one of the men was saying. "I told him sure, for ten grand. And it's worth it, because otherwise we're gonna have to replace the whole engine, and if that lets go at fifteen thousand feet, he's gonna have a big friggin' problem."

"Excuse me," Erin said, turning in her seat. "Do you gentlemen work at South Jersey Regional?"

"Yeah," the other guy said, giving her an appreciative once-over. "Bob Donahue. You looking for a tune-up?"

"He can get your engine running real smooth," the other mechanic said with a grin.

Erin didn't bother to respond to that. "Detective O'Reilly," she said, flashing her shield. "Do either of you guys know Arthur Wilder?"

"Wilder? Sure," Donahue said. "Hangar Three. Beechcraft. Pretty decent plane."

"Did you hear what happened to it?" Vic asked.

"Yeah," Donahue said. "A couple guys from the Safety Board were out here a few days ago, asking some questions."

"Pricks," the other mechanic added.

"Warner and Brickles?" Erin guessed. "A big guy and a little guy?"

"Yeah, that was them," Donahue said. "You know 'em?"

"We've met," she said. "What'd you tell them?"

"Same thing I'll tell you," Donahue said. "That plane was running fine. I checked it out the night before. Went through the whole checklist, just like Mr. Wilder told me to. Tested the engine and everything. That baby was purring."

"You ran the engine the night before the flight?" Erin repeated.

"Just said that, didn't I?" Donahue said. "And I'm telling you, that was a good plane, in good working order. I'd bet my license on it."

"Did you see anybody unusual hanging around the airport?" she asked.

"How do you mean?" Donahue asked.

"Anyone acting suspicious," Vic said. "Sneaking around, maybe being somewhere they shouldn't be?"

"This ain't exactly an Air Force base, buddy," Donahue said. "Take a look around. You see guards? Barbed wire? The hangars got doors, and the doors got locks, and that's about it. We got casual pilots here, enthusiasts. Air show guys, stunt pilots, whatever. People come and go."

"There was the babe," the other mechanic said.

"What babe?" Vic and Erin asked in unison.

"There was this chick hanging around Hangar Three that evening," Donahue said. "Ed and me, we both saw her. Figured she was one of Wilder's girlfriends."

"You'd be Ed?" Erin asked the other mechanic.

"Ed Kowalski," the man said, giving her a grin that showed a missing front tooth.

"What was this woman doing?" Erin asked.

"Not much," Donahue said. "Looking at stuff, poking around."

"Did you talk to her?" Erin asked.

"Nah, I was working," Donahue said. "Cleaning out a manifold in Hangar Two, across the way. Pulling some overtime."

"What'd she look like?" Vic asked.

"Not bad," Donahue said. "I'd say a seven easy, maybe an eight."

"Eight for sure," Kowalski said. "Great ass."

"And her face?" Erin asked.

"Didn't get a great look at that," Donahue said. "But she had on real tight pants, and she was bending over when I looked, and I gotta say, damn! That was one fine backside. You can write that down."

"Thanks," Erin said dryly. "Anything else you can tell me?"

"She was holding a bag of something," Kowalski said. "Couldn't tell what. And she had on a hat."

"What kind?" Erin asked.

"Stocking cap. With one of those white fuzzy dangly-balls on it."

"Long hair?" she asked. "Short? What color?"

"Dark hair," Donahue said. "Maybe shoulder-length?"

"About," Kowalski agreed.

"And a sweater," Donahue added.

"Yeah," Kowalski said. "She had a pair of puppies."

"Puppies?" Erin repeated, glancing at Rolf.

"Yeah, sweater puppies," Kowalski said with a leer.

The waitress arrived with their food, mercifully interrupting the conversation.

"Just one more thing," Erin said. "Can you tell me which one is Hangar Three?"

* * *

"We've got this basically solved," Vic said after lunch, as they walked across the runway toward Hangar Three. Rolf frisked at Erin's side, tongue hanging out.

"How do you figure?" Erin asked.

"We just need to put out a BOLO for a woman with a great ass and a pair of fine sweater puppies," he said with a straight face.

"This is the problem with male eyewitnesses," Erin said.

"Would you say Patience Goodspeed was an eight?" he asked.

"I don't rate suspects on a numeric scale of attractiveness, and neither should you."

"How about Regina Wilder?"

"Vic..."

"I figure you're a good baseline. Probably a seven for most guys. But if you cleaned up, put on some makeup, I think you could be a nine."

"You're screwing with me."

He grinned. "Constantly."

Vic stopped grinning when they got to the hangar. Erin knew why. The place was totally unsecured. When she put on a pair of disposable gloves and tried the small door on the side of the building, it swung open.

"No police tape," Vic said. "No padlocks. Not a single friggin' thing."

"We won't get any evidence from here," she said. "Anybody could've come and gone in the past week. We have to assume the whole thing is contaminated."

"It's not like we brought a CSU van with us anyway," he said. "But you'd think local law would've done *something*."

"Warner and Brickles have been through," she said. "Let's hope they found whatever was here."

"They're not cops," he said. "All they were looking for was mechanical crap that would explain the crash."

Erin nodded. She began walking the hangar floor, keeping her eyes on the concrete underfoot. She guessed the Beechcraft had been parked in the big open space in the middle, so she spiraled in slowly. She smelled engine grease and faint gas fumes. The place was neat and well-kept, the floor clean. Shelves along the wall held tools, spare parts, and clothing.

"Hey Erin," Vic said. "Take a look at this."

"Just a second," she said. She was nearly done with her scan.

"Take your time," he said. "I'll just wait here with my important clues."

Something crunched under Erin's shoe. She stopped. Then she backed up a step and dropped to one knee. Rolf poked his snout next to her face, wondering what she'd found that was so interesting. On the concrete lay a faint dusting of small crystals.

"I've got something too," she said, taking an evidence bag out of her hip pocket. She carefully brushed some of the crystals into the bag.

"What is it?" he asked. He was over by the equipment shelves, hands on his hips.

"I'm pretty sure it's spilled sugar," she said.

"You could taste some of it," he suggested. "Like the cops on TV."

"That's if they're testing drugs," she said.

"Because that's so much safer," he said.

"I'm not licking the hangar floor."

"Of course not. You've got your K-9 for that."

Rolf tilted his head and gave her a quizzical look.

"Okay," Erin said, standing up. "What've you got that's so important?"

"Spare parachutes," he said, cocking a thumb at the nearest shelf. Three backpacks and harnesses were lined up, ready to go.

Erin joined Vic. "They look the same as the one on Wilder," she said.

"Identical," he said. "Icarus Canopies Kraken model."

"You made that up," she said. "Icarus?"

"I did not. Look!" He pointed to the logo on the nearest chute.

"What marketing genius decided to name a parachute after a guy who's famous for falling to his death?" Erin wondered.

Vic snorted. "I never thought of that," he said. "I should've gotten a classical education, learned Greek and Latin and all that mythology crap. Instead I went to community college and acquired marketable skills. What was I thinking?"

Erin peered at the parachute. "Do you suppose Wilder had his chute already on the plane?" she said. "Or did he grab one of these?"

"And if he did, how'd our killer know which one he'd grab?" Vic replied. "My thoughts exactly."

"They didn't know," she said. "They couldn't have known. Which means either they got lucky, or the rest of these are also sabotaged."

Sure enough, Erin saw the little black stitches in the nearest pack. "There," she said.

"Yeah," Vic said. "Anybody jumps with one of these, he's gonna end up like Icarus all right. Hey, is Icarus the one who killed his dad and married his mom?"

"I think that was Oedipus."

"That's right," he said. "Then he fell off a cliff and made an Oedipus Wreck at the bottom."

"Oh my God," Erin said.

"What?"

"You're really going to be a dad. That was your first dad joke."

"You like it? I've been practicing."

"You need to practice some more. Preferably when I'm not around. Let's get these tagged and loaded into the Charger. I was wrong. We found some evidence after all."

"This is our crime scene all right," he said. "Our girl sugared the gas and stitched up the chutes. Sounds like a keeper. My mom always said a nice girl knows how to cook and sew."

"And murder. Now we just need to figure out who our girl is."

"Could be Patience," he said. "Or Regina. Or a female Mob assassin, maybe working for the drug cartels. I've heard there might be one or two of those out there."

Erin made a face. Both of them were thinking of Siobhan Finneran, who'd been a very dangerous female assassin indeed.

"Anything else we want to do here?" he asked.

"No. Let's get back to the big city."

"And the hell out of Jersey," Vic said.

Chapter 9

"You had a productive trip," Webb said, examining the updated whiteboard in Major Crimes a little after three. "We've got a solid suspect, new evidence, and a compelling narrative."

"Yeah," Vic said. "Maybe we can wrap it up before the next commercial break."

"The main thing I'm wondering is, why now?" Webb asked. "Why would she wait two years to kill the man who assaulted her?"

"Well, she is named Patience," Vic said. "I've heard that's a virtue. Maybe she was waiting for the heat to die down."

"It's true, if she'd offed Wilder right after the court case, she's the first person everybody would have looked at," Webb said. "But we found her anyway."

"There was the payoff for her college fund," Erin said. "Maybe she thought it was enough, but eventually realized she was still mad enough to kill him. But the main reason might've been that she had to wait until she was sixteen."

"What does that have to do with anything?" Webb said. Then he blinked. "Oh."

"Driver's license," Vic said, nodding. "She couldn't legally drive until recently."

"Here's what I don't get," Erin said. "When we first told her we were there about Wilder, she got upset."

"Like a guilty person would," Webb said.

"No," Erin said. "She acted guilty, but not because of anything she did."

"Right," Vic said. "She acted like she was guilty for what she hadn't done."

"Her first thought was that we were there about Wilder's sexual escapades," Erin said. "She acted like she felt responsible for other victims, because she hadn't pressed charges on her own behalf."

"An act?" Webb guessed.

"If so, it was a good one," Erin said.

"Try this on," Vic said. "Suppose our girl goes to therapy for a couple years and starts feeling better about herself. But then one day the thought hits her, what about the other girls? There've gotta be others. Rapists don't just target one girl. Now she's overcome with guilt. In a fit of remorse, she sabotages Wilder's plane and screws up his parachutes."

"I think, in all my years on the force, that's the first time I've ever heard of someone committing murder in a fit of remorse," Webb said. "Remorse usually comes after the murder, not before. But I suppose it's possible."

"Sloppy of her to send the text," Erin said.

"Even sloppier of her to show it to us," Vic said. "Unless she wants us to know she did it. But in that case, why not go all-in and confess? She seems like the type to fall on a grenade."

"You'd know all about falling on grenades, wouldn't you?" Erin replied.

"When are you gonna let that go?" he growled. "It's not like I'm some goddamn kamikaze pilot. I did that once. *Once!*"

"Most people who fall on grenades only do it once," Webb said. "That goes for kamikaze pilots, too. It's hard to kill yourself twice. And I'm not going to disregard incriminating evidence just because a suspect voluntarily shows it to us."

"When you put it that way, it sounds stupid," Vic muttered.

"That's the funny thing about stupid ideas," Webb said. "When you talk about them, they sound stupid."

"I'll start the extradition request," Vic said. "We can get it to Pennsylvania by the end of the day."

"Hold on," Webb said. "I don't think any of us believe Miss Goodspeed is about to murder anybody else. And she's not exactly a flight risk."

Vic snickered.

"What's so funny?" Webb asked.

"We're investigating a guy who died falling out of a plane," Vic said. "And you're talking about flight risks."

Webb held his poker face as long as he could. Then he chuckled. "Okay, you're right," he said. "That was pretty funny. But we don't have enough to charge her yet, so let's not jump the gun. We can be patient too. Good work, both of you."

"Thank you, sir," Erin said.

Rolf, beside her desk, sulked with his head between his paws. He hadn't gotten to do anything yet, and all he'd gotten was a car ride and a few pork rinds. All he really wanted was his Kong ball.

*   *   *

Erin stepped out of the office a little while later. She didn't want to make this call from inside a police station. She walked down the block to a coffee shop and found a table far enough away from other customers to avoid being overheard, but close enough so the buzz of conversation helped cover her voice. Then she took out her special burner cell and dialed.

"Hello," Phil Stachowski said. He'd promised he would always answer when she called, and so far he'd been a man of his word.

"Hey Phil," she said. "I'm okay."

"Glad to hear it. What's up?"

"We've got a new player in the O'Malley management."

"Oh? Who's that?"

"Declan Rafferty. Goes by Red. He's a pimp. Evan moved him into Veronica Blackburn's spot."

"Understood. You do know, what happened to her wasn't your fault."

"Of course not." Erin didn't even sound convincing to her own ears.

"I'm serious," Phil said. "Veronica destroyed herself. She was on a suicide course the moment she started dealing behind Evan's back. I wish we could've brought her in alive, but that wasn't your call."

Erin swallowed and said nothing. She still had bad dreams about the last time she'd seen Veronica, especially the ragged edge of desperation in the woman's voice and the naked fear in her eyes.

"What do you know about this Rafferty?" Phil asked.

"Not much. He runs street girls and he's a nasty-looking piece of work."

"He's in our files," Phil said, "but I didn't realize he was so high up in the organization. Do you think we have enough on him to take him off the street for a long time?"

"I don't know," Erin said. "I've been meaning to check him out with Vice."

"Be discreet."

"I know. I've been doing this a while, remember?"

"I remember. Don't get careless right before the finish line. Remember the tortoise and the hare. The moral of the story isn't persistence; the moral is, don't get cocky. Finish the race. There's plenty of time to celebrate after you've won."

"There's one other thing."

"What's that?"

"Evan wants me to grab six kilos of coke for him."

Phil laughed. "Is that all? That's only, what, a quarter of a million dollars' worth of drugs?"

"Something like that. The Long Island boys found it in a crashed propeller plane in Jamaica Bay. Evan asked me to snatch it out of Evidence."

"I thought the O'Malleys were out of the drug business."

"That was before the Oil Man got his throat cut. Now Evan's seeing an opportunity. I think he wants to expand back into Brooklyn."

"Okay. I don't see the problem."

"You don't see a problem putting six kees of coke on the street? I thought we were the good guys!"

"It'll take him some time to set up his distribution network. We're in the endgame, Erin. We're looking at a matter of weeks, not months. Evan's drug business isn't going to get off the ground. The only difference it'll make is to add another decade at his sentencing, and in the meantime, you'll look even better to the O'Malleys. Get him on tape talking about it. We'll arrange it. Then, when we sweep them up, we'll repossess the cocaine and that'll be the end of it."

"Okay," she said. "I hope you know what you're doing."

"I hope that every day," he said. "How're you holding up?"

"I'm fine."

"You always say that."

"It's always true."

"No, Erin, it isn't."

"It's true enough. I'll get through this. Later, Phil."

"Take care, Erin."

*   *   *

Erin had one more call to make before she went back to work. Normally, she would have waited until evening to call her dad, but she didn't want to talk about this from Carlyle's apartment. Sean O'Reilly was retired, so it didn't make much difference to him.

"O'Reilly," Sean said.

"Hey, Dad."

"Hey, kiddo. Everything all right?"

"That's a complicated question."

That wasn't what he'd expected her to say. "How do you mean?" he asked.

She took a deep breath. "I found out something," she said.

"Something bad?"

"I'm not sure."

He sighed. "Erin, if you called to get my advice, you should probably start by telling me what I need to know in order to give it."

"I've got an ethical dilemma," she said.

"Work or personal?"

"A little of both."

"I assume this is about your boyfriend," he said in flat, unamused tones. Sean had warmed up to Carlyle, but he'd never forgotten the Irishman's past.

"I made a mistake. I asked him a question I didn't want him to answer."

"Your mother always knew better than that when I was wearing the shield," Sean said. "Do you want me to guess, or are you going to tell me?"

"I asked how much money he had saved up."

"Why?"

Erin blinked. "What do you mean, why?"

"Why did you want to know? Did he propose?"

"No."

"Did you?"

"Dad! No!"

"Are you combining your finances?"

"Of course not."

"Then why did you ask?"

"Because I needed to know."

"But you didn't want to?"

Erin made a sound of frustration that made Rolf's head pop up in surprise. "I'm sick of secrets, Dad. I've been blindsided a few times, and every time, it hurts. If I'm going to have a future with him, we can't be hiding stuff from each other."

"Yeah, I can understand that," Sean said. "So what did he tell you?"

"What he always does; the truth."

"You say that like it's a bad thing."

"Dad, he's a millionaire."

"Really? I'm surprised."

"Why? Do you have any idea how much money's passed through his hands over the past twenty years?"

"I can imagine," he said dryly. "But as I'm sure you're aware, your average gangster doesn't save. They spend it as fast as it comes in. Most of them die flat broke. Some of them die *because* they owe money to the wrong people."

"And as I'm sure you're aware, Carlyle isn't your average gangster."

"How much does he have?"

"Four or five million, he said."

"Mother Mary," Sean said quietly. He whistled. "That's quite the nest egg he's sitting on."

"What should I do?" she asked.

"You're asking if you should report it as illegal assets?"

"Yeah, I guess."

"Is this a secure line?" Sean asked abruptly.

"It's my cell phone, Dad."

"So, no."

"Who'd be listening?"

"I think you'd know that better than I would," he said. "Do you want me to speak freely?"

Erin quickly considered. Nobody was listening in at the café. The background noise would play hell with any surveillance equipment. The only way anyone would be able to eavesdrop would be if her phone was tapped, and that would be something only Internal Affairs could do. If they were listening, she thought, she was already screwed, so what the hell.

"Go ahead," she said.

"He's got immunity for all past transgressions as part of his deal, right?"

"Right."

"So whatever crimes may have provided the money in question, the state's not going to prosecute him?"

"Right again."

"So from the point of view of the law, these ill-gotten gains don't exist?"

"I guess not."

"That takes care of the legal side of it, the work side. Now how about the personal side? How do you feel about it?"

"Weird. I never saw myself dating a rich guy, Dad. I'm no gold-digger."

"Of course you aren't. And you didn't know about his money when you started seeing him, so it's got nothing to do with your motivations. Are you worried it'll corrupt you?"

It was Erin's turn to sigh. "Maybe?"

"Did you ever hear the one about the nightclub owner and the priest?"

"You're telling a joke?"

"It's more like a parable. You want to hear it?"

"Sure."

"There's this church in this town, and it needs a new steeple. The priest stands up in front of the congregation and tells them the church needs ten thousand bucks for the construction. After Mass, a nightclub owner comes up to the priest. The club owner hands the priest an envelope. The priest looks inside and sees it's full of cash. Hundred-dollar bills. There's ten thousand dollars in it. The priest thanks the club owner and says he'll say a prayer for him.

"Another guy sees it happen. He goes up to the priest and says, 'Father, what gives? You gonna pay for our new steeple with that? That's the Devil's money!'

"The priest looks at him and says, 'I'd say the Devil's had it long enough. Let's see what the Lord can do with it.'"

"You're saying I'm doing God's work?" Erin asked. Her dad couldn't see her raised eyebrow, but he could hear it in her voice.

"I'm saying money isn't good or bad, kiddo," he said. "What matters is what you do with it. I never took a dirty dollar when I was on the Force, and neither have you."

"And I don't want to start now," she said.

"Look," Sean said. "I never wanted you seeing that guy, I made no secret of that. But he's been trying to make a go of things with you, and I'm pretty sure you love him."

"Yeah, Dad. I do. And he loves me."

"He loves you enough to leave behind the job that made him rich," he said. "He's risking his life to do right by you. He didn't have to tell you about the cash, either. He could've kept his mouth shut. He trusts you, and that's no small thing. And this isn't a payoff. You want my advice? Marriages and relationships break up over all sorts of stupid reasons, and money's one of them. Too little, or too much. Either way, it'd be a damn shame if that happened to you. So don't let the fact that it exists jam you up. See what you do with it. That'll tell you if it's a good thing or a bad one."

"Thanks, Dad."

"Forget about it," he said. "It's easy for me to talk about what to do with other people's money. Anything else on your mind?"

"Oh, the usual," she said. "Drug smuggling, rape, murder. Same old, same old."

"Some things never change," he said.

"Say hi to Mom for me, okay?"

"Will do."

"I love you, Dad."

"Love you too, kiddo."

Chapter 10

"Welcome back," Webb said.

"What'd I miss?" Erin asked.

"We had some Federal visitors," Vic said. "Tweedledee and Tweedledum."

"Warner and Brickles?" Erin guessed. "What'd they want?"

"They wanted to know if we'd solved the case yet," Vic said, rolling his eyes.

"They had some new information, too," Webb said. "Wilder didn't make a distress call to air-traffic control at JFK."

"That's not surprising," she said. "The guy was running drugs. The last thing he'd want would be first responders crawling all over his plane after a crash-landing."

"True," Webb said. "But ATC was tracking him."

"Obviously," Vic said. "Even before 9/11, you'd have had a hard time sneaking a plane into New York City. Don't give me that under-the-radar crap. Those guys know if there's extra seagulls flying around the docks."

"It looks like Wilder was trying to glide in," Webb said. "But his flight path got erratic. He was having trouble controlling the plane. It hit the ground at a pretty sharp angle. If it hadn't been cushioned by those little trees on the island, it would've been smashed all to hell."

"What does that tell us?" Erin asked. "We already knew his engine quit on him."

"That wouldn't mean he'd lose control," Vic said. "He still could've glided."

"Brickles said his rudder pedals weren't working," Webb said. "One of the cables broke."

"Man," Erin said. "What didn't go wrong for this guy?"

"They only just finished examining them," Webb said. "According to Brickles, the cable had been cut more than halfway through."

"It would've worked for a while," Vic said. "But the cable was fraying and unraveling, and our guy was probably putting some extra strain on the rudder once he was gliding, so that did the trick."

"That's got to be the same person that sabotaged his engine and parachute," Erin said.

"The girl with the bangin' bod in Hangar Three," Vic said.

Erin crinkled her nose. "That sounds like an X-rated *Hardy Boys* parody," she said.

Webb coughed. "That is not going on the whiteboard," he said. "How well does Patience Goodspeed know airplanes?"

Vic shrugged.

"I have no idea," Erin said. "She's a horse girl. I assume she knows her way around a tractor. She could definitely mess up the motor; sugar in the gas tank will wreck any engine. And she could fix the parachute. But I don't know about the rudder cables. How hard are those to get at?"

"I don't know much about planes," Vic said. "The NTSB guys seemed to think it was a pretty slick trick."

"She's still our top suspect," Webb said. "But I want to work the drug angle. Now, Agent Lorcas said Wilder was running product for the Lucarellis."

"What's left of them," Vic said.

"Do either of you have anyone who knows what's happening with them right now?"

"I might," Erin said.

"Me too," Vic said.

"You thinking the Street Narcotics guys?" Erin asked.

"Bobby the Blade," Vic said, nodding. "You?"

"I know a guy," she said.

*   *   *

"We're in the presence of greatness," Sergeant Logan said.

"Really?" Vic replied, looking over his shoulder. "Where?"

The Street Narcotics Enforcement Unit were in their office. At the moment, that meant they were curbside in Little Italy, standing near Officer Firelli's parked T-bird. The SNEU squad consisted of Paul Logan, Roberto Firelli, Zofia Piekarski, and Marek Landa. All of them were grinning at Erin, Vic, and Rolf.

"I don't see anybody much," Piekarski said. "Just a couple fancy gold shields with big egos, slumming it with us street cops."

"You know you love us," Vic said, and Erin saw the way his eyes lit up when he looked at Piekarski. The petite blonde was definitely looking a little wide around the midsection these days.

"The dog's good police, I guess," Piekarski allowed.

Firelli shook Erin's hand. He gave it a little squeeze and nodded to her.

"Good to see you, O'Reilly," he said.

"You too," she said. "How's Sandy doing?"

"She's good. She still has some dizzy spells, but the doc says they ought to pass. She says hi."

"Glad to hear it." Sandy Firelli had suffered a nasty knock on the head when a rogue NYPD detective had tried to kill her. Erin had helped Firelli save her life, and Firelli wasn't likely to forget it.

"How's things in the Five?" Vic asked.

"Like usual, only worse," Logan said.

"And the new guy?" Vic asked.

"Useless, obviously." Logan smacked Landa on the shoulder. "But we figure we'll keep him around. Somebody's got to make the coffee runs."

Landa grinned good-naturedly.

"So what do you guys need?" Logan went on.

"What makes you think we didn't just want to come shoot the shit with you?" Vic asked.

"Please," Logan said. "You work days, we're on nights. Your shift ended hours ago, we're just getting started. If you really expect me to believe you don't have anything better to do, you're dumber than you look, and that's biologically impossible."

"What've you heard from the Lucarellis this past week?" Erin asked, turning to Firelli.

"It's chaos," Firelli said. "Dario thinks we're gonna be picking up bodies all winter."

Dario D'Agostino was one of Firelli's informants, one of the rare breed of retired mobsters. He ran a small family movie theater in Little Italy and somehow managed to hear most of what happened in the ethnic enclave. For an ex-gangster, he made remarkably pleasant company.

"Did he hear anything about a missing coke shipment?" Erin asked.

"This'd be that plane that went down off Long Island?" Logan replied.

"That's the one," she said.

"Word is, Old Man Vitelli's shitting bricks about it," Firelli said. "With all the management shakeups, they're having trouble with cash flow. They can't absorb that kind of loss right now. These guys don't watch out, they're gonna have to get real jobs for a change, make an honest living just to pay the bills."

"That'll be the day," Logan said.

"Does Vitelli have any rivals?" Erin asked. "Anybody who might benefit from stopping that shipment?"

"It wouldn't have been anybody in the Family," Firelli said. "They wouldn't dare. Vitelli's gone hardcore ever since the Oil Man got clipped. With Vitelli's kid going on trial, and him trying to hold the Lucarellis together, he's on a hair trigger. Anyone screws with him this bad, he'll come down hard."

"We found a couple low-level Lucarellis in a dumpster night before last," Logan said. "Word on the street was they were going freelance and Vitelli heard about it."

"Sounds like he's scared and desperate," Erin said.

"Damn right he is," Firelli said. "I'd look at enemies outside the Family."

"One of the other Mafia organizations?" Erin guessed.

"Or the Colombians," Firelli said. "They got punched in the nose when they took on the O'Malleys last year, but I've heard they reorganized and they're back for round two. They've been nibbling at the Long Island drug trade."

"Could be the O'Malleys," Piekarski added. "They were out of the drug game for a while, but they might be making a comeback."

Erin said nothing. Evan O'Malley had told her that was pretty much his plan, but she didn't need to put that out on the street.

"Would the cartel have somebody who'd be able to sabotage a plane?" Erin asked.

"Absolutely," Logan said. "Are you kidding? Those guys have deep pockets and good connections. You think they knocked down that plane?"

"Somebody did," Vic said. "We're pretty sure it was a woman."

"Glad to see some equal representation," Piekarski said, grinning. "I gotta stand up for the sisterhood, even when they're murderous assholes."

"You heard anything about a female contract killer working for the cartel?" Erin asked.

Firelli shook his head. "But I wouldn't put it past them. Those guys will do anything."

"I'd love to stay and chat," Logan said. "But we've got to get rolling. We've got buy-and-busts to do."

"We're gonna have Landa do the buying," Piekarski said. "On account of him being so small and harmless."

"You're just glad you're not the littlest member of the squad anymore," Firelli said. Landa was muscular, but one of the shortest men Erin had ever met.

"I can bench-press you, Piekarski," Landa said. "Vest, sidearm, and all. Want to try me?"

"Maybe sometime my boyfriend's not around," Piekarski said, winking at Vic.

"You want to come along?" Logan asked. "Do some real police work?"

Erin was tempted, but she shook her head. "We need to keep working our leads," she said.

"You kids play nice," Vic said. "Don't have too much fun out there."

"There's no such thing as too much fun," Piekarski said. "On that subject, you gonna be awake when I'm done with my shift?"

"I'm a cop," Vic said. "I don't sleep."

* * *

"I feel like I've been up for a week," Vic said.

"Quit whining," Erin said. "It's only eight thirty. You've been awake for maybe twelve hours. My brother works twelve-hour shifts and he's up to his elbows in some poor bastard's guts the whole time."

"You ever think what a bad idea that is?" Vic replied. "If I'm lying on the table with a couple GSWs, the last thing I want my doc to be is tired. Why do they do that?"

"Beats me," she said. "I'm just saying, it's not that bad for us. Besides, you've got something to look forward to."

"Yeah? What?"

"Your booty call. Unless I'm totally off base, Zofia wants to see you in the morning."

"Oh yeah, that." A smile crossed Vic's face. "Where are we going now?"

"Lucky's restaurant. It's just down the way a couple blocks."

"Who's there?"

"Valentino Vitelli."

Vic stopped walking. "Hold it."

"What's the problem?"

"We're thinking about the same guy, right? The desperate, violent mobster who's knocking off his own guys?"

"That's him. I'm pretty sure we'll find him there. It's one of his main hangouts."

"In what possible world is it a good idea to lean on this guy right now?"

"It's fine. I know him."

Vic grabbed her by the arm and pulled her to one side, into a doorway. Rolf didn't like that one bit. The K-9's hackles bristled and he gave a warning rumble in his chest.

Erin twisted free of Vic. "What the hell?" she snapped.

"Listen," he said in a low voice. "You may think you're safe with these guys, but you're not."

"Vitelli thinks I'm on his side," she hissed.

"Because of that thing with his kid? You think he trusts you?"

"I'm not an idiot, Vic. Nobody trusts anybody in this business. But he believes I'm one of them."

"And you think that makes it *better*? He kills his own people! That's what these assholes *do*! The number-one cause of death of Mob guys is other Mob guys. If you think pretending to play by their rules makes you safe, you're out of your damn mind. Because when you play by their rules, you get killed. Remember Vinnie the Oil Man? Matthew Madonna? Vittorio Acerbo? Wonderbread McCrea, or whatever the hell his name was? There's been so many, I'm losing track."

"I'm not really a mobster, Vic."

"I know that and you know that, but he sure as hell doesn't! And if he did, he'd kill you just as dead!"

"Are you worried about me?"

"Damn right I am. You just run headfirst into this crap!"

"You're one to talk. I've seen you run into more dangerous situations than I can count!"

"So I know what I'm talking about! Jesus Christ, Firelli straight-up told us Vitelli's having guys whacked."

"Remember that Russian restaurant we went to? Remember when you threatened some Russian Mafia goons, just to get a reaction?"

"Yeah," he said sourly. "And I remember what happened afterwards. You wanna see my bullet scars? Are you trying to get yourself killed? Because this is one way to do it."

"I'm trying to solve the case."

"Five to one says it was the Goodspeed chick that whacked our guy and the Lucarellis didn't have jack shit to do with it."

"So what do you want to do? Arrest the farm girl because you're scared of the big-city mobster?"

"Who said anything about being scared? I'm being the voice of reason here."

They glared at each other. Five seconds turned into ten. Rolf watched them curiously. He didn't think they were going to start hitting each other, but you could never tell with humans.

Then Vic's mouth cracked into a smile. "Did you really just do that?" he said.

"Do what?" Erin felt herself trying to return the smile and resisted the impulse.

"You played the tough-guy card. Accused me of being scared. Tried to manipulate me like I was some poor mope in Interrogation trying to prove he's got the biggest dick in the room."

Erin lost her internal struggle and smiled back. "Did it work?"

"A little, yeah. But it's still a cheap shot."

"Look, Vic, I appreciate your concern. Really. It's actually kind of sweet. But this'll be fine. Vitelli will think I'm helping him. He's got no reason to come after me."

"These guys don't need a reason."

"That's where you're wrong. They're murderers, but they're not crazy. Yeah, Vitelli might try to take me out sometime, but he'd need a really good reason to clip a detective. He knows exactly what would happen if he did."

"Okay, okay. But if you think you're walking in there alone, you're the crazy one."

"I've got Rolf."

"I'm not talking about Rolf. I'll have your back."

"Okay. But Vitelli doesn't know you. He may get a little shy. If he does, and if I ask you to leave, you need to step away."

"Whatever you say, Mom."

"Call me that again and I'll kick your teeth down your throat."

Chapter 11

Some dimly-lit places were cozy and intimate. Lucky's was dark and sinister. Erin attributed most of that to the dozen sketchy-looking guys lounging at various tables, not eating anything. They were talking and playing cards, but mostly just hanging around. All of them turned to look at the detectives. Two or three slid their hands into their coats or under the tables.

"This is one big pile of parole violations," Vic said out of the side of his mouth. "How many outstanding warrants in this room, you think?"

"Doesn't matter," Erin replied in an undertone. "Not unless you want to come back with an ESU team. I think we're a little outgunned."

"These losers don't even know which end to point at us," Vic scoffed. But Erin felt his tension and knew, despite his bluster, he was primed for sudden action. His own coat hung open and she could see the butt of his Sig-Sauer within easy reach.

"I'm looking for Rudy," Erin said to the nearest goon, using Vitelli's Mob nickname. She tried to sound tough and unconcerned. Rolf helped, standing at her hip and sizing the guy up as if he was trying to decide just how much mobster he could fit in his mouth at one go.

The thug took his time about it, giving her a slow, appraising look, showing he wasn't scared of her. Then he planted his elbow on the tabletop, tilted his fist toward the ceiling, and extended his thumb toward the back of the restaurant.

Erin walked that way, keeping her eyes straight ahead. Being twitchy would only encourage the Mob guys. She knew Vic was watching her back, stalking two paces behind her and staring down every bad guy in the room, one after another.

The old mobster was at the back corner table, sharing it with another familiar face. Valentino's son Gabriel was unforgettable. The younger Vitelli was movie-star handsome, his black wavy hair perfectly coiffed, olive skin smooth and clean-shaven even at this late hour, full lips and eyelashes that stopped just short of feminine, and dark eyes that smoldered. He was polite, honorable, and a ruthless son of a bitch who'd carved up his fiancée with a butcher knife, for which crime he was currently awaiting trial.

"Well, this is a surprise," Valentino said, getting creakily to his feet. "Erin O'Reilly, living and breathing. It seems to me I oughta know you too, big boy, but I got no name coming to mind."

"Vic Neshenko," Vic said.

"Yeah, I saw you during the late unpleasantness," Valentino said. "Now that was one thing we wasn't expecting when we came to court, was it? Too bad it happened, but life goes on, right?"

"For most of us," Erin said.

"Sit down, sit down," Valentino said, gesturing to the other side of the table. "You're hungry, I bet. You won't have forgotten the pancakes, am I right? Never too late to eat breakfast. You can just say you're getting an early start on tomorrow."

"I'm good," Vic said.

"Forget about it," Valentino said. He turned to the waitress, who'd been hovering in the background. "Ricotta pancakes with strawberries for my friends here. And coffee for the young lady. What do you drink, Vic?"

"Vodka," Vic said. "But not when I'm working."

"They don't have vodka here, nohow," Valentino said. "Coffee?"

"Mountain Dew," Vic said, shooting Erin a sidelong look. He'd come half-expecting a gunfight and now he was having a late-night breakfast. The world was moving a little fast for Vic Neshenko and he was trying to keep up.

"You know my boy Gabriel," Valentino went on.

"Good to see you again, ma'am," Gabriel said, putting out a hand.

Erin took it. She'd spent some time with the Vitellis, so she wasn't shocked when the kid bent over her hand and brushed the back of it with his lips. Vic managed to swallow his derisive snort, but he couldn't quite suppress the roll of his eyes.

"Now, I'm assuming you're here on business," Valentino said. "*Chi dorme non piglia pesci*, we say in the old country. That means, the man who sleeps don't catch the fish. In other words, if you want it, you gotta work for it. So what can I do for you?"

"A plane went down a week ago," Erin said. "The pilot took a five-thousand-foot high dive into Jamaica Bay."

"Sorry to hear it," Valentino said. "It's a tough world out there."

"It was a guy named Arthur Wilder."

Valentino shrugged. "Can't say it rings a bell."

"He was carrying something you might be interested in," she said.

"Well, I wouldn't know nothing about that."

Erin smiled. Valentino's reply told her he knew exactly what Wilder's cargo had been. If he really hadn't known anything, he wouldn't have shut down the conversation topic before finding out what she was prepared to tell him.

"Of course you wouldn't," she said. "And you don't know Vic very well, either. I've been working with him a while now. We're partners. No secrets between us."

Valentino's gaze flicked back and forth between them. "I see," he said, drawing the obvious conclusion. If Erin was dirty, she was saying, Vic was too.

"He helped out with that thing at the hotel a while back," Erin said, praying Vic would play along.

"Now that's interesting," Valentino said. "What'd you say your name was, pal? Neshenko? What is that, Russian?"

"Yeah," Vic said.

"I'll remember that," Valentino said. "Now why would you think I'd know anything about this Wilder mook?"

"From what I hear, he had some cargo that was supposed to go to the Lucarellis," Erin said. "I know you didn't take his plane down; you had a very good reason not to. I was hoping you could tell me who might've wanted to get it done."

"Well, supposing, for a second, my people did have something coming in on this plane," Valentino said. "That something might've come from South America."

"Colombian coffee?" Erin guessed, raising a speculative eyebrow.

"Yeah, something like that," Valentino said. "Here's the thing. There's guys down in Colombia who don't want their coffee going to just anybody. So if there was a guy who'd been selling coffee to somebody his boss didn't want him to, that guy could get in some trouble."

"I can see how that could happen," she said.

"Unfortunately, these Colombian guys ain't exactly what you'd call friendly. They ain't the kind of guys you want doing business in your neighborhood. But I hear maybe they're looking for opportunities here. And you know what happens when these immigrant types show up. Next thing you know, they're tearing the neighborhood apart with gangs and all that crap."

"Tell me about it," Erin said.

"So if you're looking for guys who'd knock off a respectable American businessman, I'd say you oughta look at them," Valentino said. "Especially Alejandro and Dante Fuentes."

"Brothers?"

"Twin brothers. Real nasty pieces of work. I hear they're hanging around Brooklyn."

"Thanks," Erin said. "We'll look into it."

They were interrupted by the arrival of their food. Vic poked dubiously at the pancakes and took a small bite. Then he stabbed his fork into the stack of cakes and took a bigger one.

"Good, huh?" Valentino said. "You have some, it makes you want more. *L'appetito vien mangiando.*"

"What's that mean?" Vic asked.

"Appetite comes with eating," Valentino said. "Wet your beak a little, you'll want to get a good long drink. And that brings us to what you can do for me."

"What's that?" Erin asked.

"I assume whatever was on that plane has been grabbed by New York's Finest."

"That's a safe assumption."

"If that coffee were to find its way streetside, there's some people who'd be grateful."

Erin nearly choked on her pancakes. She bought time by swallowing as slowly as she could and chasing the mouthful with a sip of coffee.

"That's not an easy thing to do," she said.

"If it was easy, I'd ask someone else," Valentino said. "But I'm talking to the best. You've done some hard things for me and my boy here."

He patted Gabriel's arm. The younger Vitelli nodded.

"Just so we're clear," Erin said. "The pilot was your guy and he was carrying your cargo."

"Not mine personally," Valentino said.

"But he was delivering it to your people."

"To tell the truth, I wasn't sure what he was up to, and I was getting a little worried about him," Valentino said. "He wouldn't answer his phone."

"That's because he was feeding the fish," Vic said.

"No, before that," Valentino said. "He didn't answer the day before, neither. You know, guys in that line of work get pretty high strung. Sometimes they dip into their stash a little, fly a little higher, and next thing you know, you got a big problem. I figured something like that might've happened. So I appreciate you coming to me with this, Miss O'Reilly. We got a good working relationship. Are you enjoying your food?"

"Yeah, it's delicious," Erin said. That might have been true, but she was hardly tasting it.

"Good, good," Valentino said. "You gotta come by the house again. Milly would love to see you again. Let me know when you've cleared up this coffee business."

"You'll be the first," she said.

*   *   *

"Okay," Vic said. "What the hell was all that?"

Erin glanced over her shoulder. They'd rounded a corner and Lucky's was out of sight. There were a few pedestrians on the street, so she waited until they were out of earshot of any eavesdroppers.

"What do you mean?" she asked. "And keep your voice down."

"You pretty much told him I was dirty!" he said indignantly.

"You wanted in on this," she reminded him. "Would you rather he keep his mouth shut? Why do you care what a Mafioso thinks of you?"

"He's a scumbag."

"Of course he is. What's your point?"

He shook his head. "Okay, whatever. Too bad we didn't get a recording of that."

Erin gave him a sly smile. "Says who?" she replied. She'd triggered her hidden microphone before going in.

"You sly, sneaky bitch," Vic said in tones of profound admiration. "But that friggin' guy... can you believe his nerve? Complaining about immigrants bringing in crime? What does he call himself? What does he call the goddamn Mafia, for God's sake? They're the damn poster boys for that shit!"

"And the Irish brought gangs with them," Erin said. "So did the Russians. Hell, for all I know there were Puritan street gangs in Plymouth. Nothing's more American than crooks looking for new opportunities, and nothing's more American than being hypocrites about it to the next batch. You know why immigrant communities get targeted by organized crime."

"Because they aren't able to protect themselves," Vic said. "At least we got a couple names to run down. The Fuentes brothers. Never heard of them."

"They're probably recent arrivals," she said. "And they're definitely competition for the Lucarellis. Vitelli wants us to get rid of them for him."

"If he's expecting me to whack guys for him, he's gonna have a big surprise."

"He assumes you're working for me," Erin said. "Don't worry, if anybody gets a contract on these guys, it'll be me."

"And he wants you to get his drugs out of Evidence," Vic said. "Six kilos of coke. Then you can add 'drug dealer' to your resume alongside 'Mob assassin.' You're really moving up in the world."

"Yeah, that's a problem," she said.

"You bet it's a problem! They're never gonna let you waltz out of the One Hundred with their coke. And even if the Long Island cops are cool with it, you'd still need to get around that DEA guy."

"You don't know the half of it," she said grimly.

"It gets worse?!"

"Yeah. The O'Malleys already asked me to do the same thing."

Vic whistled. "Both gangs want the same drugs, huh?"

"Pretty much."

"And they think you're the girl to give them to 'em."

"Yeah."

"Doesn't the Bible say something about serving two masters?"

"I think it says you can't."

"Smart book. What are you gonna do?"

Erin shook her head. "I have no idea."

Chapter 12

"Sounds like you're on a tightrope," Phil Stachowski said over the phone.

"Yeah," Erin sighed. She and Vic had parted ways, Vic to get a little sleep and recharge before meeting up with Piekarski, Erin to continue her interminable day. She'd parked her car at the garage across from the Barley Corner and was now taking Rolf for a late-night walk while calling her handler.

"You haven't promised anything to anybody," he said.

"I said I'd try."

"A promise of effort isn't the same as a promise of results."

"True. And it's not like I even know if I'll be able to get the drugs released."

"About that," Phil said. "I spoke with Agent Lorcas at the DEA. He's agreed to release the drugs as long as the One Hundred's captain signs off on it."

Erin felt a rush of alarm. "Wait a second," she said. "You didn't tell him about me, did you?"

"Don't worry, Erin," he said. "I understand operational security. I didn't say a word about your arrangement with the O'Malleys. He thinks this is part of a local Narcotics op, designed to smoke out a Brooklyn drug ring. The DEA is willing to yield to the NYPD on jurisdiction. He was a lot more agreeable than I thought he'd be."

"That's awfully nice of him," she said. "What did he want in return?"

"Your cynicism is showing."

"Idealism's like concrete, Phil. It wears away over time. Cynicism's the rebar underneath."

"So idealism gives you your shape, but cynicism holds you together?"

"Something like that. And I can't help noticing you didn't answer the question."

"It's a favor between departments," Phil said with a shrug she could practically hear. "When the DEA needs something from us, they'll expect us to do it."

"In the meantime, the coke's available?"

"You'll coordinate with Lieutenant Overlin at the One Hundred. He's arranged it with his captain. With the DEA giving us cover, there shouldn't be any problem. You can pick it up—discreetly—any time during the dog watch."

Her heart sank. "Tonight?"

"That's right. Is that a problem?"

"Yeah, Phil. It's a big problem. I've been on the clock all day. I'm tired. Rolf's tired. But the main thing is, I don't have the handoff set up. You want me to carry a quarter-million dollars' worth of illegal drugs around with me in the trunk? And who am I giving the stuff to? O'Malley? Vitelli?"

"Your cover is that you're working for Evan O'Malley," Phil reminded her. "He takes precedence. The thing with the Lucarellis is a sideline."

"It was a sideline right until they started believing I'd do contracts for them," she said. "If I say no to Vitelli, what if he reminds me what happened to Teresa Tommasino?"

"He doesn't actually have leverage on you, Erin. He only thinks he does."

"And what the hell difference does that make? If I call his bluff, what happens then? What if he's not bluffing?"

"He's bluffing," Phil said. "He can't throw you under the bus without lying down in the road beside you. He won't turn you in anyway. You're too useful."

"So I make my deal with the O'Malleys?"

"I think you have to. The other point to consider is, the Lucarellis have their drug apparatus already functioning. If you put the coke in their hands, it'll be on the street in a matter of hours. We won't be able to control it or recover it. We'll have more time if you get it to Evan, and more chance it'll never hit the street at all."

She sighed again. "Okay, fine. How do I swing this?"

"I'll give you Agent Lorcas's number. You'll call him and have him meet you at the One Hundred. He'll accompany you while you go down to Evidence and sign the stuff out. You'll carry the coke and get it to Evan's people. I can't imagine Evan would take delivery in person."

"Of course not," she said. "He'd never stick his own neck out that far. But his son might."

"Richard?" Phil was surprised.

"Yeah. His dad's thinking of getting him into the family business, remember?"

"Yeah, but this the first I've heard of his direct involvement with anything. I hope you're right."

"Why?"

"Because that would let us sweep him up along with his old man when we shut Evan down. Right now, we haven't got a single thing we can tie Richard to. It's probably nothing; he's pretty ineffective, from everything I've heard about him. But I'd feel better if we got him. I don't like loose ends."

"I'll take care of it."

Erin hung up and looked down at Rolf. The K-9, unconcerned, was sniffing at the corner of the nearest building. Finding it acceptable, he cocked a leg and watered the brickwork.

"You got that right," she told him. "I wish I could just piss on this whole mess and walk away. But we're not done yet. Let's go talk to my boyfriend and get things moving on this end. Then we're going to Long Island. Want another car ride?"

Rolf's ears perked up. He knew the last two words she'd said, and his answer to that question was always "yes."

*   *   *

The first thing Erin saw when she stepped into the Barley Corner was one of the smallest men in the place. Corky Corcoran might be small, but standing on top of a table and leading a sing-along, he was hard to miss. He had a glass in his hand and a sparkle in his eye, and when he caught sight of Erin in the doorway, he hoisted the glass and winked at her as he started the last verse of his song.

"*I fear that old tyrant approaching,*
That cruel, remorseless old foe,
And I lift up me glass in his honor,
Take a drink with old Rosin the Beau!
Take a drink with old Rosin the Beau, me lads,
Take a drink with old Rosin the Beau.
And I lift up me glass in his honor,
Take a drink with old Rosin the Beau!"

Corky drained his glass and jumped down from the table amid cheers from the other patrons, landing nimbly on both feet. He threaded through the crowd to the bar, where Erin found him beside Carlyle.

"Evening, darling," Carlyle said, getting up to give her a kiss on the cheek. "All's well, I hope?"

"You could say that," she said. "I need to get a message to Evan, ASAP."

"Drink first," Corky said. "What're you having?"

"I can't, Corky," she said. "I'm working."

He shook his head sadly. "Time was, you could count on a copper to step into the pub on his rounds. What's the message?"

"I'll have what he wants," she said. "Tonight."

Carlyle raised an eyebrow. "Really?"

"Yeah. Everything's in order."

"I'll see that he hears about it at once. When are you wanting to make delivery to his lads?"

"It'll take me a couple hours," she said. "Let's say one AM?"

"Grand," Carlyle said. "Where'll you be?"

"I'm getting the stuff on Long Island," she said. "We might as well make the transfer down there. I don't want to hold it longer than I have to, and I know Evan's got people in Brooklyn."

He nodded. "I'll arrange it. Shall I call you with the location?"

"That'd be great."

"Do you anticipate trouble?"

She gave him a look. "I always anticipate trouble."

"I can send Ian along, if you'd like."

"I'd rather he not get mixed up in this," she said. "Besides, somebody needs to keep an eye on you."

"If you're certain," he said doubtfully.

"I'm going to be at a police station," she said. "And after that, it'll be your guys I'm working with. Sure, there's always some risk, but I don't think it'll be too bad. Better to play this low-key."

"As you wish, darling. Are you wanting anything to eat?"

"No thanks. I had pancakes earlier."

"Pancakes?"

"Ricotta pancakes," she said. "With strawberries. You ought to add them to the menu here. I have to get rolling now. I should be back by two."

"I'll wait up for you."

*   *   *

It wasn't paranoia that made Erin strap on her Kevlar vest before getting out of the car outside Precinct 100. It was half force of habit, half ordinary precaution. In her line of work, neglecting common-sense safety was almost the same as having a death wish. She didn't go skydiving, she didn't play Russian roulette, and she didn't go to meet drug dealers on unfamiliar ground without body armor.

The same went for Rolf. His tail started wagging as soon as he saw the K-9 vest. He knew what the armor meant; it meant work, and that meant the possibility of a foot chase and some bite work. He was more than ready.

She finished fastening the dog into his gear. Then she put on her jacket over the vest, reasoning it was best to keep a low profile. Evan's guys might not appreciate doing illegal business with a woman with POLICE stamped on her chest in big white letters. She absentmindedly put a hand on her belt, touching the grip of her Glock.

Then she laughed at herself. She was going into a police station, not a combat zone. The building was full of armed men and women who'd come running if she needed them. Shaking her head, she twitched Rolf's leash.

"*Fuss!*" she ordered. He trotted at her side into the building.

"O'Reilly!" a man called from her right. She spun, hand dropping instinctively toward her gun once more. She caught herself in time and recognized Lieutenant Overlin and Special Agent Lorcas.

"A little jumpy, aren't you?" Lorcas said with a thin smile. The DEA man looked tired. He had shadows under his eyes and lines on his face she didn't remember from the last time she'd seen him.

"Sorry," she said. "It's been a long day. Are you okay?"

"Me? I'm fine." Lorcas rubbed his eyes with one hand. "I've been working overtime and I think maybe I'm coming down with something. It's probably because of my daughter. She's not well right now. You have kids, O'Reilly?"

"Just Rolf," Erin said, nodding to the Shepherd.

"You're lucky," Lorcas said. "The little ones just tear you apart."

"Ain't that the truth," Overlin said. "I've got two of my own, and I swear I've been exposed to every cold germ in the Tri-State area. And that's not counting all the perps that sneeze and puke on me. It's a wonder any of us are still alive. You ready to take care of this, O'Reilly?"

"Ready when you are," Erin said.

Overlin led the way to the elevator and pushed the button for the second basement level. Erin suppressed the alarm that went through her when the elevator doors closed. Ian Thompson had put her off riding the damn things, with all his talk about ready-made kill-boxes. But if you were living in New York City, you could hardly avoid them.

"Where are you taking the stuff?" Lorcas asked.

"I'll find out once I've got it," she said. "What does it matter?"

Lorcas shrugged. "It doesn't," he said. "But it's a lot of coke. I'd like to have some idea where it's going. My boss is going to ask me."

"It's not his problem," she said. "It's mine."

"Of course," he said. "I didn't mean anything."

The elevator opened on a short hallway that led to Evidence. A reinforced mesh barrier kept the cops on one side and the evidence on the other. A bored-looking officer sat behind the counter on the far side of the mesh.

"Help you, Lieutenant?" she asked, recognizing Overlin.

"Hey, Stark," Overlin said. "I just need to sign out the stuff we brought in from that plane crash. I've got the forms here."

He slid the paperwork across the counter through the slot. Stark flipped through the forms.

"Says here I'm supposed to get the okay from DEA," she said.

"That's me," Lorcas said. He produced his ID and presented it.

"Okay," Stark said. "Sign here and here, initial here, here, and here."

"Bureaucracy," Overlin said with a smile. "Where'd we be without it? You need to sign this one, O'Reilly, for chain of custody."

"Got it," Erin said, waiting her turn for the pen.

Stark took the papers, double-checked them, and disappeared into the back room. She returned a short while later with six evidence bags, each one containing a kilo of fine white powder.

"Here you are," Stark said. She initialed the papers herself. "Have a good night, Lieutenant. Stay out of trouble."

Overlin produced a black duffel bag, into which he placed three times Erin's annual salary worth of controlled substances. He zipped up the bag and handed it to her.

"I'll walk you out," he said. "What's all this about, anyway?"

"Need-to-know stuff, sorry," Erin said.

"Cloaks, daggers, etcetera?" Overlin replied, laying a finger beside his nose and winking.

"Maybe you'll read about it in the papers once it's all over," she said.

They got back in the elevator and rode it up to the lobby. The Lieutenant and the DEA man flanked Erin, walking out into the parking lot.

"I've got it from here, guys," she said. "Thanks."

"You sure?" Lorcas said. "Have you got backup?"

"Right here," Erin said, patting Rolf's head.

"I could ride along," he said.

"Not a good idea," she said. "It'd spook my contacts."

"Relax, Agent," Overlin said. "This is Erin O'Reilly. Haven't you heard of her?"

"What should I have heard?" Lorcas asked.

"This is the cop who stopped the Civic Center bombing last year," Overlin said. "She caught the Heartbreaker Killer. She mowed down a bunch of Russian Mafia thugs in a gunfight. She killed Mickey Connor single-handed. She's a certified badass."

"Yeah, and I eat rusty nails for breakfast and shit bullets," Erin said, rolling her eyes. "Forget about it. I appreciate the help, guys. Have a good night."

She loaded Rolf into the back of the Charger, tossed the duffel bag into the passenger seat, and slid behind the wheel. As she drove away, she saw Lorcas watching her go.

"Goddamn babysitter," she muttered. Then she pulled out her phone. A text from an unknown number was waiting for her. It had an address on Rockaway Beach Boulevard, just down the road, and a time: 1 o'clock. She started that way. Then she paused, pulled over to the curb, and dialed Carlyle. She was feeling edgy and nervous and she didn't know why. She'd assumed the text was from Carlyle, or from another O'Malley, but did she know for sure?

"Evening," Carlyle said. "All's well?"

"Hey," she said. "I just wanted to double-check. I got an address, but I don't know who it's from."

"It's a church, aye?"

She took a second to pull up a map of Rockaway Beach. "Yeah," she said.

"That's the place. Two or three lads will meet you there, around back."

"Sheesh. You guys have no respect."

"This wasn't my doing, darling, and it's not how I'd handle it."

"I'm sorry. Your boss has no respect."

"That's better."

"Thanks. I'm on my way."

She hung up, shook her head to clear it, and started driving again.

Rockaway Beach was a long, slender finger of land shielding Jamaica Bay from the Atlantic Ocean. It was nicknamed the "Irish Riviera" on account of the large Irish immigrant population, so Erin had come out several times with her family as a girl. She'd gone snorkeling, looking for sunken ships off the coast, while her kid brother Tommy had caught waves with his surfboard. The beach had been hit hard a couple of years ago in the hurricane that had hammered Long Island, but the neighborhood had bounced back.

The tourist trade had mostly stopped for the winter and the streets were quiet this late at night. Erin drove past a few restaurants and bars that were still open, but the other buildings were dark and silent. She saw the church on her left and turned onto a side street. A space barely big enough for the Charger beckoned to her and she wiggled and jiggled the car into it. She checked the time. It was about quarter to one.

"We've got a few minutes to kill," she told Rolf. "I guess we shouldn't go to sleep."

Rolf poked his head through the window between the seats. He was fully awake and alert.

She didn't like sitting in the car. A cop in a parked vehicle was vulnerable, as had been demonstrated on more than one occasion when officers had been ambushed in their own cars. There were too many blind spots, too many ways to sneak up on her. Better to be on the street.

Erin opened her door and got out. She scanned the area and didn't see anybody suspicious. She took out the duffel bag and slung it over her shoulder. Then she popped Rolf's compartment. The K-9 jumped eagerly out to join her, prancing on his toes. He liked late-night work. They'd certainly done plenty of it in the old Patrol days.

"Let's go to church, kiddo," she told him.

Chapter 13

The church's side door was unlocked, which would have struck Erin as suspicious if she hadn't already been expecting to meet criminals inside. She eased the door open and stepped in. The place was very dark, the only light the red glow of the EXIT sign over her head. The door swung shut behind her and latched with a heavy metallic click.

She took out her pocket flashlight and flicked it on, panning the bright LED beam around the back hallway. The message hadn't indicated where in the church she was supposed to go, and she didn't know the layout, so she hesitated a moment.

"Sanctuary, I guess," she muttered. That would be somewhere on her left, to judge from the outside contours of the building. She started that direction. Rolf pranced beside her, perky and attentive. He had no idea what was going on, but that didn't bother him.

Deserted churches, like deserted hospitals, were creepy places. But Erin had gone into dozens of dark, empty buildings in her time on the Job. She wasn't scared. She was mainly conscious of a heightened sense of awareness, a slight tingling on the surface of her skin. She moved smoothly, keeping her weight balanced, ready to step quickly in any direction if anything unexpected happened. She wanted her gun in her hand, but that would send exactly the wrong message to the guys she'd come to see.

"Why couldn't we have done this at the Corner?" she wondered to Rolf. It made sense, she supposed. The Barley Corner was a known O'Malley hangout. It was entirely possible the DEA or FBI, or even some other branch of the NYPD, might have agents watching the place. That was the problem with undercover work; the whole point of it was that nobody knew what you were doing. She recalled the famous undercover FBI agent Joe Pistone, AKA Donny Brasco, who'd once found himself getting tailed by NYPD detectives who thought he was a genuine gangster. He'd freaked out because he hadn't known they were cops; he'd thought they were rival mobsters and he was about to get whacked.

The sanctuary was like the rest of the church: dark, empty, and silent. Erin, out of long Catholic habit, switched her flashlight to her leash hand, dipped the fingers of her right hand in the font, and crossed herself before entering. She and Rolf walked toward the altar, looking around and seeing nobody.

Was this the right place? It had to be. She'd double-checked the address. Carlyle had confirmed it was a church. She glanced at her watch. Still a few minutes before one. Maybe the O'Malley delivery boys just hadn't arrived yet. Mobsters weren't known for their punctuality.

Rolf stiffened, snout pointed toward the left side of the sanctuary, nostrils twitching. Erin pivoted and saw a small side door standing open. A trio of shadowy figures trooped into the room.

She brought the flashlight around. In its beam she saw two unfamiliar faces and one she recognized.

"Red," she said, feeling a rush of relief. She didn't like Declan Rafferty, but she knew he was one of Evan's guys, which meant she was in the right place after all and everything was going according to plan.

"Junkyard," Rafferty replied. "You got the stuff?" His wingmen were sticking close beside him, but they didn't seem too jumpy. Everything was going according to plan.

"Of course I do," Erin said. "All six kees." She hoped her concealed microphone was getting this.

"The boss was right about you," Rafferty said, coming toward her with a smile he probably thought looked friendly. "You get results."

"I was expecting Richard," Erin said.

"Little Dickie?" Rafferty snorted. "He couldn't wipe his own ass without Daddy's help. What, you really thought he was gonna have the narco business? You gotta have someone who knows the street handle something like that."

"Someone like you?" Erin asked.

"Why not? Hey, don't worry about none of that. I know Cars don't touch that side of things, so what do you care? You did us a solid, babe, and I won't forget it."

He came toward her, extending a hand. Erin slipped the bag off her shoulder. Rafferty took hold of the strap.

His eyes swiveled, focusing suddenly on something behind her. "Hey!" he exclaimed. "What are you—"

There was a thunderclap; a deafening, echoing roar. A massive blow slammed into Erin's back, right between the shoulder blades. Before she realized she was falling, the floor swung up to meet her. She went down on her stomach, the impact driving the breath out of her lungs in spite of her vest.

Somebody was shouting, above and to one side of her. Erin tried to move, but her body wasn't listening. She tried to suck in fresh air and couldn't. Her back was a maze of pain. There was another roar and someone started screaming.

A cold, wet snout prodded Erin's cheek. She had to get up, she knew that, but she had to breathe, too. With a desperate effort she gasped in a lungful of air that smelled of dust, old incense, and fresh blood. There were three rapid pops, like the corks getting yanked out of a row of champagne bottles.

Two roars came in quick succession, then one more. The screaming stopped. Erin recognized the sound at last. Someone was firing a shotgun. A body hit the ground beside her with a meaty thud.

She'd been shot in the back. That knowledge felt oddly disconnected from her, as if it had happened to someone else. Erin planted a hand and pushed, rolling to one side, trying to get out of the line of fire.

Rolf, standing over her, hopped sideways with her. His tail wagged anxiously. He wasn't sure what had just happened, but he knew his partner was hurt. He flattened his ears back and whined, nosing at her again.

Someone was coming down the aisle. Erin had dropped her flashlight. She couldn't see the gunman's face, could hardly see his silhouette. She fumbled at her belt and snatched out her Glock with a hand that was shaking with adrenaline, or maybe shock.

The gunman stooped and scooped up the duffel bag. He turned toward her, bag in one hand, shotgun in the other.

"Sorry," he said.

Erin squeezed off two shots. The Glock jumped in her hand. The muzzle flash in that dark room was terribly bright. In the flash she distinctly saw a face she knew.

Agent Lorcas? She thought it, but didn't have enough air in her lungs to speak. Lorcas stumbled back, spinning and running the way he'd come, beating feet for the exit.

She tried to sit up, failed, aimed between her own feet, and fired twice more in his general direction. She had no idea whether she'd hit him or not.

"*Fass!*" she gasped.

Rolf's hesitancy disappeared. He saw and smelled a running man and he'd been given his favorite command. He gave a joyful snarl and bounded after his target, a furry missile tipped with fangs.

He made it less than ten feet. Then his leash, still looped around Erin's wrist, brought him up short. His snarl turned into a yelp of surprise. The weight of the ninety-pound dog nearly wrenched Erin's arm out of its socket. Rolf's paws went up and he went under them. He turned a half-somersault and landed on his back, twisting and scrabbling back to his feet.

Erin gave a yank on the loop, managing to peel it over her hand, taking the outer layer of skin with it. Then Rolf was off and running, trailing the leash behind him, hurtling out of the sanctuary.

Erin tried to sit up again. This time she succeeded. Her back ached mercilessly, but she didn't feel any liquid soaking into her clothing. Shotgun pellets lacked the velocity to penetrate body armor, but she felt like a drummer had been practicing percussion on her spine.

"God," she said, half blasphemy, half prayer. She saw her flashlight a few feet away, its beam mostly blocked by a fallen body. She grabbed the light. The reek of blood and gunpowder filled her nose.

In the distance, Rolf started barking. That meant he hadn't caught his guy. He'd come up against an obstacle he couldn't handle, probably a closed door. Erin cursed inwardly. She wanted to be chasing Lorcas down, but with no immediate danger to anyone, her priority was to tend to the casualties around her.

Red Rafferty was the first man she got to. He'd taken a shotgun blast to the upper chest and his coat was riddled with holes. So was he. The man was still alive, but blood was bubbling in two of the pellet wounds, indicating a punctured lung. He needed emergency care, and fast.

Erin's phone was in her hip pocket. She clamped the flashlight in her teeth while she dialed.

"911, what is your emergency?" Dispatch said brightly. Erin spat the flashlight back into her hand.

"This is Detective O'Reilly, shield four-six-four-oh," she rattled off. "This is a 10-13S. I'm at the church on Rockaway Beach Boulevard and Beach 100th Street. I've got three victims, multiple GSW. I need multiple buses forthwith."

She had to pause for breath. There was a burning sensation in her chest every time she inhaled. She hoped she didn't have broken ribs.

"We copy, O'Reilly," Dispatch said. "EMTs are inbound, ETA two minutes. What's the status on the casualties?"

Two minutes was fantastic response time. There must be a hospital nearby, Erin thought distractedly. She made a quick check of the other two bodies. One of them had taken a shell to the face. There wasn't much left you could call a head. He was far beyond medical care and well on his way to a closed-casket funeral. The other was either unconscious or dead. She tried for a pulse and couldn't find one. Rolf was still barking and yelping in frustration. She imagined him jumping and clawing at the door.

"One dead," she reported. "One critical. Not sure about number three. I can't get a pulse or respiration. I've been hit, too, but I don't think it's too bad."

"Patrol units have been dispatched to your location," Dispatch said. "Are there active shooters?"

"Not right now," she said. "But put a BOLO out on DEA Special Agent Julio Lorcas. He's the one who shot everybody, including me. He's armed and extremely dangerous."

"Say again, O'Reilly," Dispatch said. "Did you say a DEA agent shot you?"

"DEA Agent Lorcas," Erin repeated. "He shot me and he did it on purpose."

"Copy that. BOLO issued. Is he on foot or in a vehicle?"

"I have no idea," she said. She could already hear sirens. That was the nice thing about getting shot only a few blocks from a police station; the backup arrived nice and promptly.

*   *   *

Four uniformed officers were the first on scene, rushing into the sanctuary with guns drawn. They found Erin performing what first aid she could on Rafferty, holding her fingers in the bubbling holes in his chest just like the proverbial little Dutch boy with his finger in the dike.

She'd called Rolf back to her side. The K-9 stood as close to her as he could get, ears flattened against his skull, tail drooping. He knew he should have been able to catch the bad guy and bite him, but he'd been thwarted, first by his own leash, then by his old nemesis, a doorknob.

One of the cops found the light switch and flipped it on, instantly transforming the dark sanctuary into a brightly-lit horror show. Erin hadn't realized how much blood was spattered on the floor and the pews. She didn't think any of it was hers, but she wasn't a hundred percent sure. Her back was really hurting.

"Holy crap," the youngest Patrolman said. He had very pale skin and a sprinkle of freckles, which stood out dark against his cheeks. "Are you okay, lady?"

"I'm fine," Erin lied. She held up her shield with the hand that wasn't engaged in keeping Rafferty's blood in his chest. "O'Reilly, Major Crimes. I need two of you on these bodies and the other two on perimeter."

"Copy that," the senior officer said. "We've got more units on the way. Saw the bus coming in. EMTs will be here any second."

He'd hardly finished when a pair of paramedics hurried in. They took a second to size up the situation, then opened their bags and dove right in.

A hand grabbed Erin's and squeezed. She looked down and saw Rafferty's eyes were open. He looked scared, and no wonder. With a pair of twelve-gauge pellets lodged in his lung, he wasn't getting nearly enough air, and the pain had to be unbelievable. He gasped and she felt faint suction against her fingertips, a very odd feeling, but a sign she was doing some good.

"You're going to be fine, Red," she told him. "We're getting you to a hospital. Don't try to talk."

"I got a gun here," one of the uniforms reported, planting his foot on a discarded revolver.

"Me, too," another said. "It's been fired."

An EMT knelt beside Erin. "I'll take over, ma'am," he said. "What've we got?"

"Shotgun to the chest," she said. "Punctured lung, probably other internal damage."

"Copy that," he said. He went to work with the calm, unhurried speed of an experienced professional.

Erin stood up and winced. One of the Patrolmen noticed.

"You've been shot," he said.

"No shit," she said.

"Seriously," he said. "Your coat's all torn up."

She shrugged out of the jacket with an effort, holding it up. Light shone through no fewer than ten holes. Lorcas had caught her with a full spread of buckshot. If she hadn't been wearing her vest, the shotgun would've turned her into ground beef. She felt suddenly weak in the knees as the knowledge of what had happened caught up with her.

"Vest doesn't look too bad," the officer said, looking at her back. "I can see some of the pellets."

"Any blood?" she asked.

"Nope. No penetration. Looks like the armor did its job. You oughta send the folks at Kevlar a thank-you note, and maybe some cookies."

"I've got a blood trail!" one of the perimeter cops shouted from outside the sanctuary.

Erin ran that way, leaving Rafferty and his guys in the hands of the paramedics. There was nothing more she could do for them.

She and Rolf dashed out into the hallway and ran smack into Lieutenant Overlin. He put out a hand and caught her shoulder.

"Easy there, Detective," he said. "What the hell happened?"

"Lorcas screwed us," she said. "He must've followed me. He shot me in the back, mowed down the other three guys, and took off with the stuff."

"That's crazy," Overlin said. "He's a career law-enforcement officer. Christ, I *know* the man. I've been to his home!"

"I don't give a damn what you think you know," Erin said. "That's what happened. I returned fire and I'm pretty sure that's his blood on the floor right there."

She pointed to the carpet at Overlin's feet. A ragged line of dark red droplets had soaked into it, tracing a path to the side door.

The Lieutenant shook his head. "It doesn't make any sense," he said. "Lorcas has been around plenty of big drug seizures. He could've grabbed a few kilos a dozen times, without shooting anybody, and probably gotten away with it. Are you sure it was him?"

"Absolutely," she said. "I saw him up close, when he grabbed the bag."

"Okay," Overlin sighed. "I'd better contact the DEA. They'll hit the roof, but they'll want to be involved. They'll want some of their own agents to help bring him in."

Erin nodded, but she was thinking hard and fast. "You're right, sir," she said. "This doesn't make sense. Either he went nuts all of a sudden, or there's something else going on. You remember what he was like at the station?"

"Yeah," Overlin said. "He was nervous. Sweating. And I thought he looked tired."

"He said his daughter was sick," Erin said. "Wait a minute. You said you've been to his house. How far is it from here?"

"Brighton Beach," Overlin said. "Just a few miles across the bay."

"We need to get there," she said.

"You think after shooting four people he's just going to go home and hang up his coat like nothing happened? You're the one who's crazy, O'Reilly. He's running. There's only a few roads out of Rockaway Beach and I'm going to put checkpoints on all of them. He might have a boat, but we still might nail him."

"I think he was telling the truth about his daughter," she said. "More or less."

Overlin wasn't listening. He had his radio in hand and was talking very quickly. "I need roadblocks at the Marine Parkway Bridge, the Cross Bay Veterans Bridge, and Rockaway Freeway at Seagirt Boulevard," he said. "Suspect vehicle registered to Julio Lorcas. It'll have Federal plates."

"He was lying," Erin said, "but he was worried about his daughter. I think that part was true. Somebody's putting leverage on him."

"Okay," Overlin said, paying attention again. "You can play your hunch. Hell, you don't need my permission; I'm not your CO. If he's quick enough to get over the bridge ahead of our checkpoint, and if he's stupid enough to go home, you'll find him at 1053 Ocean View Avenue. Fourth floor, apartment... shit, I don't remember. I think it's 402."

"Thanks," she said.

"I still think you're chasing shadows," he said. "But if you need backup, that's in the Six-One's territory. You can coordinate with them."

"Thanks," she said again, already on her way to the exit. Rolf trotted beside her, still subdued. Maybe he'd get another chance at the bad guy, but until then, he was feeling down.

"We'll need your statement," Overlin called after her. "For this shooting."

"You'll get it," she answered over her shoulder. "When I'm good and ready," she added under her breath. There was no time to deal with departmental protocol. She was following her gut, and her gut told her Lorcas was looking out for his family.

She didn't know what she'd find at his apartment. She hoped whatever it was, it would explain why a good cop would go on a self-destructive rampage, kill two people, shoot two more, and steal a whole lot of drugs. Because Overlin was right; if her hunch was wrong, what had happened was totally crazy.

Chapter 14

The Marine Parkway Bridge was Erin's only route to Brighton Beach that didn't take her miles out of her way. Overlin's roadblock made sense, assuming Lorcas hadn't already slipped through the net, but it would slow her down, too. She hoped the low traffic at this time of night meant she wouldn't get stacked up too badly.

She decided she'd better make use of the driving time and called Webb. Maybe, if she was really lucky, he'd be awake.

Nobody's luck was that good. A very groggy Major Crimes Lieutenant picked up the phone just before it rolled to voicemail.

"Webb," he said.

"This is O'Reilly," Erin said. "I'm heading toward Brighton Beach from Rockaway."

"What in God's name is going on?" Webb asked. To his credit, he'd caught the tense note in her voice and sounded more alert than he had a moment ago.

"I was in a shootout a few minutes ago. The coke we confiscated from the Wilder plane crash is in the wind."

"What?" Webb was wide awake now. "Are you hurt?"

"Only a little. But we've got two perps dead and another circling the drain."

"How many of them did you shoot?"

"None. I winged a Federal agent, though."

"How, exactly, did that happen?"

"Long story, sir. Short version is, you remember Julio Lorcas? The DEA guy?"

"What about him?" Webb asked warily.

"He's working for someone else. Best guess, the Colombian cartel. He shot up the handoff and ripped off the drugs."

"What handoff? O'Reilly, you started in the middle."

"I told you, it's a long story. Can you get to Brighton Beach?"

"I'm on my way. What's the address?"

"1053 Ocean View Avenue."

"What am I going to find there?"

"I have no idea. It's Lorcas's apartment. Overlin, the Lieutenant at the One Hundred, thinks he isn't going back there, but I think he might."

"I'll put ESU on standby," Webb said. "Just in case. You're sure this guy's dirty?"

"I don't know that I'd put it that way, sir. But I'm damn sure he murdered a couple of guys. I was there. He shot me in the back. With a shotgun."

"You said you weren't hurt."

"The vest caught the pellets. I'll be fine."

"O'Reilly?"

"Yes, sir?"

"You've got a lot of explaining ahead of you."

She saw the bridge entrance just ahead. A pair of blue-and-whites were parked across the ramp. "I have to go," she said. "I'll lay it all out for you as soon as I can."

Fortunately, only three cars were waiting at the checkpoint. Erin had her shield ready by the time her turn came. The officers waved her through. The bridge took her across the entrance to Jamaica Bay, onto Flatbush Avenue and through the Gateway National Recreation Area. It was a pleasant, green, nearly deserted route into south Brooklyn.

She made another call, praying Vic wouldn't be too grumpy at being robbed of his pitiful ration of sleep.

"Was wondering when you'd call," he said, answering immediately.

"Oh good," she said. "You're awake."

"Of course I'm awake. Webb just called me. I'm on my way south as we speak, laying rubber and breaking traffic laws."

She could hear the siren on his Taurus in the background. "I appreciate that," she said. "But I've got a head start. I'll get there way ahead of you."

"Don't you dare start without me," he said. "The boss wasn't exactly clear on the situation. He said you were in a shootout?"

"Yeah. Lorcas ripped off Wilder's coke and shot three O'Malley goons."

There was a short pause. "Erin," he said slowly, "what were you and Lorcas doing swapping bullets with O'Malley guys over a bunch of coke that, last I heard, was sitting in an evidence locker?"

"It's part of the other thing," she said. "It's all aboveboard. I cleared it through channels. And I didn't shoot any O'Malleys. I did take a few shots at Lorcas. Damn it, you don't expect the DEA guy to grab the drugs."

"Maybe *you* don't," Vic said. "I never trust the goddamn Feds. I hope you tagged him."

"I caught him with at least one round," she said. "But he's still on his feet and he's running."

"We'll get him."

"Probably. Look, I have to go."

"I'll be there in twenty," Vic promised.

"From Manhattan? You weren't kidding about breaking traffic laws."

"Those aren't the only things I'm planning on breaking tonight. See you in a few."

She wasn't done on the phone yet. Her next call was to her handler. Phil picked up on the second ring. Erin wasn't convinced he ever slept.

"Hello?" he said.

"Hey, Phil, it's me," she said. "The deal went bad. It wasn't the O'Malleys; they turned up just like they were supposed to. It was the friggin' DEA. I think somebody got to Agent Lorcas. He killed two of Evan's guys and wounded another. Plus, he shot me, but I was wearing a vest, so I'm good."

"Glad you're okay," Phil said. "This is important, Erin. Is Evan going to link you with the shooter?"

"I don't think so."

"You might be betting your life on that answer. Do you want to come in? It's short notice, but we might be able to swing it. We can get Evan, and most of his guys, if you can give me a few hours to set things up."

"No."

"You're sure?"

"I'm sure. We're this far in. Let's go all the way to the end. The best play is to run down the guy who ripped Evan off."

"This is dangerous," Phil said.

"I've had close calls with these guys before," she said. "Relax. This isn't a suicide run. Everything's under control."

"Try to at least sound like you believe that yourself," he said. "What do you need right now?"

"A couple Aspirin and a new jacket."

"I meant in terms of police resources."

"If you can keep the captain of the One Hundred off my back for the next couple of hours, that'd be great."

"Why's he going to be on you?"

"Because I left the scene of a shooting without giving a statement."

"Oh."

"That's all you've got to say about that?"

"What would you like me to say, Erin? You want me to tell you it was against regulations? That it was irresponsible and could get you in trouble? I think you know all that already."

"Yeah."

"I'll do what I can," he said. "Discreetly."

"Thanks. Now I'd better go. I've got another call to make."

"I imagine you do. Damage control?"

"Damage control," she confirmed.

Erin got onto Belt Parkway, headed west toward Brighton Beach. She took a deep breath and dialed one final number. Ironically, while this was the man she most wanted to see, it was the call she least wanted to make.

"Evening, darling," Carlyle said. In the background, something dramatic happened on TV and the Corner's patrons went wild.

"We got screwed," Erin said, speaking loudly to be heard over the hubbub. "A crooked DEA guy jumped us at the meet. Two of Red Rafferty's guys are dead, Red's in the hospital if he's still breathing, and I got banged up a little. I'm fine, but I need you to talk to Evan right away."

"What should I tell him?" Carlyle asked. He was remarkably calm.

"Tell him what I told you. We got ripped off, but I'm handling it."

"Was the lad operating alone, or in someone's service?"

"I don't know for sure, but I think the Colombians got to him."

"Not the Lucarellis?"

"What'd be the point? They already had me working the same job and they didn't know I wasn't going to hand off the coke to them. Why have him try to take me out?"

"Good point. You're certain you're not hurt?"

"I'll be sore in the morning."

"What can I do for you?"

"Why does everyone keep asking me that? I'm good. I've got the whole NYPD to call on. What you can do is smooth things over with Evan. He's going to be pissed."

"I imagine so, aye. We'll just have to make certain it's someone else he's angry with."

"My thoughts exactly."

"What's the name of this agent?"

"Julio Lorcas. But I'm not sure you should tell Evan that. The last thing I need to be doing is dodging O'Malley hitmen."

"Understood. Take care, darling."

"You too."

Erin finally finished with her phone. "You know," she said to Rolf, "they say talking on phones causes as many crashes as drunk drivers. I'm starting to believe it."

Rolf nosed her cheek. He didn't drink, drive, or talk on phones. But he was still feeling bad about letting the bad guy get away.

"You'll get another crack at him," she promised, scratching him under the chin. "Good boy."

His ears perked up a little.

*   *   *

Erin parked the Charger across the street from Lorcas's apartment. The brick building was dark and quiet. She looked for any sign of trouble and saw nothing.

"What do you think, kiddo?" she asked Rolf.

The K-9 let his tongue hang out. He thought they should stop wasting time and find the bad guy. Then they could chase him and maybe bite him.

"He was leaving a blood trail," she said. "Think you could track him?"

Rolf didn't dignify that question with a response.

Erin considered her options. She didn't have a warrant, so she couldn't just kick down Lorcas's door. Getting the warrant would take time, time she wasn't sure she had. She should have already set the request in motion, before driving up from Rockaway Beach. But that might not have helped. Judge Ferris would have signed her warrant; Ferris owed her for saving him from a particularly clever assassin. But Ferris was asleep, and whatever judge she could get at two in the morning wouldn't just blindly sign off on a warrant to bust in on a DEA agent's home. That sort of request was almost guaranteed to result in a turf squabble with the Feds. It would take hours, and multiple calls to and from the DEA, to get approval, and in that time, Lorcas might be gone, dead, or both.

There was local law. She could call up the Brighton Beach boys in blue and get two or three Patrol units to back her up. But she'd still run into the problem of needing a warrant.

"He shot me, for Christ's sake," she grumbled. That was true, but she still had to follow the rules. Maybe the rules hadn't been written with this specific situation in mind, but that wasn't the point.

She decided she could at least look the place over a little more closely. Carefully, her aching back protesting every motion, she climbed out of the Charger and unloaded Rolf. They crossed the street and approached the apartment's front door. The building remained dark and still.

Erin drew her Glock and checked the chamber. She'd fired four shots in the church. That left thirteen rounds in the gun, which ought to be plenty. She had two extra magazines on her belt, plus six bullets in her backup ankle gun. And, of course, Rolf. His teeth didn't run out of ammo.

"Ready, kiddo?" she asked.

Rolf stared up at her, ears at full attention, legs and tail stiff and rigid. He was always ready.

The throaty roar of a six-cylinder engine echoed off the walls of the surrounding buildings, closing fast. A Ford Taurus hit the corner going way faster than it should. Tires squealed in protest, laying long strips of rubber on the pavement. The car slewed sideways, drifting almost into a parked minivan, but the driver recovered with inches to spare.

The Taurus screeched to a halt less than ten feet from the apartment entrance. The driver's door flew open and Vic Neshenko bailed out. He hit the ground running, shoes skidding on concrete. He stopped in front of Erin and stood there, breathing hard. He was wearing an unzipped windbreaker over his Kevlar vest. Other than that, he appeared to be clad only in jeans and a T-shirt. He hadn't even bothered with socks, just shoving his feet into his shoes.

"Wow," Erin said. "You could've got here faster, but only if you'd hijacked a helicopter."

"Looks like I'm just in time," Vic said. "I don't see any damn backup. Tell me you weren't about to go in there on your own. And don't give me any of that crap about Rolf being your backup. I'm talking about guys with guns."

"I wasn't going to go into his unit," she said defensively. "I was just looking around. Doing my reconnaissance."

"Whatever. I turned off the siren a few blocks north. I wanted to keep a low profile."

"Good thinking," she said, poker-faced. "You wouldn't want anybody to hear you coming."

"That's exactly what I..." he began. Then he stopped and his eyes narrowed. "Cute, O'Reilly. Real cute. I jump out of bed, out of a real nice dream, thank you very much, to run down here and save your ass, and what do I get? Sarcasm. I was worried about you."

"I'm fine, Vic."

"You say that a lot."

"It's usually true."

"Keep telling yourself that. What's the situation?"

"Lorcas lives in 402," she said. "We're looking for a blood trail, or anything else that'll give us PC."

"I don't suppose we can pretend we heard a scream?"

"Not this time, Vic. This is a Federal agent's home. There's going to be eyes on this investigation."

"I love having armchair idiots second-guessing me," Vic grumbled. "What're we expecting up there?"

"Agent Lorcas. He's injured but armed."

"What with?"

"Shotgun. He'll have a sidearm, too."

"You took a shotgun hit at close range? Damn." Vic looked impressed.

"He didn't penetrate."

"That's what all the girls say," Vic said with a grin. "Anyone else up there?"

"His daughter. Possibly his wife. And maybe some Colombian drug traffickers."

"And those guys love their automatic weapons. Just a sec."

Vic hurried back to his car, leaned in, and came out a moment later with his M4 rifle. He racked the charging handle to chamber a round.

"That's better," he said. "I think we should try the super."

"Good idea," Erin said. "If he keys us in, we don't need a warrant, as long as we don't remove anything."

"Let's do this now," Vic said. "Before Webb gets here. He cramps my style."

The lobby door was locked. Erin buzzed the super. After a few tense moments a paunchy, balding guy ambled into the lobby. He had a cigarette in his hand, a mustache that belonged on a '70s porn star, and a wife-beater that didn't conceal an impressive growth of chest hair.

"This is what I love best about being a cop," Vic said out of the side of his mouth. "Dealing with high-class citizens."

"Whaddaya want?" the man demanded.

Erin tapped her shield against the glass door. Vic held his rifle in an ambiguously menacing manner.

The super didn't seem overly upset, not even by the sight of Vic's heavy hardware. He opened the door. A cloud of cheap cigarette smoke drifted out to meet them.

"Whaddaya want?" he repeated.

"Julio Lorcas," Erin said. "Is he in 402?"

"Who wants to know?" the super asked.

"NYPD," Vic said. "Either that, or we're a couple of armed assholes doing a midnight shakedown. Either way, answer the question, dickwad."

"Who you callin' a dickwad?" the man retorted.

Vic gave him an amused look. He was five inches taller than the other guy, and though they probably weighed about the same amount, it was muscle on Vic's body.

"Sir, this is important," Erin said, playing the "good cop" role she tended to slide into whenever Vic was around. "We have reason to believe Mr. Lorcas's family is in danger."

"What, his wife and kid?" the super replied, the belligerent tone leaving his voice. "Connie and Celeste? What's going on? Is this on account of their dad being a cop?"

"DEA agent," Vic corrected him.

"Whatever," the man said.

"Yes," Erin said, which was close enough to the truth. "Can you get us into their apartment?"

"Sure," the super said. "That Celeste's a sweet kid. I don't want nothing to happen to her. Yeah, it's 402. I got my keys here. C'mon, follow me."

The super led the way to the elevator, which made Erin twitch slightly, but she mastered the rush of paranoia. The elevator car looked worn and weathered, but it ran smoothly up to the fourth floor. Vic and Erin both had their weapons in hand and ready when the doors slid open, revealing an empty hallway.

The super went to 402 and pulled out a ring of keys. He fumbled with them for a moment before he found the right one. Then he paused and knocked on the door with his knuckles.

"Ms. Lorcas?" he called. "This is Bruno Orlov, the superintendent. I got a couple cops here need to talk to you."

There was no response. The super gave it a moment and tried again, with the same result. He shrugged.

"Guess they're not home."

"Sir, we need to check the apartment," Erin said.

"It's two in the morning," Vic added. "How likely do you think it is that they're not at home?"

"I guess," Orlov said. He inserted the key and jiggled it. "That's funny. This oughta work. It's jammed."

"Jammed how?" Erin asked.

"Beats me," Orlov said. "Something ain't working. I can't turn the damn thing."

Vic reached past him, took hold of the doorknob, twisted, and pushed. The door swung open.

"It wasn't locked," Orlov said. "Weird." He started into the room.

"Sir, stand back," Erin said sharply. Her Glock was now raised and ready. So was Vic's rifle.

"Whoa," Orlov said, but he obeyed, backing into the hallway.

"Julio Lorcas!" Erin called. "This is the NYPD! We're coming in! If you're here, I'd better see your hands and they'd better be empty!"

She expected no answer and got none.

"On me," Vic said. He moved in fast, rifle snugged against his shoulder, scanning for targets. Erin and Rolf were right on his heels.

They cleared the living room, kitchen, and dining room quickly, seeing no signs of life. Erin caught a glimpse of a small herd of plastic pastel ponies, just like her niece Anna had, and wondered how old Celeste Lorcas was.

"Bathroom clear," Vic said.

Erin swung right, finding a small bedroom. It was furnished in pink and had a small bed piled high with stuffed animals. She took a second to crouch and check under the bed.

"Clear," she said.

Vic was already moving to the master bedroom. He turned the knob and opened the door. Erin caught a whiff of something, a terribly familiar, sickly-sweet stench.

"Oh, no," she murmured. She already had a pretty good idea what Vic was going to find.

"Son of a bitch," Vic cursed softly. The rifle fell away from his shoulder, dangling from his right hand, forgotten.

Chapter 15

"I guess that's his wife," Vic said. "Or it was."

"Yeah," Erin said.

They could hear Orlov in the bathroom, throwing up. Neither Erin nor Vic thought any less of him for it; death scenes were disturbing. They'd been green Patrol cops once upon a time and wanted to ride the porcelain bus to get away from some of the stuff they'd seen on the Job. Sometimes they still did.

"We have to call this in," Vic said. He ran a hand over his scalp. "Jesus. Was it the Colombians, you think?"

"Probably," Erin said. "Looks like they tied her up on the bed, put a plastic bag over her head."

"Suffocation," Vic agreed. "Lousy way to go. Why not just shoot her?"

"Quieter," Erin said. "And it makes one hell of a statement. It's more personal." She took her phone out and dialed Webb.

"I'm almost there," Webb said. "Did you reach Neshenko?"

"Yes, sir," she said. "He got here ahead of you. And we've got a problem."

"A worse one than a rogue DEA agent and a couple of bodies?"

"Add another to the tally. We don't have an official ID, but looks like Connie Lorcas. Our agent's wife."

"She's dead?" Webb asked.

"Yeah. Somebody put her head in a bag."

"Good God," he said. "Do you have the rest of the body?"

Erin was confused for a second. Then she understood. "Sorry, sir. I wasn't clear. Her head's still attached. There's a plastic bag over it. She's asphyxiated."

"Are you sure she's dead?"

"She's cool to the touch. She's been dead for hours, maybe longer."

"Okay," Webb said. "I'll be there momentarily. Any sign of Agent Lorcas?"

"No."

"Understood. Stay there. I'm coming to you."

Erin hung up. Vic was prowling around the bedroom, looking for clues.

"You think he did her?" he asked. "Our suspect, I mean."

"You're asking if Lorcas tied up his wife and suffocated her?" Erin was appalled.

Vic shrugged. "Sure. I mean, the guy's obviously snapped. He's running around shooting cops and stealing drugs. Why draw the line at offing his wife? Lots of guys kill their wives. We've arrested some of them."

"No way," Erin said. "That doesn't make any sense."

"How come he just left her here, then?" Vic demanded. "This lady's room-temp, Erin. She's been dead a while. Give it another few hours and she's really gonna start to smell. What sort of normal guy hangs out with his dead wife? For God's sake, where did he sleep? She's in the middle of the damn bed!"

"I don't think he's slept," Erin said, remembering how Lorcas had looked at the police station. Why hadn't she picked up on his mood? She should've pressed harder, gotten more information from him. She'd been too distracted, too intent on the job at hand.

"The guy's nuts, either way," Vic said. "If he didn't kill her, why didn't he call the cops?"

"Because the bad guys have his daughter," Erin said. "They must be using her as leverage. I'm guessing they jimmied the lock, killed the wife, grabbed the kid, and told him he'd better get their drugs for them or they'll kill her too."

"But he knows that's bullshit, right?" Vic said. "There's no way they're letting him walk away. With him knowing they killed his wife? The DEA would come after them with everything they've got. If you're right, these guys have nothing to lose, and killing another witness won't make a damn bit of difference to them."

It was Erin's turn to shrug. "I don't know how the guy's thinking! He just lost his wife and his little girl is God knows where. He's more or less insane right now, out of his mind with grief and anxiety and all that jazz. Not to mention, like I said, he's probably been up for two or three days straight."

"NYPD!" Webb's voice came from behind them.

"Bedroom," Erin called. A moment later the Lieutenant joined them.

Orlov stumbled out of the bathroom, wiping his mouth. "Can I go?" he asked the detectives.

"Yeah," Vic said. "But before you take off, did you see anybody weird hanging around the last couple of days?"

"Probably at least two South American men," Erin said.

"I don't think so," Orlov said. "But I only work nights. I didn't see nothing that'd explain... *that*." He glanced toward the bedroom and shuddered.

"Okay, go on and scram," Vic said. "But don't leave the building. We're gonna have somebody talk to you and take your statement in a little bit."

Webb was staring at the body in the bed. "This just keeps getting worse," he said quietly. "First it's one guy falling out of a plane. Next thing we know, we've got a gunfight and a home invasion and bodies piling up all over the place."

"There's a lot of money in that white powder," Vic said.

"Are you quoting *The Godfather* again?" Erin asked.

"Usually," he said.

"Let's discuss the situation," Webb said. "Start with what we've got. One armed man on the run with six kilos of high-purity cocaine. Two dead drug dealers in Rockaway Beach, with a third in critical condition. And a dead woman in a Brighton Beach apartment, presumed to be the spouse of our fugitive. The fugitive's been on the run for what, forty-five minutes?"

"Give or take," Erin said.

"Now for the unknowns," Webb went on. "We don't know who killed this woman, why a decorated DEA agent would suddenly start murdering people and swiping drugs, where he is now, where he's going, or what he's planning to do once he gets there."

"I think we can fill in some of those gaps," Erin said. "But there's another unknown, too; the location of his daughter. She's not here. I think we can assume if the bad guys had killed her, they would've left her body with her mom, so she's probably alive, or at least she was."

"You think someone's using her as a hostage to leverage Lorcas into cooperating with them," Webb said. "Any idea who these guys are?"

"I've got a couple of names," she said. "Alejandro and Dante Fuentes, twin brothers. They're with the cartel. Word on the street is, Wilder got his coke from a crooked cartel member. I think they still consider the stuff to be theirs and they want it back."

"Along with revenge on whoever took it," Vic added.

"So we find these brothers and we solve the Wilder case, too?" Webb said.

"I hope so," Erin said. "Anyway, if they've got his kid, Lorcas is going to be desperate, but he's not a total idiot. He'll insist on seeing her and doing a trade in a way he at least thinks he can control."

"That'll be a dangerous situation," Vic said. Then he snapped his fingers. He went to the bedroom closet and opened it. "Bingo! Look what we've got here."

"That's a gun safe," Webb said.

"Yeah," Vic said. "A nice big one. I figured he'd have to have one; he's gotta have guns here, and he'd never leave them just lying around, not with a little kid in the place. It's got a keypad, though. Damn. We may have to get a guy to drill it out, and that'll take way too much time."

"Why do you want to get into his gun safe?" Erin asked.

"I want to know how much hardware this asshole is packing," he said. "Hold on, it's not locked! He didn't close it all the way."

Vic pulled the safe open. The detectives clustered around it.

"Shit," Vic said. "He cleaned the whole thing out. No wonder he didn't bother locking it afterward. All that's here is some cases, cleaning supplies, and spare empty clips."

"What can we figure about what was in here?" Webb asked.

"Three pistol cases," Vic said. "So figure on three handguns. We already know he's got a shotgun. He's got a rifle cleaning kit here, so we've gotta assume he's got another long gun, too. You're lucky he didn't blast you with an AR-15, Erin. That would've gone right through your vest."

"Yeah," Erin said, feeling an unpleasant tingle between her aching shoulder blades at the thought. "What's that box at the back? The red one?"

"Looks like a toolkit," Webb said.

Vic popped the lid. "This isn't a toolkit," he said. "At least, not for hammers and wrenches and shit. This is a grenade case. And it's empty."

"Are you telling me our guy's running around Long Island with five guns and a couple dozen hand grenades?" Webb's question started off quiet and got progressively louder.

"We don't know how many were in there to begin with," Erin said.

"But yeah," Vic said. "Let's assume that."

"I'm not sure Lorcas is planning a peaceful trade," Erin said.

"He's coming heavy, all right," Vic said.

"We'd better figure out where he's going," Webb said. "Right now. Or we're going to have more bodies by the time the sun comes up."

"Okay," Vic said. "These Fuentes punks can't be too hard to find."

"I doubt they've got a permanent address," Erin said. "From what I understand, they only got here recently."

"Then there'll be a record of them entering the country," Webb said. "I'm going to check the database and get in touch with Homeland Security."

"The Homeland boys won't know jack shit," Vic predicted. "Even if they've got them coming in, they'll have disappeared the second they walked out of the airport."

"You have a better idea, Neshenko?" Webb asked.

"I'm not an idea guy," Vic said. "I'm more in the executive arm of law enforcement."

"I've got two ideas," Erin said.

"Let's hear them," Webb said.

"The bad guys might've left some sort of note here," she said. "There's got to be a way for Lorcas to get in touch with them once he's got their product, otherwise what's the point?"

"He might've taken it with him, or been told in person," Webb said. "But it's worth a try. Your other thought?"

She was already taking out her phone. "I can talk to my people," she said. "The O'Malleys may be able to point us in the right direction."

"Use a crook to catch a crook," Vic said.

"Let's do all three," Webb said. "I'll look for a paper trail. Neshenko, start combing the scene, but don't do anything to contaminate it. I'll get CSU and some Patrol units to come help. O'Reilly, try the street angle. And see if SNEU has any idea about these guys. I'll put out a BOLO. Do you know if they've got mugshots?"

"If they're fresh off the boat, they're probably not in the system," Vic said. "What're you gonna say, 'Be on the lookout for a couple of Colombian guys?'"

Erin was calling Carlyle, giving only half an ear to the other detectives. She knew time was desperately tight.

"Darling," Carlyle said. This time there was no background noise at all.

"Where are you?" she asked.

"I'd a notion I might be hearing from you again," he said. "So I stepped upstairs to my office. What is it you're needing?"

"I have to know where the Fuentes brothers are. They've killed an innocent woman and they've got a little girl. I don't care how hard you have to push, but I need it fast and it better be accurate."

"I can put the word out," he said doubtfully. "But surely your lot have better surveillance than mine."

"We're trying everything," she said. "Just do what you can, will you?"

"I'll make some calls," he said. "I'll ring you with whatever I come up with."

"Thanks."

She hung up and immediately dialed Sergeant Logan. At least he'd be awake, she thought. The SNEU squad was right in the middle of their shift, the heart of the dog watch.

Logan's phone rang. It went on ringing.

Erin sighed. She started thinking about what message to leave on his voicemail, and whether it made sense to call one of the other squad members.

"Logan," he said, picking up just after the fifth ring. He sounded out of breath.

"Bad time?" Erin asked.

"Time of my life," he replied cheerfully. Erin heard what sounded like the tail end of a scuffle on the other line. "Say, hold on just a sec, will you?"

There was a pause, an exclamation from an unfamiliar voice, and a meaty thud. Then there was a volley of muffled profanity.

"Save it for the judge, buddy," said a woman who sounded like Piekarski.

"Sorry about that," Logan said. "I thought we had this guy, but turns out he's a slippery bastard and he tried to do a runner. It's all good, we got him. Landa's sitting on him now. That little dude's stronger than he looks."

"I heard that, Sarge," Landa called.

"Anyway, what's up?" Logan asked.

"Is Firelli with you?" Erin asked. "I need to talk to him ASAP."

"Sure," Logan said. Then, louder, "Hey! Blade! Your pal O'Reilly needs to yell at you. Get your ass over here!"

After a few seconds, Firelli came on the line. "Help you?" he said.

"I need to find the Fuentes brothers," she said, not wasting time on small talk. "Do you know where they are?"

"No," Firelli said.

Erin's heart sank. "Can you—" she started to ask.

"But Dario might," he went on. "If anybody does, he's your best shot."

"Okay. What's his number?"

"He doesn't like talking on phones. Thinks they're all tapped, that we or the Feds are recording everything. He's not far wrong, either. He won't talk business on them, especially with cops. How close are you to Little Italy?"

Erin's spirits, which had bounced back a little, sagged again. "I'm in Brighton Beach," she said. "It'd take me half an hour to get there."

"I'm guessing that's time you don't have?"

"Nope. We've got lives on the line and we're on a tight clock."

"Okay." Firelli did some quick thinking. "What I could do, maybe, is run over to his theater myself. It's just down the way, I can be there in five. Call you back in fifteen, tops. This number good?"

"Yeah. Thanks."

"Forget about it." Firelli hung up.

Erin tried to curb her impatience. She knew Firelli and Carlyle would do the best they could. The curse of being a detective was having to wait on everybody else to get back to you. She was aware of time moving both very slowly and very fast; slowly in that all she could do was wait, fast in that irreplaceable seconds were slipping past her.

Webb had gone down to his car to get on his computer. Erin decided to see how Vic was coming along. She went back to the bedroom and found him on his hands and knees in front of the closet, feeling among the clothes.

"What're you looking for?" she asked.

"The way I figure it," Vic said, "our guy comes in and finds his wife dead and his daughter gone."

"So you don't think he killed her anymore?"

"I hope not. If he did, and if he loaded up on guns, ammo, and explosives, that means he's probably planning some sort of mass-casualty blaze-of-glory bullshit, and that's something I can live without."

"Cheerful thought," she said. "So, as you were saying: he finds his wife there on the bed."

"He didn't move her," Vic said. "If he had, he would've taken the bag off her, maybe cleaned her up a little. Next place he goes is the gun safe."

"To arm up," Erin said. "Makes sense, I guess."

"So if that's what he does, maybe he's got something in his hands. He drops it when he puts in the combo on the lock, he's not thinking too clearly, hell, his family just fell apart, and maybe he doesn't think to pick it up again."

"What sort of thing are you looking for?"

"This," Vic said triumphantly, coming up with a crumpled scrap of paper in his gloved hand. He carefully smoothed it out and laid it gently on the carpet. "Light?"

Erin pulled out her flashlight and shone it over his shoulder. The note was pretty straightforward.

"'You have two days to get our *cocaina*,'" Vic read aloud. "'Or we do to your little girl what we did to your woman. We do it slow.' I guess they didn't see the need to be subtle."

"They left a dead woman with a plastic bag on her head," Erin said. "Subtlety doesn't seem to be their thing."

"'Keep your phone on. We will call you. You tell anyone, your girl dies gasping,'" Vic finished. "That's all there is. Shit."

He turned the note over, looking for more writing or any distinguishing marks.

"Were you expecting them to sign it and give a return address?" Erin asked.

"No, but I was hoping for something more," Vic said. "I guess a forensic handwriting guy could match it to a suspect once we get him in custody. For all the good that'll do. Looks like ordinary ballpoint pen, plain white printer paper. Nothing we can use."

"That's not true," Erin said. "You have an evidence bag?"

"I've always got evidence bags," he said, fishing one out of a pocket in his vest. "You thinking fingerprints?"

She shook her head. "I'm thinking we just might need to know what one of these jerks smells like," she said.

Rolf, sticking close to his partner, blinked and cocked his head.

"We might," Vic agreed, bagging the note, sealing the bag, and handing it to her.

"Find anything else?" she asked.

"No. Whatever else these assholes left behind, it's too small for me to pick out. CSU might find it."

"NYPD!" someone called from outside the apartment.

"Come on in," Erin replied, stepping out of the bedroom. A pair of Patrol cops were standing in the doorway to 402.

"We got a report of a homicide," the older one said. "Looks like the gold shields beat us here. What do you need us to do?"

"Secure the scene," she said. "And wait for CSU."

"Hurray," the younger officer said sourly. "We get to stand around twiddling our thumbs for the next two hours."

"And getting paid to do it," his partner said. "Think of it as training for your next career."

"As what?" the kid retorted.

"Security guard," the older cop said. "Once you've got your pension you can look forward to forty nice, quiet hours a week."

"Hurray," the rookie said again. "I didn't join the Force to do nothing."

"They also serve who only stand and wait," the older uniform said. "Know who wrote that? Milton."

"Milton, the weird guy who burns down the building in *Office Space?*"

The veteran rolled his eyes. "Milton the poet, dumbass. *Paradise Lost?*"

"Never saw that one," the kid said.

"Jesus. You believe this friggin' guy?"

Erin and Vic didn't stay to hear the rest of the literary discussion. They were on their way down to talk to their commanding officer.

Chapter 16

"We haven't got much," Webb glumly reported. "I found an Alejandro and Dante Fuentes listed as passengers on a freighter up from Cartagena the week before last."

"Sounds like them," Erin said.

"But you were right," Webb said. "They walked off the dock and into the crowd, and that's the last Homeland Security knows. Their names match a couple of known enforcers for one of the cartels."

"And we just let them into the country?" Vic exclaimed. "What the hell is Homeland Security for?"

"Take it easy, Neshenko," Webb said. "The Colombians don't have warrants out for their arrest and they haven't done anything in the States. They weren't on a no-fly list."

"Wouldn't that be a no-boat list?" Vic suggested.

"Whatever," Webb said. "There was no legal reason to prevent them coming in. This is still a free country, more or less."

"What was the ship?" Erin asked.

"The *Cardenal*," Webb replied. "What on Earth does that matter?"

"Is she still docked in New York?"

"I have no idea," Webb said. "You'd have to talk to the Port Authority. I tried pinging Lorcas's cell phone, too."

"Because he might be a complete idiot and have it on him and turned on?" Vic said.

"Because he might need his phone with him to talk to the people who have his daughter," Webb said witheringly.

"Oh," Vic said. "Yeah, I guess that makes sense."

"Didn't pan out," Webb said. "Maybe he already talked to them. In any case, I didn't get a hit. You two have any luck?"

"Got a ransom note," Vic said. Erin produced the evidence bag and showed it to the Lieutenant.

"I'm waiting on a couple of calls," she said.

"I filled out a request for records from the Colombian police," Webb said. "But don't hold your breath. It's the middle of the night, and I expect these take a while to process. We're not likely to see anything until it's a moot point. I also put ESU on notice, but since we have no idea where our target might be, they can't do much except stand around waiting."

"Lot of that going on tonight," Vic observed. "Milton said something about that."

"Milton who?" Webb asked.

Vic snickered.

"It's not pertinent, sir," Erin said.

"And now we wait?" Vic asked.

"Now we wait," Webb said.

"Shouldn't we be moving?" Vic asked.

"Where?" Webb replied.

Vic had no answer to that.

"Lorcas is injured," Erin said. "He was bleeding. Either I or one of the O'Malleys tagged him at the church."

"Where'd he get hit?" Webb asked.

"Upper arm, I think."

"Lucky bastard," Vic said. "Safest part of the body to get shot in."

"Really?" Erin asked.

"Yeah," Vic said. "They've done studies. Worst places are head, neck, and center mass."

"Obviously," Webb said. "You think he'll have gone to a doc? They'd have to report a GSW, even on a Fed, and I haven't heard anything."

Erin drummed her fingers on the hood of Vic's Taurus. Rolf sat down on the sidewalk and scratched an ear with his hind leg. Vic paced back and forth in front of the building, prowling like a caged tiger. Webb lit a cigarette.

"Those things'll kill you, sir," Erin said.

"Not quickly enough," Webb said and took a drag.

Erin's phone rang. Everyone started. She snatched it out and had it up before the second ring, seeing Firelli's name on her screen.

"Give me good news," she said.

"I just talked to Dario," Firelli said. "I don't have names, but word on the street is, a couple of cartel heavies blew into town a few days ago. They've been asking questions about Arthur Wilder. They've shaken down some dealers and snitches for info, broken a few fingers, scared the hell out of a bunch of guys."

"That's promising," she said. "Where are they?"

"They've been operating in Long Island," Firelli said. "Close to where the plane went down. But Dario doesn't think they've got a permanent base set up. He thinks they're moving around."

"Damn," Erin said. "How are we supposed to find them? They've got to sleep somewhere."

"Yeah, and they don't have friends in the area," Firelli said. "Dario heard from a guy called Ratface that they were hanging around the yacht club down at Sheepshead Bay."

"They're on a boat?" she guessed.

"That's what we're thinking," Firelli said. "I'll bet they chartered one, or maybe bought it."

"Which boat?"

"No idea. Sorry. That's the best I can do. Dario's gonna try to nail it down, but that's gonna take time. I might have something for you by morning."

"Thanks, Blade."

Firelli sighed. "Not you, too. I've gotta put up with this crap from my squad, and now you?"

"Lots of cops have shot guys," she said. "You're the only one I heard of who stabbed one. And you told us they used to call you Bobby the Blade."

"Used to, O'Reilly. Before I had a shield. Forget about it. I know you're gonna call me what you want. Hope this helps you catch those guys."

"Me too. Tell Dario thanks for me, okay?"

"Already did. He says you should come by sometime, catch a movie."

"I just might do that. Catch you later." Dario D'Agostino ran a little neighborhood theater in his retirement.

"Where are we going?" Vic asked as Erin hung up.

"Sheepshead Bay Yacht Club," she said. "Got a tip the bad guys might be using a boat from there."

"That's just a few minutes away," Vic said. He knew Brighton Beach's geography by heart, having grown up just down the road.

"I'll get ESU moving," Webb said. "But they'll take a while to get down here. Anyway, this is a little bit—"

"Thin," Erin and Vic said in unison.

"But it's what we've got," Erin added.

"I know," Webb said. "I'll ride with you, Neshenko. Your car moves better than mine."

"I'll follow you," Erin said. She ran to her Charger and loaded Rolf into his compartment. By the time she'd gotten behind the wheel, Vic was already rolling. She started the engine and trailed him.

"We're probably way too late," she told Rolf. "Lorcas has better than half an hour's head start. He's already done whatever he means to. Or maybe he's already dead."

Rolf didn't have an opinion. But he didn't mind if the bad guys had a lead; that just meant he got to chase them.

"No lights, no sirens," she added. "Just in case."

* * *

The yacht club was an ugly concrete structure that reminded Erin of an old hot-water radiator. It huddled next door to a seven-story brick apartment that was undergoing some much-needed repairs. Construction scaffolding surrounded the street side of the apartment. Sometimes Erin thought the entirety of Long Island was falling apart and only the desperate efforts of a few thousand contractors were keeping it from sinking into the North Atlantic.

Vic pulled over to the curb and parked illegally next to the apartment's driveway. It was a calculated risk; his police plates would probably protect him from a ticket, and at this ungodly hour it was unlikely anyone would be coming or going from the building's basement garage. Erin squeezed into the last available legitimate spot, wondering whether to scold Vic for his choice or to thank him for leaving the legal space for her.

Erin and Rolf joined Vic and Webb outside the club. Vic was carrying his rifle. Webb hadn't bothered drawing his sidearm.

The club was closed, of course; no yacht club would be open after two in the morning. The driveway was blocked by a chain-link gate.

"I could ram it," Vic offered.

"No," Webb said wearily.

"It doesn't look that sturdy."

"I said no. The city of New York is not paying for this club to get a new gate."

Erin peered over the fence. She saw a dimly-lit forest of masts clustered at the pier. "What does Lorcas drive?" she asked.

"Government-issue Chevy Malibu," Webb said.

"Like that one?" Vic said, cocking a thumb at a dark-blue Chevrolet two cars in front of his Taurus.

"Exactly like that one," Webb said.

Vic hurried toward it and knelt by the rear bumper. "Government plates," he reported. "Shit, I got what looks like a bloody handprint on the trunk. It's our guy, all right."

"He beat us here," Webb said.

"You want to wait for ESU?" Erin asked.

Webb shook his head. "They'll be another twenty minutes," he said. "Neshenko, call for local backup. We're going in."

The Lieutenant reached inside his trench coat and came out with his .38 police special. It was a classic gun, an old-school revolver; the sort they didn't issue to the new recruits anymore. It struck Erin that with all the gunfights she'd been in, she'd never seen Webb fire his weapon.

"You ever shoot that at anybody?" she asked.

"Once," Webb said. "That was in LA, before I got saddled with you kids. Let's do this."

They turned back to the gate. It was about five feet tall. Vic looked at it, then at Webb.

"You better go first," he told Erin.

She nodded, holstered her gun, dropped Rolf's leash, grabbed the fence, jumped, flexed, and swung her legs up and over. She came down on the far side, bending her knees with the impact and trying not to wince at the new pain that flared in her bruised back. She drew her Glock again.

"*Hupf!*" she said to Rolf.

The Shepherd made it look easy. He sprang up, hooked his paws over the top railing, scrambled with his back feet, and was over in less time than it had taken her. He pranced in front of her, eager to keep going.

Vic slung his rifle and cupped his hands at knee height. Webb gave him a sour look but didn't object; he was a decade older than Vic and in much worse condition. He put his foot in Vic's hands and accepted the boost to the top of the gate. He landed heavily next to Erin, shaking his head.

"Too old for this?" she asked in an undertone.

"Too bulky," he muttered.

"Gotta lay off those donuts," Vic said, vaulting the gate in a single smooth movement and bringing his rifle back in line. "Where to now?"

"They'll have a boat," Erin said. "The pier, I guess."

"Backup's on the way, but they'll be a few minutes," Vic said. "This is legal, right?"

"*Now* he asks?" Erin said.

"The suspect's vehicle is parked outside," Webb said. "Didn't you see the blood on the fence?"

"What blood?" Vic asked.

Erin blinked. She hadn't seen it either.

"I did," Webb said. "That's our probable cause right there. We're golden."

Erin glanced at the gate. Now that she was looking for it, she saw the dark stain. They wouldn't need the kidnappers' note after all. "Rolf," she hissed.

Rolf cocked his head, one paw raised, awaiting instructions.

"*Such!*" she ordered, pointing to the bloodstain.

The K-9 went up on his hind legs and snuffled at the blood. It was still wet. The fresh, coppery smell lit up his olfactory receptors like an electric current. Rolf didn't need to cast around for the path his target had taken; Lorcas might as well have marked his route with phosphorescent paint. Not only that, but dogs remembered smells. Rolf had been sent after this guy once already that night. The target had gotten away then. The K-9 was determined to see that it didn't happen again.

Rolf's whole body became a tense, muscular arrow pointing directly toward the docks. He pulled, throwing his shoulders against the resisting pressure of the leash.

Erin jogged after him. Vic and Webb followed.

They passed a sailboat, sitting high and dry on a boat trailer, shrouded in canvas. The concrete building on their left was dark and silent. A single streetlamp shone down on the parking lot with a dim, flickering glow indicative of a bulb nearing the end of its life. Rolf swung to the side and skimmed through the shadows on the edge of the light. He wasn't being stealthy; in tracking mode, Rolf didn't care one bit about sneakiness. He was following the scent, which meant Lorcas had also stayed out of the light.

A concrete driveway led straight down a short slope into the water, which lapped quietly against it. On either side, piers stretched off into the night.

Rolf angled left, rushing onto the dock, paws scrabbling on the wood with a sound like the rattle of dice in a cup. It was terribly loud in the stillness.

Erin was surrounded by the dark shapes of boats. Masts thrust skyward like a leafless forest. Any one of the boats could hide a gunman. She looked from side to side, holding Rolf with one hand, her gun with the other. She thought of her flashlight, but knew that could do more harm than good. It would mark her position for anyone who might want to take a shot at her, while only slightly improving her own visibility.

She wondered what Ian Thompson, with his Marine Scout Sniper training, would do in this situation. That was easy. He'd find a spot with a good field of fire and camp out with a rifle and an infrared scope. Then he'd pick off the bad guys with well-placed headshots. But she couldn't do that.

The cold night air filtered in through the buckshot holes in her jacket, sending shivers up her spine. In spite of the chill, she felt sweat rolling down her neck. The grip of her Glock was slippery in her fist.

Rolf made a sudden sharp turn about two-thirds of the way down the dock. He raced left and skidded to a halt beside an empty berth. The dog went back and forth along the edge of the pier, snuffling. His previous excitement dissolved. He'd lost the bad guy again. His rubber Kong ball would continue to elude him. He whined unhappily.

Vic caught up with them. Webb was a few seconds behind, puffing and out of breath.

"Where is he?" Vic asked.

Erin pointed to the empty patch of water. "Gone," she said.

"Damn," Vic growled. "Looks like a washout."

"Maybe not," Webb said. "Look out there. And listen."

They paused, all of them—even Rolf—cocking their heads. The faint sound of an outboard motor was audible.

"Could be anybody," Vic said.

"At going on three in the morning?" Erin replied. "That's got to be him."

"It doesn't do us much good, even if you're right," Vic said. "He's out there, we're here. That's one hell of a swim and that water's cold."

Webb was thinking. "We can call the Harbor Unit," he said. "Maybe get the Staties involved."

"Take too long," Vic said. "How about an air unit?"

"We're trying to save Lorcas's daughter," Erin said. "A chopper will just spook them. They'll probably dump her overboard the minute a helicopter starts closing in. But we have to do *something*. We're out of time."

A sudden burst of brilliant light washed over them.

"Hold it right there!" a man called. "I don't know what you're doing, but I'm calling the cops."

"We are the damn cops, you idiot!" Vic snapped. "Turn off that goddamn light!"

Webb held up his shield. "NYPD major crimes, sir," he said. "Who are you?"

"Bud Colton, private security," the man said. Erin saw a bulky shape at the base of the dock, holding a powerful flashlight on them.

"Mr. Colton, douse your light," Webb said. "We've got a dangerous situation here."

Colton flicked off the light. "How do I know you're really cops?" he asked.

"Oh, for Christ's sake," Vic said. "I'm carrying an assault rifle, it's loaded, and if I wasn't a cop I'd blow your thick head off because you're wasting our damn time."

"Jeez, okay," Colton said. "Cool it. What're you doing here?"

"We need one of your club's boats," Erin said, seizing on a sudden idea. "Something that runs quiet. Can you handle a yacht?"

"Well, yeah," Colton said. "But I dunno. These ain't my boats, lady."

"The NYPD can commandeer a vehicle in emergency situations, when a life's on the line," Webb said. "I'm doing that right now. If you refuse, you run the risk of liability for any injury or death resulting from your inaction."

Erin knew that wasn't strictly true. The first part was accurate enough, the second wasn't. But Colton didn't know that.

"Hey, there ain't no call for that," Colton said. "Okay, okay. But I can't get in no trouble with my boss. I need this job."

"We've got your back," Vic said. "Do this right, you'll come out of this a hero. Now will you get off your ass and move?"

"Sheesh," Colton muttered. "Okay, I guess the best one to take out is the *Lady Jane*. She just got her hull waxed and an engine tune-up. She'll run sweet, fast, and quiet."

"Okay, fine," Webb said.

"Here she is," Colton said, indicating a sleek, powerful-looking motor yacht on the adjacent mooring. "I'll get her started. You guys wanna cast off?"

"Do what now?" Vic said.

"Untie the ropes," Erin said. She was no sailor, but even she knew that much.

"Oh, yeah. Copy that."

While Webb accompanied Colton aboard, Erin and Vic began loosening the lines. In a few moments the *Lady Jane* was bobbing free, bumping gently against the fenders that cushioned her from the dock. Erin, Vic, and Rolf jumped onto the boat as the engine purred to life. As Colton had promised, it ran surprisingly quietly.

With Webb giving directions, Colton carefully steered the boat out into Sheepshead Bay.

"No lights," Webb said.

"You nuts? I gotta have lights!" Colton protested. "It's the law!"

"We don't want them getting suspicious," Erin said, joining them at the helm. "There's nowhere to hide out there. Even a blacked-out boat will be visible. It's better if we look innocuous."

"Yeah," Vic said. "We can't turn invisible, so let's look like civilians."

"Fine," Webb said. "Turn on your navigation lights."

"What's this about, anyway?" Colton asked.

"Drug smuggling and kidnapping," Vic said.

"Really?"

"Yeah. Some cartel assholes have a little kid on their boat and they're gonna kill her if they don't get a load of smack. We're gonna do your typical hero stuff."

"Hero stuff?" Colton echoed.

"Hell yes, hero stuff," Vic said. "Stop the bad guys, bust the jerks, save the kid, bag the drugs, go home, and get some freaking sleep."

Chapter 17

"How fast are we going?" Erin asked.

"About ten knots," Colton said.

"What's a knot?" Vic asked.

"Didn't your mom teach you how to tie your shoes?" Erin replied. "Okay, you start by looping the left lace under the right one and up the back..."

"Ha ha," Vic said. "I know what it is, I was hoping for specifics."

"Nautical miles per hour," Webb said. "I think it's about one and a sixth ordinary miles."

"That's right," Colton said. "You been boating much?"

"I used to know a guy in LA who was big into surfing."

"Oh my God," Vic said. "All this time I thought our Lieutenant was a middle-aged loser, but he's actually Keanu Reeves from *Point Break*. Hey, sir, when you fired your weapon, did you empty the clip into the air while screaming?"

"I fired two shots," Webb said quietly. "They weren't into the air."

"Hey, we've all killed guys in the line," Vic said in a more serious tone. "Sorry."

"Speak for yourselves," Colton said. "I've never killed anyone."

"Probably because you don't carry a gun," Erin observed.

"I've got pepper spray," Colton said.

"Well, shit," Vic said. "Might as well jump over the side right now. He's got us outgunned."

"How're we doing, Mr. Colton?" Webb asked. He squinted into the darkness.

"We're following that other boat," Colton said. "If she's the one that was docked where I found you guys, she's the *Cherry Blossom*."

"Are we catching up?" Webb asked.

"Hard to say," Colton said. "They've got a decent lead on us."

"Try to close in," Webb said. "But don't get within a hundred yards or so. Be discreet."

"Yeah," Vic said. "Whistle a tune or something."

"Where's he headed?" Erin wondered aloud.

"South," Colton said. "Around Manhattan Beach. I guess he's aimed for Breezy Point right now."

"That's it. I'm getting the Coast Guard on the horn," Webb said.

"If they intercept him, we may not be able to grab the Fuentes brothers," Erin said. "Maybe we should let him run for a bit, see where he's going."

"And let him lead us to them," Vic said. "I like it."

"I don't," Colton said. "Did you say the Fuentes brothers?"

"Yeah," Vic said. "What about it?"

"They leased a boat from the club a few days ago," Colton said. "Real nice one, red cigarette boat. Twenty-seven hundred horses, can do eighty knots on flat water. I thought those guys looked like trouble."

"How so?" Webb asked.

"They looked like drug dealers."

"Because they're South American?" Erin asked, her eyebrows showing what she thought of that.

"No, lady, because they looked like scary sons of bitches," Colton said. "What, you think I'm some kinda racist? They're twins, right?"

"That's what I've heard," Erin said. "Can you describe them?"

"Yeah, identical twins," Colton said. "Skinny, but strong, like they work out. They got beards, they wear these nice suits, but a little too flashy. And they got real scary eyes. Shark eyes, y'know?"

"Copy that," Erin said. She'd met men with eyes like that before, eyes like black marbles. They'd usually been violent psychopaths.

"And they've got guns," Colton went on.

"And it never occurred to you to call us?" Vic said.

"I just met you guys!"

"I mean the NYPD, dipstick."

"No way! I didn't want to piss them off. Besides, they weren't causing no trouble."

"They've killed one woman we know about," Vic said. "Maybe a guy in a plane, too. And they're about to kill a Federal agent and his daughter. But hey, they paid cash, and they probably slipped you a little extra to keep quiet, so no problem, am I right?"

"I don't know what you're talking about," Colton said sulkily. "I'm trying to help you guys out, do you a favor."

"Yeah, you're a real credit to your community," Vic said in disgust.

"Bring us a little closer," Webb said. "But not close enough to spook him. O'Reilly's right. We don't just want him; if you're fishing, you put the little fish on a hook to catch the big one."

"He'll see us," Colton said.

"Only if he looks back," Erin said. "I think maybe he's a little distracted. He's wounded, he just killed a couple of guys, his wife got murdered, and he's on his way to meet two really dangerous men. Plus there's his daughter to consider."

"If he starts shooting at us, I'm taking him out," Vic said. He took his pocket flashlight, clamped it in his teeth, and started checking his rifle by its light.

Webb got his phone out. "I'm calling the Coast Guard anyway," he decided. "I'll tell them to hang back, but we're not letting this dirtbag get away."

After getting bounced around a couple of times, Webb eventually ended up talking to someone in a position of authority. He briefly explained the situation and listened to the man on the other end of the line.

"Thank you, sir," he said at last. "We'll keep an eye out for you."

"Backup?" Erin asked.

"They've got a cutter on station," Webb said. "They'll stand off and wait for our signal, but then they'll come fast."

"How fast?" she asked.

"Those babies can do better than twenty-eight knots," Colton said. "Pass us like we was standing still."

"That's not nearly as fast as that cigarette boat you were talking about," she said.

He shrugged. "Cutters have to do other stuff. Cigarette boats are pure speed. Cutter's got more endurance."

"If the Fuentes boys make a run for it, we'll never catch them," Webb sighed. "But I guess we have to try. Maybe the Coast Guard can cut them off."

Erin went forward, to the bow of the *Lady Jane*. Gripping the railing, she felt the salt spray on her face. Though she'd been up for hours and it was now well after three in the morning, she felt no fatigue. She felt oddly and uniquely awake and alert. She'd never spent much time on boats, and now she wondered why not. The feeling of skimming the waves, light and almost weightless, was invigorating.

"If I grab you around the waist, we can do that scene from *Titanic*," Vic said, coming up behind her.

"Try it and you're going swimming," she said.

"You figure what they're up to?" he asked.

"Get Lorcas far from help, screw him on the exchange, kill him and his daughter," Erin guessed. "Dump them in the bay and go home with the drugs."

"Well, yeah," Vic said. "But I mean, why they're making our guy go way the hell out on the water?"

"Like I said, they want him isolated."

"Erin, I know I'm the dumb muscle, but I'm allowed to use my brain, too. How well do you know maritime law?"

"Not that well. I never worked with the Port Authority."

"I did a quick tour with them. Enrichment training, my CO called it. A pain in the ass is what I called it, but I did pick up some stuff. How far out do you figure we have to go before this water stops being the United States?"

"I have no idea, Vic."

"Twelve nautical miles. Which, I've just been informed by our knowledgeable commander, works out to a little more than that in the miles normal people use. How much you want to bet these Fuentes punks are parked just over that line?"

"What good would that do?" Erin asked.

"It'd put them in international waters," Vic said. "And therefore outside the NYPD's jurisdiction."

"So what? The Coast Guard can still grab them."

"So can the US Navy, but we don't exactly have an aircraft carrier on speed-dial. It's just like bank robbers used to do in the Depression. Rob a bank, then skip over the state line so the police can't chase you."

"I know about that," Erin said. "That's why the FBI goes after bank robbers. They can go anywhere in the country."

"I guess it's good Webb's got the Coasties on the way," Vic said. "We may need them."

"Hot pursuit doctrine applies, doesn't it?" Erin said. "As long as we're chasing Lorcas, we can still grab him."

"I intend to," Vic said. "That bastard should've seen us by now. We're not exactly hard to spot."

Erin watched the other boat. "Maybe," she said thoughtfully. "But I think he's a little distracted. He's tired, he's injured, and he's focused on his daughter. A 747 could crash-land in the bay and he might not notice."

"How will we know if he does see us?"

"He'll probably start shooting at us."

Vic rolled his eyes. "Goody."

The weird slow-motion chase went on for two dark, wet hours. They rounded Breezy Point and moved into the rougher, wilder waters of Raritan Bay. The detectives paced the deck of the *Lady Jane*. Webb smoked every cigarette he'd brought with him; a full pack, by Erin's count. Rolf enjoyed sticking his head around the pilot house into the wind, inhaling the smell of the ocean, but after an hour and a half he got bored, curled up, and went to sleep.

Finally, a little after five, as Erin was starting to wonder when the sun would be coming up, Colton whistled sharply between his teeth.

"What?" she and Webb said simultaneously.

"Look at that," Colton said, pointing straight ahead.

"What are we looking for?" Webb asked, rubbing his eyes.

"Navigation lights," Colton said.

"Aren't those stars?" Webb asked.

"Nope," Colton said. "Those are a freighter. Not as big as one of those huge cargo ships, but big enough."

"And our boy's aiming straight at it," Webb said. "You think that's a coincidence?"

"I didn't think we believed in coincidence in Major Crimes," Erin said.

"We don't," Webb said.

Vic had found a pair of binoculars in a footlocker. Muttering about the lack of infrared capability, he tried to focus on the dark shape in the water.

"Our boy's coming alongside," he reported. "Looks like there's another boat already tied up."

"What kind of boat?" Webb asked.

"Cigarette boat," Vic said. "Just like our friends the drug dealers have."

"That figures," Erin said.

"Turn out the lights," Webb said to Colton.

"But I told you—" Colton began.

"*Now.*"

Colton flinched and worked the controls. The *Lady Jane* went dark.

"Get us in close," Webb said. "As quietly as you can."

"We boarding them?" Vic asked.

"Looks that way," Webb said.

"And here's me without my cutlass," Vic said.

"You don't have a cutlass," Erin said.

"You sure about that?" Vic replied.

She wasn't.

Webb was on the radio, talking to the Coast Guard again. "Attention," he said. "US Coast Guard cutter in Raritan Bay, are you receiving?"

The reply came back crisp, clear, and professional. "We hear you loud and clear," a woman said. "This is Captain Torres of the *Raymond Evans*. Who's calling?"

"Lieutenant Webb, NYPD, aboard the *Lady Jane*. Are you apprised of the situation?"

"We are, Lieutenant. My understanding is that you're dealing with a hostage situation. We have you on scope and are standing by, range two nautical miles, south by southeast."

"Glad to hear it, Captain," Webb said. "I don't think they're aware of us. How quiet can your ship be?"

"We're a *Sentinel*-class cutter, not a rowboat, Lieutenant," Torres said. "We're big and fast, but we make a lot of noise. When we come, they'll hear us."

"Copy that, ma'am," Webb said. "We think there's a good chance they'll kill the hostage if things go sideways. Give my team fifteen minutes to see what we can do. Then come heavy. We'll be on board a cargo vessel, identity unknown."

There was a short pause. "Be advised, Lieutenant," Torres said. "The vessel in question is the *Cardenal*, flagged Colombian, bound for Cartagena."

"Damn," Webb said softly.

"So?" Vic said.

"So we're pretty close to that twelve-mile limit," Erin said. "And if that's a foreign vessel and we go on board..."

"That makes us pirates," Vic said, grinning. "I *knew* I should've brought my cutlass. And an eyepatch."

"Your eyes work fine," Erin said.

"Arrr," Vic said. "Drink up, me hearties, yo-ho."

"We copy, Captain Torres," Webb said at last. "We have reason to believe an American citizen is being held on board against her will."

"Acknowledged, Lieutenant Webb," Torres said. Both of them were speaking formally, Erin realized, because they knew what they were talking about could have serious legal ramifications. "You'd better be right about this."

"Understood," Webb said. "I'll take full responsibility."

The *Lady Jane's* engines throttled back. She was an excellent boat, in good repair, and ran remarkably quietly. The freighter loomed ahead of them, dark and brooding. They were separated from it by less than fifty yards of open water.

"Very good, Lieutenant," Torres said. "I have so noted in the log. See you in fifteen. *Raymond Evans* out."

"Our boy's right there," Vic said quietly, binoculars back at his eyes. "I can see him. He's tying his boat to the other one and he's having trouble doing it. There's some sort of stairway on the side of the freighter. I can get a shot."

"Hold fire," Webb said. "We don't want to spook the other guys."

"He shot Erin in the back," Vic said. "It'd be only fair."

"We're not here for street justice, Vic," Erin said.

"He's climbing the stairs," Vic said. "He's not using his left arm. Got it close to the chest. Must be where Erin tagged him. He's got a bag in his other hand."

"That'll be the drugs," Webb said. "Keep your voice down."

Vic nodded.

"Bring us in close enough so we can get aboard," Webb told Colton. "After that, you can hang around or get out, but don't get in our way and don't make any noise."

"Gotcha," Colton said. Erin couldn't see his face in the dark, but he sounded distinctly pale and shaky. However, he steered the *Lady Jane* with skill.

"You sure they haven't seen us?" Erin murmured to Webb.

"No," Webb whispered back. "But I figure they were watching Lorcas. And if they'd seen us, they'd probably be shooting by now. Guns ready, people. But watch your fire. There's a little kid on board."

The *Lady Jane* slid gently to within a couple feet of the freighter. Vic, at the bow, slung his rifle in spite of Webb's instructions. He tensed and jumped. Erin held her breath. It wasn't really a long jump, but if he slipped and fell, he'd either go down like an anchor or get crushed between the two boats.

Vic made the leap, grabbing the handrail of the metal staircase with one hand. With the other, he reached back and took hold of the *Lady Jane*'s rail, steadying the yacht.

"*Hupf!*" Erin said softly to Rolf. Then she jumped. Rolf was right there beside her, clearing the gap with ease. Erin turned and held out a hand for Webb, catching him and pulling him in to safety.

Vic gave a shove and the *Lady Jane* began to drift away. Erin saw Colton's silhouette in the faint moonlight. He appeared to be giving them a thumbs-up, but maybe he was using one of his other fingers. She couldn't blame him either way.

Vic pointed to Erin, then Rolf, then himself, then Webb. Erin and Webb nodded. Rolf wasn't looking at Vic; he was watching Erin.

She wrapped Rolf's leash tightly around her left hand, keeping him on a short lead. She went up the stairs one at a time, moving carefully, feeling for each step. She didn't want to trip or make a loud noise. The others followed, guns at the ready.

The *Cardenal* was an old ship. The smell of rust and spilled engine oil crawled into Erin's sinuses. The stairs creaked alarmingly, especially under Vic's heavy boots. Erin felt the throb of the ship's engines through the hull. The steel plates were vibrating slightly, which didn't speak highly of the ship's seaworthiness. Apparently the crew were making sure the ship was ready to move, though it was currently dead in the water.

They'd need more than their worn-out engines if they hoped to outrun a cutter like the *Raymond Evans*, Erin thought. If the *Evans* could make twenty-eight knots, she'd be surprised if the *Cardenal* could manage half that. The bad guys were screwed; the only question was how much damage they'd be able to do before being taken down.

Erin reached the deck and instinctively crouched against the gunwale. There were lights on deck, but only two; one at the bow, the other over the entrance to the pilot house at the stern. The amidships portion of the deck was taken up by a big set of hatches that presumably led to the cargo bay. A rusty crane stretched overhead, looking for all the world like a hangman's tree, right down to the cable dangling from its arm. There was no sign of Lorcas, nor of anyone else.

Erin eased the evidence bag out of her pocket, opened it, and held it in front of Rolf's nose. He might pick up Lorcas, or whoever had written the note. Either way, there was a good chance the guy who matched the scent was on the ship.

"*Such*," she hissed.

Rolf's nostrils flared. He tilted his head left, then right. Then he set off toward the pilot house.

Erin felt terribly exposed as they drew near, entering the circle of dim light cast by the bulb over the door. She was aware of a shrinking sensation on her skin, as if she could draw back and avoid the bullets she half-expected. But nothing happened.

The door was at the top of a short staircase on the left of the pilot house. She breathed a silent sigh of relief and scooted the last few yards, out of line of sight of the windows. Rolf pulled toward the door and raised his paw to scratch at it.

"*Platz!*" Erin said in a harsh whisper.

Rolf froze. Then he plopped down on his belly. He gave her a reproachful look. He'd done his job this time, and he really thought he deserved his Kong ball.

Vic and Webb joined them, stacking up against the bulkhead. Vic nodded to Erin. She put out a hand and laid it on the doorknob.

At that moment, Agent Lorcas's voice filtered out through the door. He sounded tired, but angry and determined.

"Okay, *hijos de puta*," he growled. "I brought the shit, just like you wanted. Now where's my daughter?"

Chapter 18

"In good time, *senor*," another man's voice replied. He sounded cool and slightly amused.

"No," Lorcas said flatly. "Now."

"Are you really in position to be giving orders?"

"I've killed three people already tonight," Lorcas growled. "You want to try for the number four spot?"

Erin held up a hand, indicating the detectives should wait. She didn't know what they'd walk into in the pilot house. It could just be Lorcas and the other guy, or it could be half a dozen armed men. She kept listening.

"Where is our product?" the man asked.

"Where's my girl?" Lorcas countered.

The other man said something in Spanish which Erin didn't understand. She caught the name "Dante" and guessed the man was Alejandro Fuentes and that he was talking to his twin brother.

"Look out the window, *senor*," Alejandro said.

Rusty metal squealed in protest. Erin turned to see what was happening. The cargo hatch was slowly creaking open. The crane swiveled and its hook began descending. Erin swallowed.

Someone was in the crane's control seat and neither she nor any of her colleagues had seen him in the dim light. Fortunately, it appeared he'd missed them, too. She blessed and cursed the darkness in the same silent breath.

Vic brought his rifle up to his shoulder and drew a bead on the crane's operating cab. He was shaded by the wall of the pilot house, so the crane operator probably couldn't see him. Webb looked back and forth between the crane and the door, trying to decide what to do.

After a moment, with a rattle of metal and a twang of cables, the hook came back into view. Now it held a metal box that looked, to Erin, like the shark cages used by divers. And in the cage huddled a little girl.

Erin had dealt with plenty of bad guys in her twelve years as a cop. She'd faced down murderers, terrorists, psychopaths, and serial killers. She'd gone up against human traffickers and drug dealers, men who profited off human misery. But seeing that scared little kid caged up like an animal, hanging in midair, Erin O'Reilly felt a sudden rush of anger she'd never felt before. It was the sort of rage that actually heated her up from the inside. Her cheeks felt flushed and sunburnt. She heard her heartbeat banging in her ears.

The girl couldn't be more than six or seven. She was wearing tights and a sweatshirt. Her dark hair was tangled and disheveled. The distance was too great to see clearly, but Erin was sure she'd been crying.

"You son of a bitch," Lorcas said. His voice quivered.

"You see, *senor*, your daughter is quite safe," Alejandro said. "Now, our property. Is it in that bag?"

"Yeah."

"You will place the bag at your feet and raise your hands."

"I can't," Lorcas said.

"Ah, yes, I see," Alejandro said. "Your arm. I hope you are not badly hurt?" He still sounded amused.

"Don't worry about it," Lorcas replied.

"Very well. You will place the bag at your feet and raise your right hand. Do it carefully. Your daughter is precariously balanced. You would not want to startle my brother and cause him to drop her."

"I've got a shot," Vic said very quietly.

"Hold fire," Webb whispered. "There may be more bad guys."

"There have to be," Erin murmured. "Somebody's running the ship."

"There's your goddamn drugs," Lorcas said. "Now you're going to put my girl down on the deck, and you're going to do it gently. Then you are opening the cage and she and I are getting back on our boat and we're leaving."

"Really?" Alejandro said with a chuckle that made Erin's skin crawl. "And just why would we permit you to do that?"

"That's the deal," Lorcas said. "If you break it, you're going to die right here."

"Oh? And who is going to kill me? You? Alone, injured, unarmed, against all of us? Or we let you go back to your agency, to bring all the power of your government down on us? I think not. I thank you for bringing us what we asked for. I think we put you in the ocean now, *Senor* Lorcas, and nobody ever finds you. And your daughter comes back to Cartagena with us. Maybe we find some use for her."

That was the final straw. Erin didn't think about whether she was making a good tactical choice. She didn't think at all, not even about her own safety or survival. The only thing in her mind was an image of her niece Anna, not much older than Celeste Lorcas. She grabbed the doorknob with her left hand, the one with Rolf's leash around the wrist, and flung it open.

The pilot house was about fifteen feet across, lit by an overhead bulb. On Erin's left was a console with the controls for the ship. Directly in front of her stood four men. Julio Lorcas had his back to Erin. His right arm was raised, hand empty. His left was in a sling. At his feet lay a black duffel bag. Opposite him were three men with guns in their hands. The one in the middle, a slim, bearded guy holding a pistol, had a smirk on his face that instantly told Erin he was the leader.

One good thing about being a cop was that you always had something you could say in awkward situations. It was unoriginal, but definitely appropriate.

"NYPD! Drop your guns!" Erin shouted. And a lot of things happened at once.

The man on Alejandro's right had a submachine-gun. Vic, who knew guns, would've instantly identified it as an MP5-K. Erin, who didn't care what it was called, saw the muzzle tilt toward her, so she fired twice, aiming for center of mass. The bullets punched the gunman back against the far wall, blood blossoming on his white button-down shirt. He squeezed his trigger as he went down. The submachine-gun rattled, a long burst spraying a random diagonal line across the room. One pane of the pilot-house window shattered in sparkling shards. Sparks fountained from the console.

Simultaneously, Alejandro sidestepped behind his other goon and fired his own gun three times. Two of the bullets whipped through the air between Erin and Lorcas, one buzzing past her ear with a high-pitched zipping sound. The third went through Lorcas's throat. A spray of blood spattered Erin's face.

Lorcas lurched forward, his left arm coming jerkily out of the sling. Erin, with the odd slow-motion clarity granted by a massive adrenaline boost, saw something very small wrapped around his index finger. It looked like a thin metal ring with a wire or pin protruding from it. He stumbled toward Alejandro, blocking her line of fire.

The other gunman, panicking in the sudden chaos, fired several wild shots from his handgun, hitting nothing but sheet metal.

Outside, Vic's rifle cracked once.

"Cover me!" Webb shouted.

Rolf was tensed at Erin's side, ready to spring into action. But he was too well trained to do anything yet. He was waiting for orders.

"Out of the way!" Erin yelled at Lorcas, trying to draw a bead on one of the other two. But he either didn't hear or didn't listen because he kept going forward, charging straight at the two armed men.

Alejandro and his buddy kept shooting. The range was far too close for even untrained shooters to miss every time. Erin saw Lorcas shuddering as bullet after bullet struck him. He was going to fall, he had to fall, but somehow he stayed on his feet and kept going, spreading his arms as if he intended to grab the two gunmen and bang their heads together.

If she'd had a clear shot, Erin wouldn't have paid any attention to the DEA agent. She would've been doing her best to drop the shooters. But he was still blocking her line of fire. She opened her mouth to order Rolf to bite, but then her brain caught up with her eyes and she realized what the thing on Lorcas's finger was.

It was the pin from a hand grenade.

"Shit," she breathed. How long were the fuses on those things? Five seconds, more or less, she thought. But she wasn't sure. Besides, she didn't know exactly when he'd pulled the pin.

"*Raus!*" she snapped at Rolf, spinning and throwing herself through the doorway, back the way she'd come. It was his command to get out. The K-9 obeyed, scrambling out of the pilot house. Erin landed on the steel deck with a hard impact that drove spikes of pain into her knees and elbows.

"Grenade!" she gasped, hoping Vic and Webb could hear her. She hadn't quite gotten the word all the way out when the explosion came.

The remaining window-glass blew out with a gigantic roar. There was no fireball; that was the stuff of movie special effects. There was only a storm of shrapnel and debris, a cyclone of steel and smoke. Shards of metal tore through the thin walls of the pilot house over Erin's head, leaving jagged holes and stunned silence in their wake.

Erin cautiously raised her head. Just in front of her, Vic was flat on his face. He wasn't moving. Rolf, beside her, was crouched low, ears flat against his skull, tail tucked between his legs. She didn't see Webb.

Her ears were ringing. She wondered how badly she'd been hurt. The only pain she felt was in her knees, elbows, and back, but that didn't mean a thing. The worst injuries were often so deep, so serious, that you didn't feel them right away because of the shock. That was okay; she didn't have time to be hurt.

She forced herself onto hands and knees, crawling to Vic's side. She saw blood on his scalp, staining his short blond hair. His vest was peppered with fragments of metal and was actually smoking.

"Vic!" she shouted, shaking his shoulder. Her own voice sounded tinny and echoing in her ears.

He stirred and groaned. Relief washed through her like water down a thirsty throat.

"Vic!" she said again. "Are you okay?"

He put his hands against the deck and did a slow push-up, getting his legs under himself. He got onto one knee, cleared his throat, and spat on the deck.

"Holy *fuck*," he said with quiet emphasis. "What *was* that?"

"Grenade," she said. "Where's Webb?"

Vic blinked and pressed a hand to his head. "Out there," he said, nodding toward the crane.

"*Platz*," Erin told Rolf.

The Shepherd flattened onto his belly and put his chin between his paws.

She shook his leash off her wrist and wrapped both hands around the grip of her Glock. She leaned around the corner of the pilot house and looked down the length of the deck. Webb was standing at the crane's cab, pointing his gun through the windshield. Erin noted that the windshield was a mass of cracked glass. In midair, the cage swung slowly to and fro. Celeste Lorcas was holding two of the bars.

"Clear!" Webb shouted, looking back at them. "What on Earth just happened?"

"Sir! Look out!" Erin yelled back. She'd seen movement toward the bow of the ship, a glint of metal in the moonlight.

A lot of guys would've wasted a second standing still, trying to figure out what she was talking about. Webb, more street-savvy and sensible, did the right thing and dove for the deck. It probably saved his life. There was a strobe-light flash of an automatic weapon, a sound like tearing cloth, and a burst of bullets skipped and whined off the deck plating around him.

Erin squeezed off three shots, aiming for the muzzle flash. She had no idea whether she'd scored a hit or not. Another burst of fire answered her. Several rounds ricocheted around her. She ducked back reflexively, bumping into Vic.

"Where is he?" Vic asked. He'd recovered his rifle and was kneeling close behind her.

"One o'clock," she said, meaning the shooter was just to the right of straight ahead.

Webb's revolver barked twice and was met with another volley from the unseen shooter.

"You get the guys behind us?" Vic asked.

"They're down," she said. She wasn't a hundred percent sure of it, but couldn't imagine anyone surviving a blast like that without any protection. "You ready?"

"Hell yes," Vic said. "Let's get this bastard."

Webb had managed to crawl behind the cab of the crane. He was crouched next to it now, revolver in hand. He was in the middle of a buzzing hornet's nest of bullets.

"Shoot!" Erin told Vic. Then, as the Russian started working his gun, she looked at Rolf. *"Fass!"*

Rolf had been waiting and hoping she'd say exactly that. He came up out of his down posture with liquid speed, streaking out onto the deck. He ran flat-out, tail straight behind him, ears plastered against his skull, a streamlined furry guided missile homing in on the shooter. The man was behind cover, using a pile of crates to screen himself, but that didn't matter to the K-9. Dogs had much better night vision than humans, and there was no hiding from Rolf's nose.

Erin joined Vic, blasting away in the gunman's general direction, aiming high to avoid Rolf. She wasn't really trying to hit him, just get his attention and encourage him to keep his head down. The flat, hard crack of Vic's M4 tore holes in the night, the distinctive starbursts of its muzzle flash leaving afterimages on her eyeballs.

The gunman shifted aim, spraying a handful of rounds their way, but he was rattled and his aim was at least as bad as theirs. A few shots hit the wall they were hiding behind, but none came too close. Then Rolf went in, low and hard, and the shooting stopped and the screaming started.

"That's what I like to hear," Vic said, lowering his gun. "I'll check inside."

"I'll get the guy up front," Erin said, nodding. She ran toward her dog.

A deep rumble, like the bottom note on a really powerful pipe organ, passed through Erin. She felt it in the soles of her feet and the fillings in her teeth. It was a ship's horn, making a noise so powerful it was more sensation than sound. The night flared and vanished in the glare of an enormously bright spotlight.

"Attention!" came the voice of an angry goddess, amplified by a massive bullhorn. "This is the United States Coast Guard! Heave to and prepare to be boarded!"

Erin ignored the announcement. She followed the cries of distress instead, which led her to her dog. Rolf was standing over a man, teeth clamped on his arm, tail wagging excitedly. Next to the man lay a submachine-gun.

She kicked the gun away and covered the guy. "You're under arrest," she said. She could feel the shakes coming, now that the danger seemed to be over. She suddenly felt very, very tired.

Chapter 19

Contrary to Vic's piratical fantasies, the Coast Guard boarding party didn't bring any cutlasses when they boarded the *Cardenal*. They came with rifles, flashlights, and questions. Fortunately, they also brought a medic.

Erin was happy to let Webb handle the questions. She left Vic in the care of the Coast Guard medic, the Russian grumbling that he felt just fine and to leave him alone. While a couple of Coasties figured out how to get Celeste down to the deck, Erin went back to the pilot house. She didn't really want to see what was there, but knew she needed to.

It was at least as bad as she'd feared. One look was enough to tell her the medic wouldn't be needed in this room. All four men were way beyond the skill of any doctor. The duffel bag had also been blown to kingdom come. Erin figured a fair amount of the dust the explosion had scattered was actually high-purity coke. She made sure not to let Rolf into the room. The K-9 could inhale the stuff without even meaning to.

"That was one expensive grenade," she muttered. Her ears were still ringing and she'd added a headache to her backache. She was exhausted and depressed and wanted nothing more than to lie down somewhere dark and quiet for a day or two. But she couldn't do that; the job wasn't finished yet. She took Rolf back toward the crane to see how the Coast Guard was getting on with their rescue.

The cage settled to the deck. It was secured with a padlock. One of the Coasties went to work on the lock with a set of bolt cutters. He made quick work of it and opened the door. Celeste shrank back from him.

"C'mon, kid," the Guardsman said, extending a hand. "It's okay. You're safe."

Celeste shook her head and backed into the corner.

"Jeez," the Guardsman said. "It's fine. We're the good guys."

"Mommy?" Celeste said.

Erin's heart gave a twinge. "Hey," she said to the Guardsman. "Can you move for a second?"

"Who're you?" he demanded.

"Detective O'Reilly, NYPD Major Crimes."

"This isn't New York, O'Reilly," he said. "You don't have jurisdiction."

"We can have our turf war in a minute," she said. "Can I talk to this girl, please?"

"Fine," he said, throwing up his hands. "She's all yours."

Erin got down on one knee, ignoring the flare of pain from a fresh bruise. "Hey, Celeste," she said. "I know you're scared, kiddo. But we're here to help."

"Want mommy," Celeste said stubbornly.

"Your mommy's not here," Erin said, forcing herself not to think about how Connie Lorcas had looked the last time she'd seen her. "Do you know what your daddy does for his job?"

"He's with the DEA," Celeste said, pronouncing the letters with the emphasis of a girl who'd recently learned to spell and was proud of it.

"Do you know what that means?"

"He goes after bad guys."

"That's right," Erin said. "So do I. I'm a police detective."

"Show me your badge," Celeste said suspiciously.

"Sure thing," Erin said, unclipping her gold shield and holding it out. "I met your daddy earlier tonight. It's because of him that my friends and I came here to help you."

"Really?" The girl was hopeful but still wary.

"I promise," Erin said. "That cage looks really cold and hard."

"It is."

"Wouldn't you like to come out and go somewhere softer?"

Celeste thought it over. She nodded.

"Do you like dogs?" Erin asked.

Celeste looked at Rolf and nodded again.

"This is Rolf," Erin told her. "He's a police dog, so he's really well trained. He's a good boy. And he likes kids. Why don't you come out and meet him?"

Celeste carefully stepped out of the cage. She awkwardly patted Rolf on the head in the manner of small children everywhere. Rolf, who was accustomed to Erin's niece and nephew, submitted to the clumsy petting with good grace. He licked her hand. She giggled, which Erin took to be a very good sign.

Webb joined them, accompanied by a slender, hard-faced woman in a Coast Guard uniform. The woman gave her a cool once-over and nodded politely.

"O'Reilly, this is Captain Torres," Webb said.

"Good to meet you, ma'am," Erin said, most of her attention still fixed on Celeste. "Thanks for the help."

"Looks like your team did the heavy lifting," Torres said. "We're just the cleanup crew. You understand this is going to be a shitstorm, don't you?"

"We're used to it," Erin said.

"Tell me about it," Vic said, strolling over and attaching himself to the group. "This is nothing." He had a bandage wrapped around his head but seemed otherwise none the worse for wear.

"It's a long way from nothing, Detective," Torres said. "This is more along the lines of an international incident. What did you do to this ship? The helm looks like a bomb went off."

"Hand grenade," Erin said.

"More than one, I'd guess," Vic said. "But they weren't ours."

"They weren't?" Torres asked.

"Of course not," Vic said. "We're the NYPD, lady. We aren't even allowed to use flashbangs. You think they'd issue us grenades?"

"DEA Agent Lorcas brought them on board," Erin said. "He had at least one hidden in his sling. He yanked the pin when the shooting started."

"And blew himself up?" Torres asked doubtfully.

Erin glanced at Celeste again. The girl was holding Rolf, her arms wrapped around his neck. She didn't seem to be listening, but you could never tell with kids.

"He took a round in the throat," she said in an undertone. "Either he didn't think he'd make it, or he'd already decided to take as many of them with him as he could."

"Kamikaze style," Vic said. "Strap grenades to yourself and give the bad guys a hug. I gotta say, it's a badass way to go."

"It's a stupid way to go," Webb said. "He had a kid."

"And he'd committed several major felonies on his way here," Erin reminded him. "Best case, he was going to spend the next twenty years in prison. I think he figured he didn't have much to lose."

"Are you defending him?" Webb asked. "He tried to kill you."

"No, he didn't," Erin said. "He told Alejandro he'd killed three people tonight."

"So?" Vic said.

"So four of us got shot," Erin said. "Three O'Malleys plus me. It was dark in that church. He couldn't possibly tell how badly hurt all of us were, but he thought he'd taken three of us out. I was wearing my vest under my coat, but at the station I was standing pretty close to him. He would've seen I was wearing it. He aimed for my center of mass and he used a shotgun."

"It wouldn't penetrate," Vic said, nodding. "That's why he didn't use a rifle. He didn't want to kill a cop. I bet it hurt like hell, though."

"You have no idea," Erin said.

Torres was looking at them with intense curiosity. "What's this all about, anyway?" she asked. "It sounds like the DEA was involved. But did you say an agent shot you? Why?"

"It's complicated," Erin said. "We're investigating the death of a guy who was running drugs. The drugs were stolen from a Colombian cartel. The cartel kidnapped the kid to use as leverage to get the stuff back. She's the agent's daughter."

"They kidnapped a DEA agent's child?" Torres was obviously a tough woman, but she was shocked. "What did they have, some kind of death wish?"

"Didn't work out great for them," Vic observed. "But nobody said these guys were geniuses. How many of them did we get?"

"Rolf and I grabbed the one at the bow," Erin said. "He's a little chewed up, but basically fine. None of the guys in the pilot house made it."

"Everybody aft is DOA," Torres confirmed. "And there's another body my guys pulled out of the crane."

"Yeah, that was me," Vic said. "I figured once everybody started shooting, he was gonna drop the kid or some shit, so I took him out. Figured I better go for the head."

"Good shooting," Erin said.

"Why'd you have to open that door?" Vic asked. "You could've at least warned us."

"They were about to kill Lorcas," she said. "I didn't think we had any more time."

"These drugs you were talking about," Torres said to Erin. "Where are they now?"

"All over the place," Erin said. "The grenades sprayed them every which-way. You might be able to sweep some of the powder up if you send a guy with a broom."

"Between that, the guns, and the American kid, I don't think the Colombians will protest too much," Torres said. "I still need to write all this up, though, and I'll need statements from the three of you."

"We understand," Webb said. "We're not going anywhere for a while."

"You got that right," Vic said. He was looking over the rail on the port side of the ship. "You know that goddamn rent-a-cop?"

"The guy from the yacht club?" Erin said. "Bud?"

"Yeah, him. He must've taken off once the lead started flying. He's long gone."

"We should've grabbed him," Torres said. "But we were focused on the freighter and the firefight. You want me to send a launch to bring him back?"

"No point," Webb said. "We know who he is and where to find him if we need him. He's peripheral."

"Besides, he may be an asshole, but he gave us a hand," Vic said. "No point in making his life any harder than it's gotta be."

"We need to identify the bodies," Webb said.

"That'll be a little tricky," Vic said. "It's a big bowl of chunky salsa back there."

"They'll have passports," Torres said. "And probably enough intact fingers to give us prints."

"Jesus," Erin muttered.

"I'd like to interrogate our survivor," Webb said. "O'Reilly, can you keep an eye on Miss Lorcas?"

"I'd like to help with the interrogation, sir," she said.

"And I'd like our prisoner to speak English, but it appears he doesn't," Webb said. "How's your Spanish?"

"Not great," Erin admitted.

"That's because you weren't with the LAPD," Webb said. "It comes in pretty handy out there. Don't worry, I'll let you know what I find out. I don't think he knows much in any case. I think he's one of the little fish."

"That's probably right," Erin said. "I think the guy on the crane was Dante Fuentes, and one of the guys Lorcas took out was Alejandro."

"Think that last perp can help close our case?" Vic asked. "You know, the one that got us started with this whole goddamn mess? The playboy pilot with the stitched-up chute?"

"That's what I'm going to find out," Webb said.

"So you're doing police work," Vic said. "And Erin's babysitting. What do I get to do?"

"You get to find a quiet spot and relax," Webb said. "You just shot and killed a man and you've been injured. Either thing earns you some time on the bench."

"Seriously? You call this an injury?" Vic pointed to his head. "It's a lousy scratch. The shrapnel bounced right off my skull."

"Now that I believe," Erin said. "You've got the thickest skull of any guy I know."

"And you two were shooting guys too," Vic went on.

"I'm pretty sure I didn't hit anyone," Webb said.

"That doesn't surprise me, sir," Vic said with a straight face.

"Why don't I go ahead and take your statement for my report, Detective?" Torres asked Vic, deciding to inject some diplomacy. "It's a necessary part of the process, and it'll make your CO feel better."

"Fine," Vic grumbled. "Damn it, now IAB is gonna take away my M4."

"You'll get it back," Erin said.

"Yeah, but they'll screw up the sights when they test-fire it. I don't like other people touching my guns."

Erin shook her head and returned her attention to Celeste. The girl was really clinging to Rolf. His warm, furry presence was a tremendous comfort to the kid. Rolf seemed to realize this. He was leaning into her embrace, staring at the small human with his steady brown eyes.

Erin blinked. Celeste's eyes were closed. She appeared to have actually fallen asleep, sitting right there on the deck, arms wrapped around the dog. The poor kid must be all used up. When fear started wearing off, one of the main symptoms was exhaustion.

Smiling in spite of everything that had happened, Erin knelt down and gently gathered the child up, carefully disentangling her from the K-9. Celeste shifted and, without waking up, circled Erin's neck with her little arms.

Celeste would wake up all too soon, to a world in which she no longer had parents. But for now, Erin could keep her warm and safe, so that was what she would do.

The eastern horizon was starting to turn pink. The night was almost over at last.

Chapter 20

Five hours later, Carlyle came downstairs to find Erin sitting at the bar in the Barley Corner. It was just past eleven, a little early for the lunchtime crowd, and the room was mostly empty. A soccer match was playing on the big TV, a couple of truck drivers watching and eating sandwiches. Erin had two empty shot glasses and half a glass of Guinness in front of her. Rolf was lying under her stool, fast asleep, the tip of his tongue protruding from his mouth and his front paws twitching slightly.

Carlyle slid onto the stool next to hers. She didn't turn her head. She just kept staring at the polished wood of the bar, hands wrapped around her glass.

"Morning, darling," he said quietly, laying a gentle hand on her wrist. "You've had the devil's own night, I'm thinking."

"How do you figure?" she asked, looking up with the best smile she could muster. It didn't even feel convincing to her.

"You've been awake nearly thirty hours, if my reckoning's right," he said. "You've not changed your clothes, nor showered, and rather than come up to bed, you went straight to the bar.

Two glasses of whiskey before noon tells a publican his customer's either a drunk or a lass who's had a difficult time."

"Yeah," she said.

"I don't know what you've heard from your people," he went on. "But Red Rafferty's going to pull through. Aidan Rierdon and Brian McGovern weren't so lucky, but you know that already."

"I didn't know their names," Erin said dully.

"Since you're not at the hospital yourself, I'm thinking your own wounds aren't too serious," he said. "But I've been worried about you, darling."

"I'm fine."

"I can see that, aye. Can't imagine why I'd think otherwise."

She raised an eyebrow. "Really? Sarcasm, from you? I thought you were better than that."

"Were you able to track down the lad who double-crossed you?" Carlyle asked.

"Yeah," she said. "But it won't do Evan any good."

"What happened, darling?"

Erin wasn't sure whether to laugh, cry, or scream. She took a drink instead. The two shots of Glen D and half-pint of Guinness she'd already drunk had steadied her a little. Carlyle was watching her with concern in his eyes.

"The stuff's gone," she said. "And practically everybody's dead. I shot a guy. Up close. Two rounds, right in the chest."

"Oh, darling," he said, squeezing her hand.

"Not that it mattered," she said. "He'd have been blown to bits a few seconds later anyway. That happens to me a lot, have you noticed? We've got four dead Colombians on a freighter, one dead DEA guy and his dead wife, and a little kid who's an orphan. I left her with Child Protective Services. And it was all for nothing."

"How do you mean?"

Erin took a quick look around the room. Nobody was paying the slightest attention to them, and the only one who might be near enough to overhear was Matt, Carlyle's early-shift bartender. Matt had been working at the Corner long enough to develop a good case of selective deafness.

"The coke got blown up too," she said, keeping her voice down just in case. "So nobody's getting it."

"Perhaps that's for the best," Carlyle said. "Filthy stuff."

"I couldn't agree more," she said. "But it's such a damn waste. We've got nine bodies now, all because of one goddamn stupid plane crash."

"Nine?" Carlyle said.

"There's Wilder, the pilot," Erin said, counting on her fingers. "Then Rafferty's buddies, Aidan and Brian; that makes three. Then there's Agent Lorcas and his wife, the Fuentes brothers, and two gunmen they had on their boat. Nine."

"It seems things got out of hand," Carlyle said.

"Yeah, you could say that. And you know what the worst of it is? The Colombians didn't have a damn thing to do with killing Wilder."

"Really?"

"Really. We got one of their guys alive, thanks to Rolf." She caressed the dog with her foot and gave him an affectionate glance. "I didn't think he'd talk, but Webb got to him. I guess he figured he was dead anyway, once word got back to the cartel about how badly everything got screwed up, so his best chance was WitSec. Plus, between Rolf and Vic, and with all his buddies dead, the poor guy was practically shitting himself. He spilled everything he knew."

"I'd expect you to be happier about that," Carlyle observed.

"They knew about Wilder," she said. "The cartel had a traitor, a guy who was dealing on the side. They found out he was selling to this other guy in Panama, who had a contact in

Puerto Rico, who got the stuff to Philadelphia, where it ended up in Wilder's hands. It was complicated. And I guess there's more than nine bodies, come to think of it."

"I'd rather not think what happened to the other lads who were involved," Carlyle said dryly. "The cartels aren't known for being merciful to traitors and thieves."

"Wilder was next," Erin said. "They were going to kill him and take the stuff back, but they never got the chance. Alejandro and Dante were actually at JFK, waiting for his plane to land. They were planning to snatch him the moment he walked out of the airport. I guess he was luckier the way it worked out. I think, whatever they were planning on doing to him, it wasn't going to be quick."

"I imagine not," Carlyle said. "A Colombian necktie isn't an article of apparel."

"Isn't that where you cut a guy's throat and pull his tongue out through the slit?"

"That's my understanding. I'm not speaking from personal experience, obviously."

"The timing is crazy on this," Erin said. "Here's this jerk, trying to ship his drugs to New York to sell to the Lucarellis, and there's guys lined up around the block to murder him. I mean, what are the chances? You've got a bunch of cartel thugs waiting on the ground, but someone else kills him in the air, and it all happens right after the girl he raped sends him this sweet message of forgiveness? That's one hell of a coincidence."

Carlyle nodded. "From the sound of it, this lad spent his last bit of goodwill, and the bill came due. It was his time to go. You've the right of it, darling."

"No," she said. "No, nothing's right about it. There's no way all this is coincidence. You know what Ian says about coincidence?"

"I don't recall," Carlyle said. He stood up and waved to the booth at the far corner. "Lad! Can you join us a moment?"

Ian Thompson got out of the booth and walked briskly to join them. Erin hadn't even known he was there.

"Morning, sir," he said. "Erin. What's the situation?"

"Just needed to pick your brain," Erin said. "What did they teach you in the Corps about coincidence?"

"Once is happenstance, twice is coincidence, three times is enemy action," Ian said without hesitation.

"Exactly," she said. "We've got three things going on here. Number one is the drug smuggling. Number two is the assault. Number three is the sabotage of the plane. No way are they all separate. Now, we know the drug smuggling isn't connected to the sabotage; the Colombians wanted their drugs back and expected the plane to land. They didn't want to wreck it. So the other two must be linked somehow."

"You're saying the girl he victimized took her revenge?" Carlyle said.

"Not necessarily," Erin said. "She sent him a text message, forgiving him for what he did to her. I could see her getting pissed and taking him out if he'd said something back to her, some asinine macho bullshit. But he didn't."

"What did he say to her?" Carlyle asked.

"Nothing," Erin said. "He didn't reply at all."

"Perhaps his silence angered her," Carlyle said.

"Sounds like a comms screwup to me," Ian said.

They both looked at him. The former Marine shrugged slightly.

"Happens all the time," he said. "If you send a message and the recipient doesn't copy, you assume he didn't receive. So you re-send if it's important."

"But the text did go through," Erin said. "Patience showed us her phone. It went to his number. He read it."

"Making a couple assumptions there," Ian said.

Erin thought about it for a moment. Then she smiled. It was more genuine than the one she'd put on for Carlyle earlier. She slipped off the barstool, leaned in, and kissed Ian on the cheek.

"What's that for?" he said, startled.

"If you ever get tired of being a bodyguard, you could join the Department and work cases," she said. "You're absolutely right. I was making assumptions. And now I'm not, and I just cracked the case."

"What assumptions?" Carlyle asked. He was smiling too, enjoying Erin's sudden burst of energy, though he didn't understand what had just happened.

"I assumed Wilder was the one looking at his phone," she said. "Excuse me. I need to go."

"Go?" Carlyle repeated. "Where?"

"Philadelphia."

"Hadn't you best have something to eat first?" he asked with a smile. "And this isn't delicate of me, but might I suggest a shower and a change of clothes?"

Erin's stomach growled. Rolf looked up at her, head cocked. Food sounded good to him, too.

"A shower," she said grudgingly. "And clothes, sure. I'll grab food on the way."

*   *   *

The shower revived her a little, and a bowl of kibble refueled Rolf. Erin hurried downstairs again, went out the back way, and headed for the parking garage. She was waiting for the light at the street corner when she realized she was being followed. The man had come up behind her so smoothly and silently, she'd had no idea he was there. This wasn't surprising;

he'd been a quiet guy to begin with, and Scout Sniper school had taught him to be basically invisible.

"You can't drive to Philadelphia," he said.

"Like hell I can't," Erin said. The light changed and she started across the street. "I don't take orders from you, Ian."

"Not giving orders. Stating facts." He fell in step beside her and Rolf. "You've been awake thirty hours, been wounded, got three drinks in you. Best case, you get pulled over by one of your guys before you make the Holland Tunnel. Worst case, you fall asleep at the wheel or you're a little slow to react. Then you're wrapped around some soccer mom's minivan."

"What do you know about road safety?" she snapped. She hadn't meant to speak sharply. Fatigue gave an edge to her voice.

"Drove Humvees through Fallujah," he said. "Wasn't like New York driving, I guess. Not as many taxis and bikes, more snipers and IEDs."

Erin forced herself to think, to consider the situation logically. For just a moment, everything had been clear and sharp. But now exhaustion, coupled with a whole buffet of aches and pains, was reasserting itself. Ian waited, giving her time. Like the sniper he'd once been, he could be excruciatingly patient.

"I don't need to go to work today," she said, speaking slowly. "I'm not getting any new assignments until IAB clears me for the shooting on the boat. But that'll take a few days, maybe longer. It happened in international waters and it involved the Coast Guard and a Colombian ship, so the Feds will have to get involved. Hell, maybe the State Department. That means more delays. But the NYPD didn't put me on modified assignment yet. They should've, but it's not clear I actually killed anyone. As soon as they dig the bullets out of that bastard and match them to my Glock, I'll be stuck riding a desk."

"Your point?" Ian asked politely. They'd reached the parking garage across from the Corner. Erin's Charger was on the second level. She started up the stairs. Ian stayed with her.

"I can put this one to bed now, or it'll take a week or more," she said. "I don't know what'll happen in that time. I've got a window, but it's only a few hours wide. I don't have time to rest. I've driven tired before. It's always come out okay."

"You don't have to," he said. "Bring backup."

"I can't haul Vic into this," she said. "He's already on a desk. There wasn't any doubt about his shooting. He blew a guy's head off with his rifle. Webb watched him do it. Everybody knows it was a clean shoot, but he can't go into the field until he's officially cleared. And Webb's wiped out. You think I should grab some poor random uniform and haul him along?"

"I'll drive you."

"Are you nuts? All the way to Philly?"

"Won't be a problem. Already cleared it with Mr. Carlyle. Taking a vacation day."

"A vacation day," she repeated. "Ian, this is going to be a miserable trip. Two and a half hours each way, and that's if traffic's good, which it won't be. I'll have to coordinate with Philadelphia PD, since it's their jurisdiction, and that means a ton of red tape. Assuming I can cut through the bullshit, I'll have an interrogation to conduct, which won't be pleasant, and if it goes well, I'll have a murderer riding back with me. You really want to put yourself through all that?"

He shrugged. "Had worse trips."

"Are you talking about your helicopter crash? Yeah, yeah, I know; five days, no sleep, carrying your wounded buddy, Taliban trying to kill you. I've heard the story."

"Was worse than driving across Jersey," he said. "Even for a kid from Queens."

Erin shook her head. "Okay, fine. Are you going to insist on driving your car?"

"Isn't mine. Mercedes belongs to Mr. Carlyle."

"You know what I mean."

"Yours is fine. Better engine, has a spot for Rolf. It okay with the Department if I drive?"

"It's unmarked, so as long as you don't use the flashers or siren, it's fine. Anyway, you've got me in the car, and I suppose I'll be on duty, technically speaking. You're covered."

Erin fished out her keys and handed them over. Ian stooped and looked under the car.

"You know, I do have a bomb-sniffing dog," she reminded him. "Rolf, *such!*"

Rolf made a circuit of the Charger, inspecting the wheel wells and undercarriage. He finished his search and looked up at Erin, wagging his tail uncertainly. He hadn't found anything.

"Good boy," she said, rubbing his head. It was a silly, pointless ritual, right up until the one time it wasn't. That was the thing about precautions. You didn't need them until you couldn't live without them.

Ian slid behind the wheel, adjusted the seat, and checked his mirrors. "Where's the objective?" he asked.

"Philadelphia police headquarters," Erin said. "Wake me up when we're close."

Rolf's compartment made it impossible to recline the seat more than a couple of inches back, like a chair on an overcrowded commercial airline. Erin did the best she could. Then she closed her eyes and let herself drift, hoping sheer exhaustion and alcohol would keep nightmares at bay.

She ought to call Webb and let him know what she was doing. She ought to contact Philadelphia law enforcement and get the ball rolling with them. She ought to be tackling the massive pile of paperwork from the incidents that had happened during that endless night. And she ought to be at home, in bed, getting a solid eight hours. Instead, here she was, letting a civilian—no, that wasn't right, a non-police veteran—drive her beloved Charger, chasing a hunch across two state lines in the hopes of closing her case before the NYPD bureaucracy caught up with her.

God, but she was tired.

Chapter 21

"Ma'am?"

"Don't call me that," Erin said sleepily.

"Sorry. No excuse."

She opened her eyes and wished she hadn't. Golden-white light speared through the windshield into her brain. Could you get a hangover before noon, if you'd only slept a couple of hours and had a couple of drinks? Apparently you could. Maybe it was the aftereffects of the concussion from the explosion. She groaned and closed her eyes again.

"Where are we?" she asked.

"Police HQ, Philadelphia," Ian said. "Orders were to wake you when we got here."

"Yeah. Thanks." She didn't move.

Something cold and wet nuzzled her ear. She flinched. The cold, wet thing was replaced by a warmer, wetter thing as Rolf upgraded his nose to his tongue.

"Okay, okay," Erin said. "Let's do this."

"Want me to stay with the car?" Ian asked.

"Why don't you come in?"

"Not a cop."

"You don't have to wear a shield to go into a police station."

"Not under arrest, either."

"Or that. Come on."

Ian took a moment to unbuckle his shoulder holster and stow his sidearm in her glove compartment. That was probably a good idea. He was legally licensed to carry in New York, but the Philly cops would get twitchy if a non-officer carried a Beretta into their house.

Erin had never been in a police station in Philadelphia, but it wasn't that different from New York. She presented her credentials to the desk sergeant, asked around, and got directed to Captain Franklin's office. Franklin was a big, bald, muscular guy who looked like he spent more time at the gym than behind a desk. He had a bone-crushing handshake and a big smile that showed perfect dentistry.

"Detective O'Reilly," he said. "I've heard a lot about you."

"I'll take that as a compliment, sir," she said, returning the smile as well as she could. Her head was really pounding.

"This must be your K-9," Franklin went on. "It's unusual for a detective to have a police dog."

"This is Rolf," she said proudly. "Rolf, *sitz.*"

Rolf sat bolt upright on his haunches, looking at least as proud as his partner.

"I can tell he's an asset to the Force," Franklin said. He turned to Ian. "And you are...?"

"Thompson," Ian said. "Detective O'Reilly's driver, sir."

Franklin looked him over, taking in his haircut, the scars on his scalp and neck, and the way he talked. "You were in the Service," he said. It wasn't a question.

"Yes, sir," Ian said.

"What branch?"

"Marine Corps, sir."

"Where'd you serve?"

"Scout Sniper, sir. Sergeant. Two tours, one in the Sandbox, one in the 'Stan."

"Semper fi," Franklin said, grinning even more broadly. Belatedly, Erin noticed the Captain's lapel pin. It was red, with a metallic emblem of an eagle, globe, and anchor; the symbol of the USMC.

"You were in the Corps, sir?" she asked.

"Did my time in the first Gulf War," Franklin said. "Long time ago now. I was a First Lieutenant, but I hope Sergeant Thompson can forgive me for that."

"No problem with officers, sir," Ian said, poker-faced. "They draw fire away from the noncoms."

Franklin laughed. "Can I offer the two of you some coffee? I think there may be a donut or two left in the break room."

"Coffee would be great, sir," Erin said. Her stomach rumbled loudly, reminding her that she'd slept through her chance at a meal. "I wouldn't say no to a donut."

Franklin had a pot behind his desk. Erin soon held a steaming cup of coffee with cream. Ian took his black. Franklin added cream and two lumps of sugar to his. The donut had chocolate icing and multicolored sprinkles. It tasted wonderful.

"Now," the Captain said. "What can I do for you?"

"We're here about the death of a Philadelphian," she said. "Arthur Wilder."

"That'd be the guy who died in that plane crash?" Franklin asked.

"He jumped out of the plane before it hit the ground, so technically, he didn't die in the crash."

While Franklin listened, Erin laid out the short version of what had happened. She left out a lot, omitting some of the shady dealing with the O'Malleys and Lucarellis, but explaining how Wilder's drugs had led to the deaths of Julio Lorcas, his wife, and various underworld thugs.

"Damn," Franklin said when she'd finished. "I was in firefights in Kuwait that had fewer casualties. So you're following up the drug angle?"

"Actually, no," Erin said. "I don't think Wilder's murder had anything to do with the drugs. At least, not directly."

"So you want to arrest and extradite that young woman you mentioned? Miss Goodspeed?"

"She's a suspect," Erin said. "But I don't want to arrest her either."

Franklin spread his hands. "Then I don't quite see what you're doing here, Detective."

"I'm pretty sure I know who killed Wilder," she said. "But I don't have proof. I do have an eyewitness, but both the witness and the killer are outside my jurisdiction. I'd like to request your department's assistance."

"Of course," Franklin said. "Who's the witness?"

"An airport mechanic. I think he can identify our killer."

"And you want to bring this mechanic in? Give him a look at the murderer's face?"

"Almost." Erin smiled. "It's not her face he remembers."

"I'm intrigued," Franklin said. "What did you have in mind?"

*   *   *

An hour later, Erin found herself in the unpleasant position of waiting while other cops did the legwork. She, Ian, and Rolf were camped out in the break room. Erin found and devoured another donut. Rolf had spent the first few minutes sniffing around the room, acquainting himself with the new odors. Satisfied, he was now curled up at her feet, snout tucked under his tail.

"Lucky break," Erin said. "Running into another former Marine."

"Lot of us out there," Ian said. "Don't think it mattered. He would've helped anyway."

"Maybe. But the connection helped. Did you ever think about it?"

"About what?"

"Becoming a cop."

Ian didn't startle easily. The only indicator he gave was a slow blink of his eyes. "No," he said.

"Why not?"

"Seen a lot of combat," he said. "Did lots of shooting. You think I should be going around with a badge and a gun?"

"You carry a gun," she reminded him.

"As a precaution," he said.

"You've used it more than once since you got back," she said, feeling a little irritated.

"Would've used it more if I was wearing a uniform," he said. "Got all the wrong instincts and reflexes. Some drunk idiot would take a swing at me some night, I'd blow him away. You don't want me as a police officer."

"What *do* you want to do, Ian?" she asked, turning to look him in the eye. "You don't want to be a driver and bodyguard your whole life, do you?"

He shrugged. "Got no problem with it."

"How about your girlfriend? And her kid?"

"What about them?"

"Where do you see that going?"

He didn't smile; that wasn't Ian's style. But his eyes held a faint mischievous spark. "Interrogating me because you don't have a suspect to grill?"

"Okay, fine," she said, holding up a hand. "Sorry. I guess I worry about you a little."

"Really?" Now he was genuinely surprised. "Why?"

"I expect one of the things you learned in combat was not to think about the future."

"Affirmative," he said. "It's dangerous. Gets you distracted from what you're supposed to be doing. Can get you killed."

"But you're not in combat anymore, and I think you still don't think about it. You still act like you could get killed any moment."

"You *can* get killed any moment. That's the way the world works."

"Believe me, I know," she said. "I got shot last night. Thank God for my vest. But there's a pretty good chance we'll both be going home at the end of the day tonight, so it might be a good idea to spare a thought for what happens tomorrow."

He nodded. "Been thinking about it, a little."

"And?"

"Think maybe I'll ask Cassie to marry me."

"What?" The word came out louder than Erin meant it to. Rolf perked up his ears and raised his head to look at her.

"I say something wrong?" Ian asked.

"No! I just... I mean, that wasn't what I was expecting."

"Not sure she's ready," he said. "She still misses her husband. Cries about him sometimes. Hasn't let go all the way."

Erin put out a hand and touched his arm. "Ian, if you wait until she doesn't miss him anymore, you'll wait forever. You don't stop missing people who die. You learn to live with it. Just because she still loves him doesn't mean she can't make room in her heart for you."

"Don't want to be disrespectful," he said.

"I sometimes think you get a little too wrapped up in being respectful."

"Think that, do you, ma'am?"

She swatted his shoulder. "Stop that!"

"No excuse," he said, and now he had a faint but unmistakable smile at one corner of his mouth.

"You're serious? About proposing?"

"When we're ready. And when Ben's ready. Don't want to mess up the kid."

"Ian, Ben loves you," Erin said, speaking with every bit of sincerity she could muster. "I've seen you with him. He needs a dad in his life, and I think you're the one he needs."

"My dad's a total fuckup," Ian said, the unexpected vulgarity making Erin flinch in surprise.

"But you're not," she said. "You're nothing like your father."

"You don't know him."

"I don't need to. I know you. You'll be the best husband and father that family could hope for. So get off your ass and get that girl a ring."

"Giving me orders again?" he said. The twinkle was back in his eye.

"I'm giving you advice. Good advice."

"Can I give you some?"

"Sure."

"Stop worrying about me and start worrying what you're going to say when they bring in your suspect."

"Oh, I know what I'm going to say," Erin said. "I just get impatient, so I'm using the time we've got. I hate waiting."

"I might have made a bad cop," Ian said. "But you'd have made a worse sniper. Got to have patience. You'd run in, guns blazing, get everybody shot."

"Maybe," she admitted.

Her phone buzzed. She saw Webb's name on the screen and sighed. After briefly considering letting it roll to voicemail, she swiped the screen.

"O'Reilly," she said.

"How fast can you get to the Eightball?" Webb asked.

"If I leave right this minute? About two and a half hours."

"Good. We've got the DEA, the Coast Guard, and Homeland Security breathing down the Captain's neck, and that's not even counting the Colombian consul, so we want to make sure... Wait, you said *hours*?"

"Yes, sir."

"Where in the hell are you? Miami?"

"Philadelphia."

"Philadelphia? The one in Pennsylvania?"

"Is there another one, sir?"

She heard Webb take a slow, deep breath on the other end of the line. "This is not a good time to be a smartass, O'Reilly," he said. "Who's with you?"

"Rolf. And Ian Thompson."

"Ian Thompson," Webb repeated. "This would be the same Ian Thompson who moonlights as a vigilante and has shot and killed one Irish assassin, one Colombian cartel gunman, and two O'Malley associates that we know of?"

"That's the one."

"Subordinates like you are the reason they make economy-size bottles of antacid, did you know that?"

"I wasn't aware of that, sir." Erin kept her tone carefully neutral.

"What are you and he doing in Philadelphia?"

"I'm trying to close the Wilder case. Ian's my driver."

"Did you lose your driver's license in some incident I haven't seen the paperwork for?"

"No. But I was up all night and I'd had a couple of drinks after that gunfight we were in, so I figured it was safer for someone else to drive."

"That's the one sensible decision you've made since the last time I saw you," Webb said. There was a pause, and Erin could practically hear the gears moving in the Lieutenant's brain. "Do you have a good lead?" he finally asked.

"I know who did it," she said. "Do you need me to head back to Manhattan right now?"

"Don't bother. By the time you'd get here, the bureaucrats ought to have things sorted out regardless. Neshenko and I will handle this. When were you planning on telling me about your little out-of-state jaunt?"

"I was just getting around to it," she said, which was almost true. "I slept the whole drive."

"I'm sure you needed it. How much longer will your investigation take?"

"A couple hours, probably."

"Good. Let me know how it comes out. Call me when you're on your way. Oh, and O'Reilly?"

"Yes, sir?"

"IAB has determined it's not possible to tell whether the shots you fired were lethal or not, given the condition of the body of the man you shot. You'll be cleared, Lieutenant Keane is sure of it, but in the meantime they have no choice but to treat it as a fatal shooting. You can consider yourself on modified assignment as of the moment you hit the road back to New York."

"Then? Not now?"

"You have to be informed of your status for it to take effect," Webb said blandly.

"Didn't you just do that? In this conversation?"

"What conversation?" he said and hung up.

"I think we're rubbing off on him," Erin said to nobody in particular.

Ian said nothing.

Captain Franklin rapped on the open door with his knuckles and leaned into the break room. "Detective?" he said.

"Yes, sir," Erin said, coming to her feet. Rolf jumped up beside her, instantly ready for action.

"We've got your suspect in Room One. Mr. Thompson can wait here. If you'd like to leave your dog with him, that'd probably be best."

She nodded. "Rolf, *platz. Bleib.*"

Rolf sank back down to the floor, planted his chin between his paws, and gave her a mournful, reproachful stare. But he was a good boy, so he didn't protest. Ian rubbed the base of his ears. Rolf was not placated. He didn't know exactly what went on in interrogation rooms, since he was never allowed into them, but he was pretty sure he ought to be there. What if a bad guy needed to be bitten? Erin's teeth weren't remotely up to the task.

Chapter 22

"I'll be joining you in the interview," Franklin said. "My jurisdiction, after all."

"Of course," Erin said. "I really appreciate your help, Captain."

"My pleasure," he said. "My guys have your witness and they're bringing him here. How do you want to use him?"

"Can you have them keep him outside? Where he can see us when we come out?"

"Sure," Franklin said. "Planning an ambush?"

"Yeah."

"I like it. This is my house, but it's your investigation, so you'll take the lead. I'm looking forward to seeing how you handle this."

Erin grinned. "Me too."

* * *

Interrogation rooms were designed to make suspects uncomfortable. They were all cold colors and hard surfaces, suggesting a faceless dystopia. Erin felt right at home. Franklin showed himself to be a gentleman, holding the door for her and following her in.

"Finally," the woman in the room said. "Maybe one of you will tell me what I'm doing here."

"I apologize for the inconvenience, Ms. Wilder," Erin said.

"Wait a minute," Regina Wilder said. "I know you."

"We've met," Erin said.

The other woman was stylishly dressed in a hip-hugging dark red skirt and matching blazer over a cream-colored silk blouse. Regina was wearing a lot of expensive-looking jewelry, her model-perfect cheekbones enhanced with the clever application of various cosmetics. She looked like she'd walked right off a Parisian runway, except for the expression on her face; that was a cross between irritation and confusion.

"You're one of those New York detectives," Regina said.

"The ones looking into your husband's murder," Erin said. "That's right."

"Are you sure?" Regina asked. "I thought there was a possibility it was an accident."

"His plane was sabotaged," Erin said. "So was his parachute. He was murdered."

"That's dreadful," Regina said. "But I really don't see what more I can do to help. I've told you everything I know. Have you looked into that tramp of a farm girl?"

"Patience Goodspeed?" Erin said. "Yes, we've talked to her. She was very helpful."

"I'll just bet she was," Regina said. "The shameless little slut."

Erin fought down a wave of anger. An interrogation wasn't about being polite; it was about getting the subject to talk. You had to let insults slide off you, even the ones directed at innocent girls, and keep your eyes on the objective.

"It's interesting," Erin went on. "Patience was assaulted two years ago. Why would she suddenly decide to take revenge on the man who'd attacked her?"

"Maybe she'd been planning it the whole time," Regina suggested.

"Maybe," Erin said. "But in spite of her name, patience really isn't the strong suit of very many teenage girls. She'd been going to therapy, trying to come to terms with what happened to her. You know why her family dropped the complaint, of course."

"Because they knew the truth would come out in court," Regina said spitefully. "And their precious little angel's reputation would get torn to shreds."

"They dropped the complaint because your husband wrote them a very large check," Erin said. "Her family isn't poor, but this was a chance for her to really get ahead in life, to afford to go to a good college."

"She blackmailed us," Regina said. "The little bitch. Maybe she had that in mind from the start, teasing him and leading him on just so she could get her payoff."

"Have you ever met a rape victim, Ms. Wilder?" Erin asked. "I talk to a lot of them in my job, unfortunately. They struggle with guilt over the little choices they felt led to their attacks, but I haven't met a single one who wanted it to happen. And none of them thought a few thousand dollars would make it okay. Patience has been struggling with what happened to her for years. And she finally made peace with it. She hadn't spoken to your husband since his arrest, but she sent him a text message. It was a message of forgiveness."

Regina rolled her eyes.

"But you knew that already," Erin went on. "Because you're the one who saw the text on Arthur's phone."

"I don't know what you're talking about," Regina snapped.

"It gave you an idea," Erin said, ignoring Regina's retort. "You hated your husband, because you knew exactly what he was; a thrill-seeking playboy who raped teenage girls, went skydiving and bungee jumping, and was running drugs. Let's face it, Ms. Wilder. Arthur was a lousy guy. I don't blame you for hating him."

Regina said nothing. She just sat and seethed, her perfect lips pressed so tightly together that the only color in them came from her lipstick.

"Here was your chance to get rid of him," Erin said. "You knew the police would look at you for the murder; we always check out the spouse when somebody gets killed. But you had layers of protection. You could make it look like an accident. If the investigation successfully determined the plane had been sabotaged, you had the perfect fall guy—or fall girl. You had a girl with the perfect reason to kill him, and you could even point us at her, knowing we'd find the message she'd sent him right before his death."

"This is wild speculation," Regina said. "I don't have to listen to this."

She stood. Captain Franklin held up a hand.

"I don't!" Regina insisted. "She's a New York detective. This is Philadelphia. She has no right to keep me here."

"That's correct, ma'am," Franklin said. "She doesn't. However, I'm a Philadelphia police captain, and you're here at my request. I do have the right, and the authority. Please sit down and let Detective O'Reilly finish."

He phrased it as a request, but it sounded like an order, and Franklin had the physical and psychological presence to enforce it. Regina sat down, looking daggers at him.

"You had one more possibility to fall back on," Erin said, picking up where she'd left off. "You knew about the cocaine. If all else failed, you could try to pin Arthur's death on the

Colombians he'd stolen the drugs from. The irony is, if you hadn't done a thing, they would've taken care of him for you. They were waiting for him at the airport, and not to congratulate him on a successful flight."

Erin was watching as she said this, and she caught the reaction she'd been looking for. Regina's eyes widened slightly at the revelation. The woman's hands clenched on the tabletop, her crimson-painted nails digging into her own palms.

"Here's the problem," Erin said. "We know the Colombians didn't kill him. Like I said, they wanted to. They planned to. But they hadn't had the chance. Plus, they didn't just want him; they wanted their drugs back. They wanted them badly enough to take hostages and kill. They never would've deliberately crashed the plane that was carrying their product. Even if the coke survived the crash, the government would seize the drugs.

"That left Patience Goodspeed. She did know engines, and maybe could've doctored the airplane's motor to make it crash. But then there were the parachutes."

"You're spinning quite a story," Regina said. "I don't know what you think you know, but it's nonsense."

"The killer had to know Arthur well enough to realize he wouldn't try to land a plane without an engine," Erin said. "She had to know he was a skydiver, that he'd have a parachute with him on the plane, and that he'd use it when the plane started going down. He might've survived if he'd stayed with the plane, but he thought he had a safer way out, so he took it. Only the chute didn't open. We estimate it took thirty seconds for him to hit the ground. That's a really long time when you know you're about to die."

"So what?" Regina said. "I suppose the killer found the parachute on the plane and stitched it shut when they sabotaged the engine."

"That's when it happened, I agree," Erin said. "Only two problems with that theory: the parachute wasn't on the plane. It was on a shelf in the hangar, along with several others."

"How do you know that?" Regina said.

"Because the killer didn't know which chute would go on the plane," Erin said. "So you doctored all of them. We went to the hangar, Ms. Wilder, and we found the other chutes."

"That doesn't prove a thing!" Regina said.

"And the other thing," Erin said, feeling a smile trying to break through her stern façade. "I never said the parachutes were stitched shut. To know that, you'd have to be the one who did it."

"Of course you said that," Regina said.

Erin shook her head.

"She didn't," Franklin said. "But you don't have to take my word for it, ma'am. This interview is being recorded."

"You must have said it the last time we talked," Regina said.

"We didn't know it then," Erin said. "I couldn't have."

"Am I under arrest?" Regina demanded.

"This is your jurisdiction, Captain Franklin," Erin said. "So it's your call."

"I'm afraid so," Franklin said. "Regina Wilder, you're under arrest for the murder of your husband Arthur Wilder. I'm going to take you into custody here, pending extradition to New York. I'm going to advise you of your rights."

"I know my rights and I want my phone call and my lawyer," Regina said.

"I still have to read them to you, ma'am," Franklin said. "You don't have to listen, but I have to talk. It's the law. Then we'll take you to Booking and you can make your call."

After Franklin had Mirandized Regina, he stood up. Then he paused, embarrassed.

"I usually work a desk, Detective," he said to Erin. "I seem to have left my handcuffs upstairs."

"That's fine," Erin said, pulling out her bracelets. "You can borrow mine. You can ship them to New York along with her when she's extradited."

"This is circumstantial evidence," Regina said. "All you have is a single word, no proof. It'll never stick."

"We'll see," Franklin said. "It's amazing how much evidence shows up once you start looking for it. Place your hands together, please, ma'am."

As Franklin led their prisoner out of the interrogation room, Erin saw a familiar face sitting next to a detective's desk. She'd last seen Bob Donahue in the café at South Jersey Regional Airport. She was glad the Philadelphia cops had been able to coordinate with New Jersey law enforcement to get him here so fast.

Erin steered the procession past the desk. Donahue watched them, raising an appreciative eyebrow as they went by. He openly checked out both Erin and Regina. For once, the male gaze didn't annoy her. She'd been counting on it this time.

"Mr. Donahue," Erin said, stopping. "Does this woman look familiar?"

"Oh yeah," Donahue said. "That's an ass I'd remember anywhere."

"I beg your pardon!" Regina said indignantly.

"Where did you last see her?" Erin asked.

"Hangar Three," Donahue said, licking his lips at the memory. "She was doing something with the plane, bending way over. She was wearing a skirt a lot like that one. Not a good one to wear for aircraft maintenance, but I'm not complaining. And yeah, it's her face, too, come to think of it."

"Now we've got one word and an eyewitness," Erin said. "The problem with taking so much trouble with your appearance, ma'am, is that people remember when they see you."

The look in Regina's eyes reminded Erin so strongly of Siobhan Finneran, the assassin who'd nearly killed both her and Carlyle, that she reflexively felt for her gun. Her holster was empty; her Glock was in the possession of the NYPD's Internal Affairs department.

"Nobody's going to miss Arthur," Regina said coldly. "He was a son of a bitch. You want to know why he was smuggling drugs? You want to know how much of my money he blew through? He was a man-child who never grew up; a stupid, reckless little boy. And he was a lousy lover. I'm glad he's dead."

"What about the others?" Erin retorted.

"What others?" Regina snapped.

"Connie Lorcas. Julio Lorcas. Aidan Rierdon. Brian McGovern. Alejandro Fuentes. Dante Fuentes. Two more we haven't identified yet."

"Are those names supposed to mean something to me?"

"Those are people who died because of what you did," Erin said. "Because of you, six bad men and one decent one are in the morgue, along with an innocent woman. Because of you, a little girl will grow up without her mom and dad. Because of you, one of my best friends had to kill a man last night. It was necessary, but he'll live the rest of his life second-guessing himself."

"I don't know what you're talking about," Regina said haughtily. "That has nothing to do with me."

The burst of anger had drained what little energy Erin had been able to muster. "I know you don't," she said wearily. "And you probably wouldn't care if you did. But it matters."

"Enough of this," Regina said. "I want my phone call."

"You'll get it," Franklin said.

Chapter 23

Ian drove Erin and Rolf back to Manhattan. They didn't have Regina Wilder with them; the Philadelphia police were holding onto her until the respective cities could sort out the extradition paperwork.

Erin knew it'd be a good idea to get some more sleep, but despite her fatigue, she was annoyingly, stubbornly awake. To rub it in, Rolf was blissfully snoozing in back, making the cute little yipping sounds that indicated good doggie dreams. Ian had found a radio station playing '80s rock. Bruce Springsteen was singing about being born in the USA.

"Can I ask you something?" she said.

"Just did," Ian said.

"Ha ha. You don't have to answer if you don't want to."

"What's the question?"

"It's about the war."

He nodded, keeping his eyes on the road. "Figured."

"When you were over there, did you ever see anyone die on purpose?"

"All the time. Hajjis love that stuff. Pack a truck full of explosives, ram a checkpoint, go straight to Paradise. Take as many Marines with them as they could."

"Oh. Right. I wasn't thinking. Sheesh, that's what started the whole thing. 9/11. Those hijackers knew they'd die."

"Affirmative."

"When you were shooting it out with Mickey Connor and his guys, did you think you were going to die?"

"Wasn't thinking about it," Ian said. "Didn't care. Important thing was the mission. Why?"

"I'm trying to figure Julio Lorcas out," Erin said. "He had a kid, for God's sake! But he still strapped a bunch of grenades to himself. Did he want to die?"

"Not the right question."

"What is the right question?"

"What was more important to him than survival?"

"He wanted to save his daughter," Erin said. "And kill the guys who killed his wife. I guess he thought he might be able to take all the bad guys down. But it was a damn stupid plan."

"Sounds brave to me," Ian said. "Sometimes you can salvage a bad plan by being brave enough. Happens all the time in the Corps."

"That's no excuse for being stupid," she said sharply.

"You still talking about him?" Ian asked. "Or me? Or maybe yourself?"

"What do you mean?"

"Done plenty of dumb things. So have you. Doesn't matter if they're dumb. Matters if they're the right thing to do."

"You believe that?"

"Wouldn't be a Marine if I didn't. Got a saying in the Corps; know what MARINE stands for?"

"Tell me."

"Muscles Are Required, Intelligence Not Essential," Ian recited. He said it with a completely straight face.

"If your mission required it, you'd throw your life away, just like that?"

"What'll you do if your job calls for it?" he countered. "You run toward the fire, just like me."

"Yeah," she said. "Why do we do that?"

"Have to die of something," he said. "Might as well be doing something worthwhile."

"Ian?"

"What?"

"Did you ever want to die?"

He was silent so long she figured he wasn't going to answer. He kept driving, guiding the Charger between the lines on the highway, staring straight ahead. Just when she'd given up and was about to apologize for asking, he spoke up.

"Not exactly."

Erin waited, knowing there'd be more.

"Didn't care if I died or not for a while. Figured I deserved to. Took chances. But that's not the same thing."

"No, I suppose it isn't."

"Don't feel like that anymore."

"I'm glad to hear it. Because of Cassie?"

"Affirmative. And Ben."

"You're telling me this woman and her kid make your life worth living?"

"That's accurate."

"And you're hesitating about proposing to her? Ian, you weren't kidding. You're a goddamn idiot!"

That did the trick. Ian's stony expression cracked into a slight smile. Then the smile faded.

"What if she says no?" he said quietly.

"If you can take chances dodging bullets, you can damn well take this chance, too," Erin said. "It's worth it."

"How would you know?" he answered, and though the smile didn't come back to his lips, she saw it in his eyes.

"We're talking about your love life, not mine," she said. It was a weak answer and they both knew it.

"If you say so," he said. Then, changing the subject, "We going back to the Corner? Or your station?"

"Better go to the Eightball, if you don't mind," she said. "I've got a lot of paperwork to take care of. I'd better call the Lieutenant and let him know what to expect."

"Not a problem. I'll drop you with the car. Catch a cab or walk to the Corner."

"I really appreciate this. You've been a big help."

"Just doing my job."

"I knew you'd say that," she said, grinning.

* * *

The normal workday was over by the time Erin and Rolf dragged themselves into Major Crimes. But police stations didn't keep nine-to-five hours. Plenty of cops were around, taking care of the normal business of a metropolitan law-enforcement agency. Webb had gone home, but Vic was still at his desk. He had two empty Chinese takeout boxes and three empty Mountain Dew cans lined up next to his computer.

"Welcome back," he said. "How was your vacation?"

"It wasn't a vacation," she said. "I caught our murderer."

"So the Lieutenant told me," Vic said. "Awfully convenient that you were off having fun while we had to deal with the international incident."

"How bad was it?"

"Not too bad. Webb and Holliday handled most of it. The Captain's pretty good at that diplomacy bullshit when he sets his mind to it. You should've heard him sweet-talk the Colombian consul."

"What's happening with the freighter? The *Cardenal*?"

"The Coast Guard impounded it. If the owners want it back, they'll have to file a court claim. Poor bastards, I almost feel sorry for them. That court's got an eight-month backlog; I checked. I swear, if the people who wrote the Eighth Amendment could see our modern judiciary, they'd have apoplexy. That's what they all used to die of, isn't it? How come nobody gets apoplexy anymore?"

"I think it's an old word for a stroke," Erin said. Being a trauma surgeon's brother meant having the chance to absorb weird medical trivia. "How about Celeste Lorcas?"

"Her folks had a plan in place," Vic said. "The dad knew he might get whacked, having the job he did. The mom, Connie, has a sister who becomes the legal guardian until the kid turns eighteen. The sis lives in Boston. Last I heard, she was on her way down here with her husband. So the girl doesn't go into the system."

"That's something, I guess," Erin said. "How're you holding up?"

He shrugged. "I'm up to my ass in paperwork. Why do you think I'm pulling unpaid overtime?"

"Did you make your breakfast date with Zofia?"

"You kidding? I've been here all damn day. I haven't slept, and I haven't eaten or drunk anything that didn't come out of a box or a can. Zofia gets it, she's not mad. It's the Job, but not getting laid isn't making me feel any better."

"Sorry, but I can't help you out there."

He smiled. "I wasn't asking. Don't take this the wrong way, O'Reilly, but I'd rather jerk off with sandpaper."

"Is there a *right* way to take that?" she said, making a face. "But when I asked how you were, I was asking about the other thing."

"What other thing?"

"You had another OIS," she said, using the shorthand for Officer-Involved Shooting.

"I had the shot," he said, shrugging. "Then all hell broke loose and I took the shot. What else could I do? That asshole had a little kid. I wasn't gonna sit there with my thumb up my ass and watch him kill her."

"Of course not. You did the right thing, Vic. I know that. Everybody knows that. I just wanted to make sure you knew it."

He nodded. His eyes were unhappy. "How come that stupid bastard made me do it?" he asked, not expecting an answer. "Every SOB who goes suicide-by-cop is a goddamn cowardly scumbag. They can't hack it, so they gotta lay that shit on us? Like we don't have enough crap to deal with. And don't get me started on these goddamn Colombian cartel jerkwads. You notice every time they come up here, there's some crazy-ass gunfight and half a dozen people get killed? What's it gonna take for them to knock it the hell off?"

"I don't know," she said.

"Maybe if every batch of losers they send ends up dead or in prison, they'll get the message," he said. "Or maybe they'll run out of bad guys."

"Vic, if you think the world's ever going to run out of bad guys, I've got real bad news for you."

"You're right about that," he said. "Being a cop has plenty of job security. Speaking of which, did you come up here to bitch, or do you want to grab a chair and some DD-5s and get some work done?"

"That's why I'm here," she said. "I need to fill out the extradition request for Ms. Wilder. And I've got use-of-force forms, arrest reports... God, I don't even know what else. We're going to be here all night."

"Caffeine," he advised. "Lots and lots of caffeine."

"And takeout," she agreed.

*   *   *

It was nearly midnight when Erin was finally done with her paperwork. She rubbed her burning eyes, stretched her aching back, and wondered if she was really running on less than three hours of sleep. Vic had stumbled out at eleven, muttering something about the wrong people getting murdered. Bureaucrats and paper-pushers, according to him, made the best targets.

Erin stared at the whiteboard. It was covered with names, photos, and notes. Webb had put most of them up during the day, making sure the drug case made sense. She and Vic had added the remainder that evening, wrapping up Regina Wilder's part of the story. In the morning one of them would box up the notes and clear the board for the next case.

She could hear some sort of ruckus going on downstairs in the lobby; probably a drunken idiot fighting a half-dozen cops and adding "resisting arrest" to whatever else they'd be charging him with. If Rolf had been there, she didn't think there'd have been a fight. Even a big guy with ten beers in him knew better than to tangle with a German Shepherd.

"Time to go," she told her K-9.

Rolf lifted his head, blinked, and slowly stood up and stretched. He yawned hugely.

"Detective O'Reilly," a man said from the stairwell. "Glad I caught you."

Oh, shit, she thought. "Evening, Lieutenant," she said.

Lieutenant Keane, Internal Affairs' own Bloodhound, walked into the Major Crimes office. Despite the lateness of the hour, his suit was neatly pressed, his cheeks showing no hint of stubble. His smoothly handsome face gave nothing away, showing only polite interest.

"I hope I'm not interrupting anything important," he said.

"I was just leaving," she said.

"Oh, good," he said. "I won't keep you long. There was something I wanted to discuss with you."

"Sir, I'm really tired," she said. "It's been a hell of a couple of days and I'd really like to get home."

"This will only take a moment," he said.

"Do we need to go upstairs?" she asked, resigned.

"Oh, no," he said. "My office is locked up for the night. I was actually on my way out, too. Walk with me."

I'd rather go for a stroll with Jack the Ripper, she thought. "I don't have my car here," she said. "I'm going to take a cab home."

"That's fine," Keane said, waiting for her and falling in step beside her and Rolf.

"You can start talking, sir," she said.

Rolf, at her hip, watched her quizzically. He didn't think there was any danger, but he could feel the sudden tension radiating off her. He decided to be ready, just in case someone needed biting.

"As I understand it," Keane said, "you signed off on the release of six kilograms of high-grade cocaine from the Precinct 100 evidence locker."

"It's in my report," she said wearily. "And we shouldn't be talking about that operation."

She meant that she'd been working for the O'Malleys, an undercover operation of which Keane was well aware.

"Two O'Malley associates were killed and a third wounded," Keane said. "In a church sanctuary. I guess it's true;

nothing is sacred anymore. It's funny; I was under the impression Evan O'Malley was out of the drug game."

"That might've changed," she said.

"It's a pity the drugs were destroyed in the incident on that freighter," he said. "They *were* all destroyed, weren't they?"

"Yes, sir. I guess you could recover a few grams with a broom and a dustpan. The Coast Guard might've swept some of it up, but you'd have to check with them."

He nodded. "Who gave Evan the idea, I wonder?" he said.

Erin stopped. They were on the landing between the first and second floor of the Eightball. The scuffle downstairs was still going on, masking their conversation.

"What does that matter?" she asked.

"I was just wondering who was wielding the influence in the O'Malleys these days," Keane said. "They've had so much turnover in their middle management. After Evan, who would you say is in the best position to call the shots?"

Like you don't know, she thought. "Morton Carlyle," she said. "But he's never been involved in the drug trade."

"Ah yes, the gentleman gangster," Keane said with his cold, reptilian smile. "So good at keeping his hands clean. So it must be someone else. James Corcoran, maybe? He's a skillful smuggler, so they say."

She shook her head. "Not a chance. Carlyle would know. And we really shouldn't discuss this here."

"I suppose that leaves Gordon Pritchard, Declan Rafferty, and Kyle Finnegan," Keane said. "Of those, Rafferty is the obvious one. He was there last night, and he's got the bullet holes to prove it."

"Why do you care?" she asked.

"I don't," he said. "I'm just trying to sort everything out. You continue to do excellent work, Detective. I'm continually thankful I decided to bring you up from Queens."

Erin felt a sudden chill that had nothing to do with the temperature. "Captain Holliday brought me here," she said.

"At my suggestion," Keane said, still smiling. "Which probably saved your shield. And I'm glad I've been able to extend you the professional courtesy of smoothing over some of the, ah, rougher spots in your rather spectacular career. It really would have been unfortunate if your path had been derailed by one of your more impulsive decisions."

Erin fought down the impulsive urge to punch Keane in his clean-shaven, perfect, hateful face. "What's your point, sir?" she said, forcing her jaw to unclench.

"It's important in this job, as in any, to know who your friends are," Keane said. "When your current assignment concludes, I expect we'll have a great deal to discuss. I look forward to it."

The old Erin O'Reilly, the straight-shooting Patrol cop from Queens, would have told him where to stick his conversation and his friendship. But the Erin O'Reilly on the landing had spent months convincing thoroughly bad men that she was just as bad as they were. She'd graduated from a master course in disguising her feelings.

"I'll look forward to hearing what you've got to say, sir," she said. "I'm sorry, I'm not at my best right now. I wasn't kidding about the long hours. I slept a little in the car on the way to Philadelphia, but that's it. I'm dead on my feet."

"Of course," Keane said. He put out a hand and laid it on her shoulder. "I'm sorry to impose. Go home, get some sleep. And don't worry; this will keep. I'm not going anywhere."

Chapter 24

Erin was at the end of two very long days. The Barley Corner, on the other hand, was in the middle of a typical night. The sport on the TV was ice hockey. It would be difficult to say whether the crowd at the arena or the one in the pub was more raucous. The roar of happy, intoxicated voices that met her when she opened the door nearly drove her back out onto the street.

She wanted no part of it. All she wanted was sleep. She should've gone in the back way, she realized. But circling around now would be silly. Besides, if anyone noticed, it would hurt the street image she'd worked so hard to create. So she squared her shoulders and started threading through the crowd toward the back stairs.

She'd made it halfway when an arm looped itself around her shoulders with easy, friendly familiarity.

Her reactions were dulled by fatigue, but her self-defense instincts kicked in. She grabbed the offending hand just below the wrist with her opposite hand and squeezed hard. As she did, she twisted the hand down and back and spun away, rotating to face her assailant and applying pressure to the awkwardly-contorted arm. The motion forced the man to his knees. He went down; it was that or have his wrist broken.

"Glad to see you too, love," Corky Corcoran said. His tone was light, showing only slight strain from the joint-lock. "Rough evening, I take it?"

"Corky," she growled. "Not tonight."

Rolf added a warning rumble of his own, letting the Irishman know he was lucky Erin had gotten to him first.

"If you'll let me up, I'll buy you a drink by way of apology," Corky said.

"I drink here for free," she reminded him. But she let go anyway.

He stood up, rubbing his arm. "True enough," he said cheerfully. "I'll let you buy me one, then."

"For your apology?"

"Nay, love, for yours. You near yanked my arm out of its socket, and for what?"

"You should know better than to grab a cop by surprise. Or a woman. Especially one from Long Island."

"Fair point," he said. "But will you have a wee nip with me?"

"I'm pretty tired—" she began.

"And a nightcap will help you sleep," he said, heading for the bar. To Erin's own surprise, she found herself following him. Corky had a way of making you want to go with him, if only to see what he'd do next.

They found Carlyle sitting at his usual barstool. He got up to greet her with a glow of delight in his eyes that warmed Erin clean through. She could feel his pleasure at seeing her, coupled with relief that she was all right. Her anger at Corky drained away.

"One drink," Erin said, holding up her index finger. "One. Then I'm going to bed."

"Evening, Erin," Danny the bartender said, appearing as if by magic. Erin thought he might have a trapdoor under the bar. "What'll it be?"

"Double Glen D, straight up," she said.

"I'll have the same, lad," Carlyle said.

"I'm feeling adventurous," Corky said. "Since Erin's buying, I'll have whatever she orders for me."

"Really?" Erin said. "Even if it's some pink girly drink with a little umbrella?"

"If you're woman enough to order it, I'm man enough to drink it," he said with a grin.

"Danny," she said, "help me out here. What would you recommend for a guy with a death wish?"

"Lots of choices there," Danny said. "Plenty of cocktails with the right vibe. Let's see, there's brain damage, atomic bomb, screaming death, white death, kamikaze—"

"That's the one," she said. "Get him a kamikaze."

"Have you any idea what's in that?" Carlyle asked.

"That's Corky's problem, not mine," Erin said.

"Vodka, triple sec, and lime juice," Danny said. "Coming right up."

In a matter of moments, their drinks were on the bar in front of them. Corky hoisted his glass and winked at Erin.

"Here's to you, love," he said. "Nothing is past, nothing is lost."

"I have no idea what that means," Erin said. "And it sounds like bullshit to me. But I'll drink to it."

They drank. Carlyle and Erin, who appreciated good whiskey, sipped theirs. Corky knocked his whole drink back at one go. He coughed once, eyes watering, and smiled.

"Not bad," was his verdict. "Now I'm off. I've a girl to call. Long-distance."

"Corky," Erin said. "You aren't seriously calling... *her*, are you?"

"Unless you're a mite more specific, I can't possibly answer that," Corky said. "Ta, love."

Erin and Carlyle watched him go. Then, without a word, they left the pub and went upstairs, locking Carlyle's apartment door behind them.

"Jesus Christ," she said once they were safely behind the soundproofed steel door. "He's calling Teresa Tommasino."

"I imagine so," Carlyle said. "He's in love with her, darling."

"And she's in hiding after being declared dead! If he's not careful, he could blow the whole case! Not to mention getting himself killed, along with her and the rest of us! I was joking about the death wish!"

"He doesn't want to die," Carlyle said. "I've been watching the lad ever since he came back. He's changed. Something happened to him out there."

"Great," she muttered. "As if we don't have enough to worry about. He's out of control."

"I don't think so," he said. "The lad's more focused than I've ever seen him. He's determined to see this through. Don't you understand, darling? The only way she can come back to New York is if both the O'Malleys and the Lucarellis are out of the picture. We ought to be grateful to Miss Tommasino. She's given Corky the finest motivation he'll ever have. But we've something to discuss ourselves."

"Can it wait till tomorrow?"

"I fear not."

"Then at least let me get ready for bed. I'm about to fall over."

"Of course."

In the bedroom, she stripped off her clothes and changed into a baggy old NYPD T-shirt that had once belonged to her dad. It came down almost to her knees and made a good nightshirt. She went to the bathroom and brushed her teeth. When she came back to the bedroom, Carlyle was sitting on the side of the bed.

"We need to talk about Red Rafferty," he said. "And what happened at the church."

"I figured," she said, sitting on the bed and curling her feet under herself. Rolf climbed up beside her and settled on the mattress, resting his chin on her thigh.

"Rafferty's in custody at the hospital," Carlyle said. "It looks like he'll live. He's not as badly hurt as he ought to be. But he's under arrest."

"For what?"

"A weapons charge. That's actually the whole of it. Since the lad wasn't in possession of narcotics, nor did he shoot anyone, all they can pin on him is his gun. But since he's a convicted felon, the gun's rather a serious matter. Evan's hoping you can get that pushed aside."

"That shouldn't be a problem," she said. "I'll talk to Phil about it in the morning. We ought to be able to get him released by the time he's out of the hospital."

"Grand," Carlyle said. "And as for the cocaine?"

"It's gone," she said flatly. "Blown to bits, scattered all over the Atlantic. Unless he wants to get a fishing pole and try to catch some coked-up codfish, Evan's shit out of luck. And that's probably for the best."

"I'm inclined to agree," he said.

"Especially since now I don't have to decide who to give it to; Evan or Old Man Vitelli," she said.

"There's that," Carlyle said, nodding. "Evan's expecting a call from me tonight. I'll explain the situation. He won't be happy, but I think he'll understand."

"At least we took out some of his competition," she said. "The Fuentes brothers were going to be trouble. Tell Evan your attack dog wiped out a few more goons and call it a day."

"I'll do that," he said. "Are you all right, darling?"

"Not really," she said. "I killed another guy. I mean, the grenades would've killed him anyway, I guess, but I shot him. It's getting easier, damn it, and I don't want it to. Killing a man should be a bigger deal."

"It was a big deal to him, I'd imagine," Carlyle said dryly.

"That's not what I mean," she said. "And there was a little girl out there. She almost died. And Vic killed Dante Fuentes, and he says it doesn't bother him, but it absolutely does. We're coming loose here. We have to finish this. Soon."

He leaned in and kissed her forehead. "We will," he promised. "Just a wee bit longer. Then no more pretending. It'll be over before we know it. Now, get your sleep. It'll all look better by daylight."

*   *   *

Erin woke up with no idea where she was or what she was doing. She felt drunk on sleep, groggy and incoherent. Her eyelids were gummy and didn't want to open. Her hair was a tangled mess. "Whiskey would've been better," she muttered.

"Beg pardon?" Carlyle murmured sleepily.

She rolled over and found him there beside her, warm and comfortable. She slipped an arm around him, nestled in close, and went back to sleep.

The next time she woke up, she felt slightly more human. By a great effort of will, she raised her head off the pillow and craned her neck to look at the clock. It read 10:36.

AM or PM, she wondered. Then she wondered if it even mattered. Carlyle was still asleep under her arm. It felt so damned good having someone there, someone she could love and trust. Maybe she'd just stay in bed with him for a while.

She lasted almost ten minutes. Then she became aware of eyes on her. She slowly turned and saw Rolf's head, resting on the mattress next to her own. He was staring at her, silently but meaningfully.

"Right," she sighed. The dog needed his walk and she had things to do. Reluctantly, she disentangled herself from Carlyle and got up. As it turned out, it was morning, so she'd slept about eleven hours. That was a lot, but it wasn't ridiculous, considering the amount of catch-up she'd needed to do.

A quick shower revived her a little. Walking Rolf in the crisp, cold late-morning air finished the job, especially since her perforated jacket was still letting cold air flow across her back. By the time she got back to the Corner, she was wide awake and ready to face the rest of the day.

She had a text on her phone from Webb. He'd sent it at ten. It said, "Come in when you're alive again." That made her smile. It was nice having a commanding officer who understood the Job.

First she ordered breakfast; bacon, eggs, and coffee. She took her food upstairs and gave Rolf his kibble. Then she called Phil Stachowski and set up a meeting for 11:30 at Zuccotti Park.

It wasn't much of a park. Most of it was concrete or stone. A few token patches of greenery were hemmed in by blocks of masonry. Now, in the New York winter, the plants were scraggly and disreputable. The place was full of benches, but the average New Yorker had no interest in sitting out in the open on a stone bench when the temperature was in the low thirties. The park was therefore almost completely deserted.

There was, however, a falafel cart by the curb, set up by an enterprising and optimistic young Middle Eastern man. Erin found she was still hungry, in spite of her big breakfast, so she went over and bought some falafel. She'd never known exactly what was in falafel, but it was hot and tasty, so she didn't care.

Munching away, she turned back to the park and saw Phil in the act of sitting down on one of the benches. He had a copy of the *Times* in one hand and a wide, flat cardboard box under his other arm. He set the box on the bench next to his hip, opened the paper, and started reading, looking for all the world like a completely harmless middle-aged man; a professor at a low-tuition community college, or maybe a junior-high teacher.

Erin took a seat beside him, leaving some space between them. Rolf sat on the ground in front of the bench, watching the falafel in case it made a bid for freedom. You could never tell with street food.

"Morning," she said.

"Good morning," Phil said, folding the paper and setting it aside. "I know I'll be getting your report today or tomorrow, so I won't ask you to go into too much detail now. You called the meeting; what's on your mind?"

"The drugs aren't hitting the street," she said. "They got destroyed."

"I can't say I'm sorry to hear that," he said.

"It means I don't have to give in to Vitelli or O'Malley," she said. "I was wondering how I was going to juggle that."

"Good."

"Declan Rafferty got shot. He's in the hospital, but should be out in a few days. Evan wants me to get his weapons beef dropped."

"Rafferty is a multiple offender," Phil said. "He's got a jacket two inches thick. If he had a gun on him, that's a major parole violation. I don't think we can get a judge to just look the other way."

"Then we need to finesse something," she said. "Can't we mislay the paperwork, buy a little time? It doesn't need to be much. All these guys are going to be in jail in a few weeks."

"True," he said. "That's a good idea with the paperwork. I can create a little bureaucratic confusion. We'll still have the charges on the books, but he'll be released. If we do it right, he won't be able to tell the difference."

"Good. That's the only major business with the O'Malleys."

"What about the Lucarellis? How angry do you think they'll be about missing out on the drugs?"

"We took out the Colombians for them," she said. "I can spin it with Vitelli. It won't be a problem. He'll know I fought his rivals. Hell, I nearly got killed."

"About that," Phil said. "I've got something for you."

He handed her the box.

"What's this?" Erin asked. "Are we swapping gifts now?"

"I asked what you needed," he said, smiling. "I try to look after my people."

She lifted the lid off the box. Inside, neatly folded, was a black leather jacket next to a small white bottle. She picked up the bottle and turned it so she could see the label. It was Aspirin.

"I said I needed a new jacket and some pills," she said, remembering. "You don't miss much, do you?"

"It pays to listen," he said.

"I was joking."

"You didn't need a new jacket?"

"Yeah, I did," she said. She shrugged off her coat and handed it to him. While he examined it, she tried on the new one. It was a perfect fit.

Phil whistled softly. "Looks like you took a full spread of buckshot," he said, holding the tattered garment up. Sunlight shone through the holes.

"It's not a big deal," she said. "Lorcas aimed for the vest. He was trying to knock me down, not kill me. I didn't know that at the time, of course, so I returned fire and winged him. What else could I do?"

"Nothing," he said. "I wouldn't worry about getting in trouble for that."

"Trouble?" she said and laughed bitterly. "I don't see how I could possibly get in more trouble."

"It's always possible for things to get worse," he said mildly.

"Is that supposed to make me feel better?"

He shook his head. "You're doing great, Erin. I've never been so impressed by one of my officers."

"I shot another guy."

"Was it necessary?"

"Absolutely. He was about to shoot me."

"Then you did what you had to do. I'm sorry he made you do it. That's a weight nobody should have to carry."

"This is a nice jacket," she said, zipping it up.

"There's a wire sewn into the lining," he said.

Erin rolled her eyes. "Of course there would be."

"You activate it by squeezing inside the right-hand pocket."

"Phil, why did you put a wire in my new coat?"

His smile broadened. "That way I could charge it to the Department as an operational expense," he said.

Erin blinked. Then she laughed. "You look so harmless, I forget what a sneaky bastard you can be. I guess you'd have to be, doing what you do."

"I have my moments," Phil said. "Anything else I should know?"

"Corky's in contact with Teresa," she said quietly.

"What sort of contact?" he asked.

"Phone calls."

"Do you think it's dangerous?"

"It's a risk," she said. "But maybe it's okay. I just thought you should know."

He nodded. "Is she safe?"

"Corky wouldn't have left her alone if she was in trouble. He can be careless, but he knows when something's important."

"I still can't believe we used him to guard a witness." Phil shook his head. "Desperate times."

"It all worked out. So far."

"That's all any of us can say." He stood up. "Good seeing you, Erin. Take care of yourself. It's almost over."

"I keep hearing that," she said. "But it keeps on going."

"Where are you off to now?"

"The Eightball. I still have a day job."

"Remember to watch your back."

She flexed her shoulders and winced. She still felt bruised all over. "I'm not likely to forget. Look what happened when I didn't. Be seeing you, Phil."

Chapter 25

Half a day of modified assignment left Erin wanting to climb the walls. Vic was even worse; Erin thought the custodians might be wondering about tooth marks in the edge of the Russian's desk. It wasn't that they didn't have things to do. The fallout from the gunfight aboard the *Cardenal* was still showering them with paperwork. So was the extradition of Regina Wilder. They still had plenty of reports to write. Erin also had to request warrants to search the Wilder home and to take another look at the hangar. Then there were reports from the NTSB regarding the plane crash that had started the whole thing, more reports from the Coast Guard, and still more reports from the DEA.

When she finally shoved the remaining paperwork into a file cabinet and got out of there, she had to fight the urge to look over her shoulder to make sure a wave of official paper wasn't rushing after her. She made herself walk, not run, to the garage.

Rolf hopped happily into his compartment. He'd had a boring afternoon, but now that they were in the car, anything might happen. He poked his head between the seats to see where they were going.

Erin herself wasn't sure. She wanted to go home. A stiff drink and a bowl of Marian's Irish stew would really hit the spot. But she was restless and edgy. She kept thinking about the Lorcas family, especially the little girl. So it wasn't really a surprise when she steered north and drove to Midtown, stopping in front of a familiar brownstone.

Three locks clicked open in answer to her finger on the doorbell. Then the door opened to reveal Michelle O'Reilly.

"Hey, sis," Michelle said. "Is everything okay? I didn't know you were coming."

"Everything's fine, Shelley," Erin said. "This is a spur-of-the-moment thing. Can Rolf and I come in for a minute? If it's a bad time, I can go."

"Nonsense," Michelle said. "Come on in. I'm starting dinner in a little while, but don't worry. You're family. You can come anytime."

The rest of the family was in the living room. Sean Junior was sitting in his armchair, reading a medical journal. Anna and Patrick were on the carpet, playing with Lucy. The pup was running back and forth between them in a clumsy, shambling motion thanks to his oversized paws.

"Rolfie!" Anna called. "Come play with us!"

"Go on, kiddo," Erin said, nodding to the Shepherd.

Rolf gave her a look of long-suffering patience. He'd rather be chasing bad guys than dealing with a puppy, but he knew his duty. He trotted over to join the group. Lucy raised her black, fluffy head and sniffed noses with him. Then she licked his snout.

Rolf, with great deliberation, licked the pup in return and poked her with his nose. She rolled over onto her back and wiggled her paws in the air.

Anna giggled.

Watching them, Erin swallowed a sudden lump in her throat. Without fully knowing why, she crossed the room in five quick strides and scooped Anna up into her arms.

"Hi Auntie Erin," Anna said.

Erin didn't say a word. She just held her niece close, hugging her tightly.

"Auntie Erin?" a muffled little voice said after a moment. "You're squishing me."

"Sorry," Erin said, setting her down again. "Wow, you're getting big. I'm not going to be able to do that much longer."

"Good to see you, kiddo," Sean Junior said. "Keeping the streets safe?"

"Some of them," Erin said. To her astonishment, she had to wipe her eyes with the back of her hand.

"Erin?" Michelle said. "What's wrong?"

"Nothing," Erin lied. Michelle had been kidnapped in June and her kids had narrowly escaped the same fate. The last thing they needed was for her to bring up bad memories. They were all together and safe, thank God, and that should be good enough for her.

"It doesn't look like nothing," Michelle pressed.

Erin shook her head. "It's just work," she said. "I wanted to see you... all of you. Sometimes I need to remind myself what I've got, I guess."

"Count your blessings?" Michelle said.

"Something like that, yeah. I'll get out of your hair. You've got things to do and—"

"Erin," Michelle interrupted, laying a hand on her arm. "Why don't you stay for supper?"

"You don't need to do that," Erin said.

"You're family," Michelle said again. "I'll have it ready in an hour. Unless you have somewhere else you really need to be."

"No, I don't." Erin said. She looked down at her niece and nephew. They'd incorporated Rolf into their game. The big German Shepherd and the little Newfoundland puppy were getting on well. Lucy was following Rolf wherever he went, grabbing at his tail with her sharp white puppy teeth. Lucy succeeded in latching on. She dug in her paws, but Rolf was so much larger and stronger that he just dragged her across the carpet, making Anna squeal with laughter. Even quiet little Patrick was giggling softly.

"Come on," Michelle insisted. "Stay with us."

"I'd like that," Erin said. "I'd like that a lot."

Here's a sneak peek from Book 22: Jackhammer

Coming 12/11/2023

Flashing emergency lights made an oddly festive multicolored halo above the crime scene. It was the Christmas season and the blinkers reminded Erin of holiday displays, particularly since this scene was illuminated not only by the familiar blue-and-red police flashers, but by golden-orange lights indicating a construction zone.

"Great," she muttered. "Road work."

"Nothing wrong with a bit of urban renewal," Carlyle said. "I'm sure you'd agree Brooklyn can use all the repairs it can get."

"How close you want me?" Ian asked.

"Stop at the first squad car," she said. "I can walk the rest of the way."

"The weather..." Carlyle began.

"Look around," she said. "It's a damn parking lot. Not a roof within thirty yards. I'm going to get wet anyway. I might as well get a head start."

Ian pulled the Mercedes to a halt as a uniformed officer waved him to the side of the road. The gray sedan wasn't a police vehicle, so he would've had a hard time getting closer in any case. Erin got out of the car, followed closely by Rolf. The Shepherd, shielded by his coarse outer coat of fur, didn't mind the wet, clinging sleet.

"I'll see that Marian has a fine hot toddy waiting for you," Carlyle said.

"What the hell is a hot toddy?" she retorted, but she'd already started closing the car door and didn't hear Carlyle's reply. Ian backed the car into a U-turn and headed back the way he'd come, leaving her to trudge through an inch and a half of slush toward the latest urban atrocity.

She found the rest of her squad standing around a jagged hole in the concrete of the parking lot, accompanied by a half-dozen men in reflective vests and hard hats. The lot was littered with construction equipment. Erin recognized an air compressor and jackhammer, an industrial-sized circular saw, and various hand tools like pickaxes, crowbars, and shovels. Lieutenant Webb held an umbrella; his trademark trench coat and fedora were, as a result, only a little damp. Vic was wearing a wool watch cap and fleece-lined jacket. He looked cold, wet, and grumpy.

"What've we got, sir?" Erin asked.

"You got here fast," Vic said. "There's no way you could've got here from that hole-in-the-wall bar you hang out at."

"The Barley Corner isn't a hole in the wall," she retorted. "It's an upscale Manhattan business. How'd you get here so fast?"

"I was visiting my mom," Vic said. "Down in Brighton Beach. It was a quick drive."

"I was in the neighborhood too," she said absently. "Maybe I caught the scent of fresh blood."

"Unlikely," Webb said. "There's nothing fresh about these."

"Old bodies?" Erin guessed.

Webb nodded.

"How old?" she asked.

"They're way past their sell-by date," Vic said.

"Doc Levine's on her way," Webb said. "She'll have answers for us."

"You said there's three bodies?" Erin asked.

"At least," Vic said.

"You don't *know* how many?" she asked incredulously.

"Have a look," he said, pointing to the hole. "Utility crew was breaking up the ground. They're going to be replacing this lot with some sort of fancy building. Then they found these three poor schmucks in the cement and freaked out."

"Wow," Erin said, peering over the edge. Vic aimed a flashlight. The bodies weren't fully unearthed; the work crew must have stopped when they'd realized what they'd found, and no wonder.

"Know what it reminds me of?" Vic said. "What's that place in Italy that got wiped out when that volcano blew up? You know, back in the Roman Empire?"

"Pompeii," Webb said.

"Yeah, that's the one," Vic said. "And the ash cloud rolled down the mountain and cooked everyone right where they were standing. They got basically petrified, and then people found them a couple thousand years later. Freaky shit."

Erin nodded. She felt a cold shiver down the back of her neck, but that might have just been the sleet rolling down her collar. The bodies were only visible up to the shoulders, but one had its hands raised. And she'd noticed something on the hands.

"Take a look there," she said, pointing. "The wrists."

"They're tied together," Webb said. "Looks like a zip-tie."

"That makes it a homicide for sure," Vic said. "As if there was any doubt. It's not like three guys pitched head-first into cement by accident. And this is a lot thicker than it'd need to be for a parking lot. Somebody dug this hole extra deep and dumped the poor bastards in."

"It's worse than that," Erin said. She swallowed, trying not to think too hard about the implications of what she'd seen. "Hands tied, standing up... these men were still alive when the cement got poured in on them."

There was a brief silence.

Vic broke it. "Okay," he said. "That's horrible."

"It's murder," Webb said. "If it wasn't horrible, we'd be out of a job. Every murder victim is alive until someone kills them."

"You're a philosopher, sir," Erin said.

"I'm a detective doing his job," Webb said. He turned to the workmen. "Do you guys have something we can use to cover this hole?"

"I got a tarp in my truck," one of the workers said.

"Could you get it, please?" Webb asked. "We don't want the scene getting more contaminated than it already is."

"No kidding," Vic said. He stooped and picked up a handful of gray slush. "You know that song? The one about Bette Davis and her eyes?"

"What about it?" Erin replied.

"There's a line in it about a girl being 'pure as New York snow.' I always got a kick out of that. Look at this shit. You say a girl's pure as this, she's probably turning tricks behind the 7-Eleven for drug money."

*   *   *

By the time Sarah Levine finally arrived, Erin's teeth were chattering. She, Vic, and Rolf had retreated to the shelter of

Vic's Ford Taurus, but it was too late. She'd already been soaked to the skin and the sleet had sucked the warmth right out of her flesh. Vic had the heater going full blast, but the only thing that seemed to do was fog up the windows. The car interior steamed and smelled of wet dog.

The Medical Examiner parked her Prius between a pair of squad cars, got out, and walked straight to the excavation, paying no attention either to the weather or the people already on site. Give Levine a dead body, Erin thought, and she wouldn't notice a nuclear explosion in the background.

"Want to go talk to her?" Erin asked.

"You think she wants to talk to us?" Vic retorted.

"Not really," Erin admitted. "I think she wants to look at some corpses."

"I say we give her a little quality time with the stiffs," Vic said. "Extra stiff, on account of being locked in concrete for God knows how long. When do you figure they got stashed here?"

"When the concrete was poured," Erin said. "Obviously."

Vic rolled his yes. "I know that," he said, speaking slowly. "I mean, how long do you think the concrete's been here?"

She shrugged. "It'll be in the city records."

"Yeah," he said. "Because I'm sure this was completely legal and aboveboard. You think they went to City Hall and applied for a body-dumping permit? Hey, do they actually have those, you think?"

"Of course they do, Vic," she said. "That's how cemeteries operate."

"What makes a place a cemetery?" he wondered. "It's not the dead bodies. Hell, there's dead bodies everywhere. Half the tenements in the five boroughs would be cemeteries by that definition. It can't be that they're holy ground, because then you'd have no place to dump the atheists. Is it the headstones? 'Here lies So-and-So?'"

"Vic?"

"Yeah?"

"You're being creepy."

"I am?"

"Yeah. Stop it."

"Sorry."

"No you're not."

"So, what were you doing on Long Island tonight?" Vic asked, changing the subject rather than continue addressing his lack of remorse.

"Working," she said.

"We aren't working a case down here," he said. "I mean, we weren't until just now. And I'm pretty sure I saw your sugar daddy's Mercedes driving away."

"That reminds me," she said. "I need a ride back to Manhattan when we're done here. And next time you call Carlyle a sugar daddy, I'll kick your ass."

"Love to see you try," he said, grinning. "So, putting two and two together, if you were working, and if your... *distinguished older gentleman* was providing your transportation, that means it was that other thing."

"Distinguished older gentleman?" she repeated.

"Yeah," he said. "I like the acronym."

"What acronym?"

He motioned with his head toward the panting German Shepherd in the backseat. "D-O-G," he said, still grinning.

Erin smacked him on the shoulder. It had no effect whatsoever.

Knuckles rapped on the driver's side window. Vic swiped his hand across the glass, clearing the condensation to reveal Lieutenant Webb. Webb motioned for them to get out. They complied, Rolf more cheerfully than the other two.

"Let's see what the good doctor can tell us," Webb said. "Then we might as well get indoors. This is a cold case, no doubt about it."

"Cold enough," Erin said, suppressing a shiver. "It's thirty degrees out."

"Ha ha," Webb said.

"I thought you liked getting out of the office onto the street," Vic said.

"As long as the street isn't covered with ice," Erin said.

A pair of unhappy-looking Patrol officers were holding the tarp a few feet above the hole so Levine could kneel there and conduct her initial examination. She'd brought a pair of floodlights and mounted them on either side. The ME was in a pool of bright LED light, surrounded by old corpses, and couldn't have been more at home.

"What've we got, Doctor?" Webb asked.

"Three adult males," Levine said without looking up. "Decomposition is not as advanced as might be expected, due to encasement in concrete."

"So they're mummies?" Vic asked.

"Of course not," Levine said, sounding annoyed. "Mummification requires a process of embalming, including removal of internal organs. These bodies have undergone none of the necessary procedures. They were, however, entombed in a largely anoxic environment. Despite the considerable age of the bodies, soft tissue has not fully decomposed."

"Yeah, we know," Vic said, wrinkling his nose. The smell of death was wafting up out of the hole.

"Cause of death?" Webb asked.

"I have not yet ascertained it," Levine said. "I see no external signs of traumatic injury, but all three will require a detailed postmortem examination."

"What about the age of the bodies?" Erin asked. "Any idea how long they've been down there?"

"Not yet," Levine said. "As I previously stated, decomposition has been retarded by the medium of suspension."

"How about the concrete itself?" Erin asked. "Can you tell how old it is?"

"No," Levine said flatly. "Concrete is effectively impossible to accurately date, except by wear and erosion, neither of which is sufficient for a determination in this case. However, I can determine that the concrete is of fairly high quality and was laid with skill."

"How can you tell?" Webb asked.

"No cracking around the bodies," Levine explained. "The concrete was wet-cured and consolidated."

"Meaning what?" Vic asked.

One of the construction workers stepped forward. He'd been hanging out around the fringe of the site, smoking soggy cigarettes and talking things over with his buddies. "You know concrete, lady?" he asked Levine.

"I understand its chemical composition and industrial applications," Levine said.

"Me too," the worker said. "What she means is, if you want the concrete to set right, you gotta put curing blankets over it after you pour it."

"Explain it to me like I'm an idiot," Vic said. "What's a curing blanket?"

"Like?" Erin said quietly.

"It's a sheet of curing paper or polyethylene," Levine said.

"Yeah, what she said," the worker said. "You put the blanket over top and you keep it wet. You hose it down for a while. That keeps the concrete from cracking."

"How long is a while?" Webb asked.

The man shrugged. "You want it done right, four weeks."

"You're saying the killers came back to hose down this place for a damn month?" Vic said.

"I ain't saying that," the worker said.

"I am," Levine said. "If the concrete had cracked, it would have allowed entry of water and escape of decomposition gases. These bodies would be fully skeletonized, unless they were very recently interred."

Webb turned to the workman. "Do you guys know how long this slab's been here?" he asked.

The man shrugged again. "Years," he said. "Dunno how many, but it's kinda worn down. Concrete gets a look when it's been there a while, y'know? You get a feel for it. I had to guess, I'd say maybe ten, give or take."

"Ten years is a possible timeframe, given the state of preservation," Levine said.

Webb rubbed his temple with one hand, keeping his umbrella above his head with the other. "We've got a mass murderer who buried three guys alive and then visited the grave for a month, just to make sure the bodies were properly preserved?" he said.

"I can't speculate as to the motive," Levine said. "But that is a reasonable hypothesis for the chain of events."

"There's nothing reasonable about this," Webb said.

"Oh, good," Vic said. "It's been a while since we had a total lunatic to chase down. Who was the last? That wannabe serial killer college boy?"

"Don't get your hopes up," Erin said. "If this was a decade ago, our perp could be long gone. Hell, he could be dead."

"Nah," Vic said. "This guy was careful. A guy like that doesn't just die. He's still out there. For all we know, he's spent the last ten years putting other dudes in cement. Half the buildings in New York might have dead guys in the foundations."

Erin made a face. "Thanks for that, Vic. I'm sure we'll all sleep better thinking about that."

He smiled nastily. "It's what I'm here for."

Ready for more?

Join the Clickworks Press email list
for the latest on new releases, upcoming books and
series, behind-the-scenes details, events, and more.

Be the first to know about new releases in the Erin
O'Reilly Mysteries by signing up at
clickworkspress.com/join/erin

About the Author

Steven Henry learned how to read almost before he learned how to walk. Ever since he began reading stories, he wanted to put his own on the page. He lives a very quiet and ordinary life in Minnesota with his wife and dog.

Also by Steven Henry

Fathers
A Modern Christmas Story

When you strip away everything else, what's left is the truth

Life taught Joe Davidson not to believe in miracles. A blue-collar woodworker, Joe is trying to build a future. His father drank himself to death and his mother succumbed to cancer, leaving a broken, struggling family. He and his brother and sisters are faced with failed marriages, growing pains, and lingering trauma.

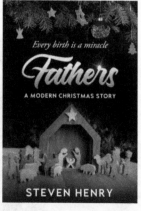

Then a chance meeting at his local diner brings Mary Elizabeth Reynolds into his life. Suddenly, Joe finds himself reaching for something more, a dream of happiness. The wood-worker and the poor girl from a trailer park connect and fall in love, and for a little while, everything is right with their world.

But suddenly Joe is confronted with a situation he never imagined. What do you do if your fiancée is expecting a child you know isn't yours? Torn between betrayal and love, trying to do the right thing when nothing seems right anymore, Joe has to strip life down to its truth and learn that, in spite of the pain, love can be the greatest miracle of all.

Learn more at clickworkspress.com/fathers.

Ember of Dreams

The Clarion Chronicles, Book One

When magic awakens a long-forgotten folk, a noble lady, a young apprentice, and a solitary blacksmith band together to prevent war and seek understanding between humans and elves.

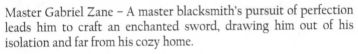

Lady Kristyn Tremayne – An otherwise unremarkable young lady's open heart and inquisitive mind reveal a hidden world of magic.

Robert Blackford – A humble harp maker's apprentice dreams of being a hero.

Master Gabriel Zane – A master blacksmith's pursuit of perfection leads him to craft an enchanted sword, drawing him out of his isolation and far from his cozy home.

Lord Luthor Carnarvon – A lonely nobleman with a dark past has won the heart of Kristyn's mother, but at what cost?

Readers love *Ember of Dreams*

"The more I got to know the characters, the more I liked them. The female lead in particular is a treat to accompany on her journey from ordinary to extraordinary."

"The author's deep understanding of his protagonists' motivations and keen eye for psychological detail make Robert and his companions a likable and memorable cast."

Learn more at tinyurl.com/emberofdreams.

More great titles from Clickworks Press

www.clickworkspress.com

The Altered Wake
Megan Morgan

Amid growing unrest, a family secret and an ancient laboratory unleash long-hidden superhuman abilities. Now newly-promoted Sentinel Cameron Kardell must chase down a rogue superhuman who holds the key to the powers' origin: the greatest threat Cotarion has seen in centuries – and Cam's best friend.

"Incredible. Starts out gripping and keeps getting better."

Learn more at clickworkspress.com/sentinel1.

Hubris Towers: The Complete First Season
Ben Y. Faroe & Bill Hoard

Comedy of manners meets comedy of errors in a new series for fans of Fawlty Towers and P. G. Wodehouse.

"So funny and endearing"

"Had me laughing so hard that I had to put it down to catch my breath"

"Astoundingly, outrageously funny!"

Learn more at clickworkspress.com/hts01.

Death's Dream Kingdom
Gabriel Blanchard

A young woman of Victorian London has been transformed into a vampire. Can she survive the world of the immortal dead— or perhaps, escape it?

"The wit and humor are as Victorian as the setting... a winsomely vulnerable and tremendously crafted work of art."

"A dramatic, engaging novel which explores themes of death, love, damnation, and redemption."

Learn more at clickworkspress.com/ddk.

Share the love!

Join our microlending team at kiva.org/team/clickworkspress.

Keep in touch!

Join the Clickworks Press email list and get freebies, production updates, special deals, behind-the-scenes sneak peeks, and more.

Sign up today at clickworkspress.com/join.

9 798889 000129